Praise for Ray Loriga and
Tokyo Doesn't Love Us Anymore

"Loriga, a cult figure in Europe, constructs a bewildering dystopia dominated by multinational conglomerates, chemical dependency and sexual excess. Both disturbing and funny."
—*New Statesman*

"A fascinating cross between Marguerite Duras and Jim Thompson."   —Pedro Almodóvar

"This weird, wonderful tale is as detached and decadent as novels get."   —*I-D*

"Loriga is set to join that select band of writers—like Michel Houellebecq and Haruki Murakami—who are busy retooling fiction for the twenty-first century." —*The Big Issue in the North*

"*Tokyo Doesn't Love Us Anymore* reminds you of several other dystopian visions, from Orwell to Philip K. Dick. It is a measure of Loriga's talent that this disquieting, striking novel bears comparison with both."   —*Arena*

"Despite his youth, [Loriga] has captured the attention of both Europe and America. *Tokyo* . . . confirms the astonishing maturity of his narrative skill and strengthens his reputation as one of the boldest and most original voices in modern European literature."   —*El Correa de las Letras*

"Romantic desperation and indifference, as well as happiness, brutality and lyricism . . . An elusive and shocking novel from an outstanding talent."   —*El Pais* (Spain)

"Ray Loriga has found in his direct, simple and fragmented expression a rhetorical nakedness that allows him to set off the haste and madness of our time."   —*El Cultural* (Spain)

TOKYO DOESN'T LOVE US ANYMORE

TOKYO DOESN'T LOVE US ANYMORE

RAY LORIGA

TRANSLATED FROM THE
SPANISH BY JOHN KING

GROVE PRESS
New York

First published in the UK in 2003 by Canongate Books Ltd, Edinburgh

Printed in the United States of America
Published simultaneously in Canada

Library of Congress Cataloging-in-Publication Data

Loriga, Ray, 1967–
[Tokio ya no nos quiere. English]
Tokyo doesn't love us anymore / Ray Loriga ;
translated from the Spanish by John King.
p.   cm.
ISBN 0-8021-4147-1
I. King, John, 1950–   II. Title.

PQ6662.O77T6513 2004
863'.64—dc22   2003069104

Grove Press
841 Broadway
New York, NY 10003

04 05 06 07 08   10 9 8 7 6 5 4 3 2 1

To my wife,
and to my son

CONTENTS

THE LIGHT FROM
THE SWIMMING POOL
IN THE MIDDLE OF THE DESERT

It wasn't snowing.

It really was snowing but it was pretend snow. Astrud Gilberto was singing in front of a Christmas tree and that's why there was pretend snow. And then the song finished.

Ever since the newspapers started saying that the world is going to end, songs have seemed shorter and the days longer. I called in at your house but they told me that you weren't there, they told me that you were somewhere else, in Tokyo.

She left years ago. That's what they told me. I wouldn't be surprised if it were true.

I watched *The Girl from Ipanema* on the classic movie channel. Astrud Gilberto was singing almost without moving, the artificial snow, the daiquiris, the band, the young ladies lined up next to the small stage.

Last week, at the fair, they sold two old cars. We were in Phoenix, Arizona and your mother wrote something on the window, on the windowpane and then rubbed it out before we could read it.

What do you think they're all doing now that you're not there? They share out your things amongst them, they mimic your gestures, they strip your bed.

In the hotel room there were plastic flowers, two hundred TV channels, green carpet covered with fish and all sorts of crazy designs. I was tired and my eyes were closing, and so

I slept for three or four hours and then I woke up, opened the curtains and watched the planes until dawn.

I bumped into your mother in Phoenix and she said we should take you flowers and I said no, we shouldn't. Then I went up to my hotel room. I had a bath. I slept for a while and afterwards I stayed there watching the planes.

Your mother only gambles on roulette and she swears that she wins, she swears that she wins more than she bets and she looks good for a woman who has tried her luck in five different continents and who now only gambles in Phoenix, Arizona, and writes things on windows with her finger and then rubs them out with her fist. A fine woman, your mother, and good-looking, nice tits as well, a real laugh, lively. She places her bets and wins, great, isn't it?

Let's get back to sleep darling and look at the planes.

No need for flowers.

Goodnight.

I went downstairs for the newspaper at ten in the morning but then I stayed in the bar drinking a non-alcoholic beer, a man asked after you and I told him that you were dead, that you had died, it's not true of course, but you've got to say something. Died in an accident. A car accident? No, not a car accident.

There were two identical girls in the swimming pool wearing identical yellow swimming costumes. When one of them dived into the water the other one would get out, so that there was always the same girl in and out of the water at the same time.

At twelve o'clock I lay down on my bed again but I didn't go to sleep. The room was freezing cold.

In Puerto Rico I spent three days in an even worse room, I had to open the windows to let the heat in. This room was not as cold. I also saw your mother in the casino in Puerto Rico and in one of those floating casinos in New Orleans. She didn't see me. That's right, it was in Puerto Rico, New Orleans. The Mississippi is brown. I don't know why but I thought that it would be different. What happened is that the lawyer called me up and told me that if I knew how to find you I should find you and tell you that some documents urgently need your signature. I told him that I didn't know how to find you and that, anyway, you had probably died in an accident and this last bit alarmed the lawyer and he asked, 'A car accident?' And I simply said to him, 'No, not a car accident'.

The Mississippi is brown because it drags all that earth along with it, because it's a vigorous and nervous and long and brown river. A good river, all the same. After talking to the lawyer I went down to the bar again and when I passed by the swimming pool there was absolutely no sign of the girls, so I had a daiquiri or a mojito or both and everything began to get better so quickly that I was all for going up for my swimming trunks and celebrating but then, I don't know why, I didn't do it and carried on drinking until three or four, until someone suggested that we should go to visit the Indian reservations, well, it seemed a good idea to me because I can't drive, which in a certain respect is almost a sin in this country, but I know that there's a lot to see in Arizona. So in next to no time the four of us were on the road, a chubby little Apache and his girlfriend, a chubby little Apache girl and me.

Kayenta.

Welcome to Kayenta. Thanks a lot. Are you a foreigner? Yes, I'm one hundred per cent foreign. At least when I'm here. Are you single? Widowed.

Time for lunch. There we are, having lunch and this big

dark-haired man with sideburns and braces shows up and tells me that he's Spanish and I tell him that's great and he tells me that he's descended from the family of the *Cid*, wow, I'm amazed, I'm really amazed and the man almost goes wild and I tell him that I'm genuinely surprised but that I don't doubt him and he tells me that there's no reason why I should doubt him and then his girlfriend, who's an Indian, gets out some corn tortillas and enchiladas, with chicken, marinated meat and guacamole. And my Apache friends, who don't know who the *Cid* is, wolf it all down in a second and then ask for more, and beer and then tequila and then more beer and so on until the big guy brings us the bill and I pay it all.

We go back to the car and take a drive around the town, which is a tiny town with prefabricated houses and a mall and one of those American canteens just like the ones we saw in the east before the fall of communism and which are probably called Macdonalds here.

Poverty is multi-coloured in America, like the International Pancake Shop.

We carry on bound for Fort Apache and we cross some breathtaking mountains and a breathtaking forest and even a breathtaking lake, we smoke grass and they ask me about this and that and I do the same, I mean that I ask them things as well and we reach the city, we drive past the casino, I remember your mother and I think that it would be great to meet her here, in the only Apache casino on earth and then, I don't know why, I'm convinced that she's in there and I decide that we're not going to stop. People are looking at us. The fact is that some people look at us and others don't, but I said that to cut it short and to make it clear that some of them do look at us.

The house is a bit better than the houses in Kayenta but

a dump nevertheless and the boy explains to me that the dump's a present from Social Security and I tell him that that makes it a marvellous dump and I mean it.

My Apache friends have got the biggest TV set in the world and a poster of Geronimo pinned up to the right above it and a picture of Johnny Hallyday to the left. We smoke more grass and drink beer. When the beer runs out she goes to the car and brings another case of it that must have been in the boot of the car and that's warm, but it doesn't matter, and we drink all of that as well. When there's no grass left the boy goes out and I hear him starting up the car and leaving and he comes back a bit later and while he's been out my Apache friend and I have hardly spoken.

She asked me about my wife and I told her that my wife's dead.

She became very sad so I told her that it isn't really true, that it's a joke.

She got angry and told me that it was a disgusting joke and I could only agree with her.

What can have become of that girl in Hong Kong who lived in a shop surrounded by plastic buckets and trays and baskets and washing-up bowls of every imaginable colour?

My friend the Apache doesn't know what I'm talking to him about. We're sitting smoking next to the lake. Two shots ring out. Duck hunters, my friend says. Then another Indian goes by in a boat. He smiles. We smile back.

Night falls and then it's day again. The girl has disappeared and now there's a very large dog and two kids sitting in front of the TV set. My friend says they're his brothers and that he's got another older brother who's in gaol. What's he there for? For going into a liquor store with a shotgun. He's also got a sister who's married to a Navajo. He pulls a face at the word Navajo. Apparently, Apaches and Navajos don't get on too well together. Navajos are lazy, Apaches aren't. It's just as well to know that.

When we get into Phoenix it's five or six in the afternoon.

The girl in Hong Kong, the one in the shop selling plastic trash, used to sit at the window and instead of looking at the colours inside she would look at the ones outside.

Behind the till there was a photo of a girl, even prettier, wearing a green kimono, leaning on a white balustrade on which there was a china vase with red and yellow flowers on it. Clearly, the girl in the photo and the one in the shop, sitting at the window, were the same girl.

This morning I woke up on hearing a shout, on going out into the corridor I saw a little man wearing an alpaca suit, I closed the door and went back to bed. I don't know if the man had anything to do with the shout. Above the TV there's a photo of a naked black woman, exactly the same photo that the chef from *The Shining* had in his room, the guy who crossed the country in a hellish snowstorm just so Jack Nicholson could stick an axe into his heart the moment he went in through the door.

The fact is this room and the one belonging to that man are almost identical, with walls covered with thin wooden panels and red carpet on the floor.

The TV is switched on, and there appears on it a man just like the one I've just seen in the corridor.

It's all coincidences this morning.

Incidentally, it's not true that women find me boring because yesterday I brought a woman up to my room and she couldn't stop laughing. She was about forty and wasn't pretty but she had a good body, at least with her clothes on, I didn't get to see her without them because we had drunk a lot, especially me. When she left my room she was still laughing and I heard her laughing until she got into the lift.

As a matter of fact I went to sleep with the sound of her laughter and woke up with the shout.

There were loads of people in the swimming pool and I was surprised to see just one of the identical girls.

I didn't have breakfast. I had a non-alcoholic beer and then another one with alcohol.

Yesterday they said on TV that this has been the warmest and at the same time the coldest January of the century.

Sadness has no end, happiness does.

This morning I received a message from the Company, they want me to go back to Brazil. They say that it's necessary.

Necessary has always seemed an overstated word to me.

They say that our man in Rio has disappeared. They say that they need someone there for *Carnaval*. People always do everything that they shouldn't during *Carnaval* and afterwards they need the help of chemistry in order to forget it all.

I swore never to go back to *Carnaval*.

I don't remember exactly how Marcel Camus' film *Orpheus* ended, the girl electrocuted herself and everything went red. Then Orpheus, dressed more or less like a Roman, went to the hospital and ran up the stairs and the hospital was full of victims of *Carnaval*. Wasn't it in Sao Paulo Airport that they seized my suitcase and all my merchandise all because of a mistake made by the Company? Yes, that's where it happened. They set the dogs on me with absolutely no proof, the chemical keeps an eye on things and thinks that it knows everything, but the chemical also makes mistakes and now they want me to go back, no way, to Rio. I couldn't give a toss about *Carnaval*.

So our man in Rio has headed off into what's left of the jungle with his suitcase under his arm. He's taken them for a ride, he's got enough chemical there to keep him going for a year. Then he'll turn up leading a tribe of vindictive natives like that poor wretch who stirred up half of Algeria to revolt just to end up roasted by fundamentalists on the Moroccan border. Now I remember, Orpheus found Eurydice in the morgue and carried her out in his arms singing songs to her. They then let fly with a hail of stones to his head and he fell over a cliff.

Let that be a lesson to you.

At the end the children got the sun to come out by playing their guitars.

Tucson is celebrating the diamond fair, which can't be bad. A traveller in diamonds offered to swap his case for mine and we both laughed a lot about this.

Today is Monday. I'll work the fair until Friday.

The worst thing about fairs are the whores. Whores in the lifts, whores in the corridors, whores everywhere, as well as guys going in and out of motel rooms like gusts of wind. A precious stones saleswoman invited me to have dinner with her, she was French and had a couple living in her room, a big, blond farmer and a fairly attractive Mexican woman, she had them waiting there just like I always leave the TV on. We had dinner, we drank, she bought a huge dose of memory eroder from me, we went up to her room and I ended up with the farmer, it wasn't bad, my hotel is near so at least I showered in my room. When I went past the swimming pool I thought I saw something at the bottom and I suddenly remembered a guy who drowned in the lake

on a golf course trying to recover lost balls so as to be able
to sell them at a third of their original price.

Of course there was nothing in the pool.

Tucson is full of palm trees and palm trees always put me
in a good mood.

I don't know how many diamond dealers there are in
the world but they're all here. I closed five more deals.
Mostly STM, short term memory eroder. Then I went for
a walk and went to bed. Oh yes, I also downed a bottle of
champagne.

I couldn't prevent myself from going down to the swimming pool just to make sure that there was nobody at the
bottom of it.

An urgent message from the Company. Apparently my sister
has killed herself with a shotgun. The strange thing is that
I can't recollect having a sister. At home they're wondering
if I'll attend the funeral. I'm wondering the same.

On Friday before leaving Tucson I took the test. Negative.
Despite this, as usual, I got nervous. I suppose that I'm the
kind of person who on seeing the photofit of a murderer on
TV always finds an absurd resemblance with himself. The
hotel was certainly the height of luxury. The bathroom was
pale blue and the bedroom carpet, yellow. Yes indeed, very
pretty. I think that I had already been there but there's no
way of establishing this. They tell me at the Company that
my decision to say no to the place at Rio on the eve of
Carnaval didn't go down at all well. That can't be helped.
By the way, what do you make of a Polish police car parked
outside a cemetery? I dreamt it last night and I don't know
why but it seems to me that I had already dreamt it before.

That wouldn't be unusual, the same hotel, the same
dream.

*   *   *

February in Arizona, not too cold as long as you keep a long way from the mountains during the day and far from the desert at night. Very pleasant temperatures in Phoenix and quite a lot of fuss because of the end of the American football season. People from all over the world and the strangest looking hats. Nothing to forget for the time being and so I spend the night at Sedona on the way to Flagstaff and when I get off the bus with a group of English tourists the first thing that I do is to have a really cold beer in one of those tin diners which are still left over from the fifties. Pastries and ice-creams of every imaginable colour and hicks with their gazes lost half-way between suspicion and the most complete ignorance. Short-sighted murderers like the ones we saw in the swamps of Louisiana, clinging on to the end of their rifles with the same faith as a man clinging on to a branch on the edge of a precipice. Another cold beer while the sun sets over beautiful Sedona, surrounded by red stone, deep in the red canyon, covered by a vast red cloud. In short, the pearl of the desert. A small town at the foot of a dead river filled with empty motels, because tourism doesn't pick up until the spring, when the route towards the Grand Canyon becomes the main destination in the area. There are just two cinemas in Sedona, so it doesn't take me long to choose a film. I sit down in the cinema ready to be entertained, but before a strange monster from hell destroys San Diego, I'm sleeping peacefully. Then there occur a whole lot of strange and immensely boring things like all the things that only happen in dreams, whether it's dragons on the roof or volcanoes under your bed.

When I wake up the film hasn't yet finished but, of course, I've lost track of the plot, so I leave the cinema through the emergency exit and go out into the street, which is the main street in Sedona and almost the only one because Sedona is one of those little towns bisected by a main road going somewhere else. A town one passes through cut down the middle like an orange. It's already night and there's hardly any moonlight, the rocks around the town are no longer red but black like a pile of hooded men. I cross the road over to the diner, which is the only bar that's still open. I have a beer and the waiter asks me whether the film was any good, and I tell him that it was fine, just to say something, and he says that he's fed up with monsters and that he still remembers when real people appeared in films and he also tells me that once, his wife, may she rest in peace, went on foot the whole way between Sedona and Lake Moctezuma to see him and that he was working on the building of the airport next to the lake and that many Indians and whites flogged themselves to death working on the wretched airport all for a politician in Phoenix to decide to scrap the project just a year after it was started.

Naturally I ask him how his wife died and he tells me, without getting particularly sad, that his wife died giving birth to their second daughter and that their second daughter is called Helen and that the first one is called Andrea and that without a moment's hesitation he would give his life for his daughters. On the way to Sedona along Highway 17 you can see the remains of the abandoned airport. It's at least twenty kilometres from Sedona to the disused runways.

Then, before I leave, the barman who's on the other side of the bar tells the latest customer:

We've had two dreadful years.

The other man, who's wearing a fishing cap, with hooks stuck around it on a tape, and who's old enough to be my father, doesn't reply. He just looks down as if confirming that indeed they've been terrible days.

The English tourists have checked into the Gran Sedona

Hotel on the way out of the town, which is where groups always stay because it's cheaper and because at dawn the view of the red hills is magnificent. I'm staying in the bungalows in the valley, where the golfers stay, or those who already know the view. The bungalows are a lot better, not just the food and service, also the pay-per-view channels on the TV and of course the fake fireplaces. Flames that go up and down behind the glass by just pressing a button on the remote control. All the little houses give the impression of being adobe huts but once inside you have to be careful not to fall into the huge jacuzzi. One miniature of whisky and off to bed. On TV I saw a man crying at the trial of his daughter's murderer. The man was saying something about the girl, had mentioned her name, Molly, six or seven times but when he reached a particular word he couldn't go on. The District Attorney asked him if anything was missing from the girl's room. The man replied that at first they didn't notice anything but that afterwards, checking through the girl's toys and clothes, they hadn't been able to find her . . . that's when he couldn't go on and he began to cry and he cried so much that the judge had to suspend the hearing for a time.

Of course I fall asleep thinking about what it could be that the poor man wasn't able to say and why they didn't find it.

When I wake up I'm still thinking about the same thing.

How are things in Flagstaff?

The question couldn't be more innocent but despite everything I don't reply because I don't like to talk to strangers unless there's money at stake. So the good lady who, apart from anything else, is a delightful old Indian, looks away while I get off the bus and starts to brush the hair of a little girl who's undoubtedly her granddaughter and who's sitting peacefully playing with one of those little handheld computer games. And here I am in Hollbrook looking at the River Colorado from the bridge, next to the bus station, despite the fact that I ought to be in Winslow, thirty miles to the east, probably because I've gone to sleep on the bus or because these towns in the desert are all the same. Incidentally, things aren't great in Flagstaff. A quick deal with a couple of Coconino Indians and a surprise meeting with one of the Company's operations controllers who reminded me that the good folk in administration are worried by what they term 'dead zones' in my diary and by the inconsistency of the explanations that I've given. Arizona is a very big state. That's what I said to him and he replied that of course they understand but that they don't have more people available at present and that what's more the two things are totally unconnected. That might certainly be true. Despite their suspicions, I tested negative and all the records of chemical and sales were fine, so that in the end the situation calmed down a bit. Be positive and persevere. These were his final words, as he got into a Japanese car with darkened windows at the door to my hotel. Afterwards I took the bus towards Winslow Airport but I carried straight on and ended up in Holbrook, once more in Apache territory, near the petrified wood, far from home. The Company is concerned by unwarranted absences, the temporary disappearance of agents on duty who reappear within a short time and continue to carry on their assignments as if nothing had happened. The Company ought to know, by this stage, that with chemicals like this in one's possession everything tends to be more or less unjustified, and that oblivion is, however fiercely they resist the idea, an inevitable part of this job, just like wrist injuries in the career of a professional tennis player or the smell of smoke in the life of a fireman. Back to Winslow anyway since I've still got six hours before I take my flight, naturally there isn't another bus until that night so I spend the afternoon fucking an Indian girl in the Sahara Inn. In fact she's half Apache and half Mexican and we don't fuck all afternoon. We do it for less than twenty minutes and I spend the rest of the time looking at the swimming pool.

On the plane a woman tried to make a purchase but I reminded her that it's forbidden to deal in things other than those belonging to the airline. She took exception to this. She says that in planes everything is adulterated, not just chemical, but also films, alcohol and sandwiches. She's probably right. By the way, am I the only person who realises that planes are flying lower and lower? I almost manage to read the number plate on a red convertible that was crossing the Mexican border.

Naturally on reaching Tijuana I saw your mother on the back of a pick-up truck surrounded by Mexican labourers, all of them drunk, all singing, all happy. If she saw me she pretended not to have noticed. It seems that the good woman is still making a living.

Tijuana stretches out into the desert like a stain of oil on an ice rink.

A huge commercial success. There are a group of Germans here who are making a fortune building hotels. All very solid and serious, very Bauhaus. So, gentlemen, you have to forget. Each needs to forget his own problems, as usual. Franz wanted to forget a love affair and Otto wanted to forget a promise made without thinking. Germans are extremely bad at keeping secrets, they tell everything, whatever it is, after three beers. Poor Otto, staring at his shoes. What's more, ridiculous shoes. Red and white, like golf shoes, but without spikes. Otto should first of all forget all about those shoes. They're worried and want to know if it's reliable stuff and I tell them that it's the only reliable stuff. They ask this because apparently a friend of a friend in Old Europe forgot the name of his dog while he was trying to forget a tune that had got stuck in his head and which he couldn't stop humming for a single moment. I agree that's very funny but don't worry about it, it's is as sure as killing a canary with a baseball bat. So a few more beers and the ten Germans disappear into the Tijuana night ready to carry on dancing and forgetting and tomorrow, needless to say, more hotels.

Congratulations from the Company for an amazing deal, amazingly quick and amazingly clean. A bonus and your name, my name, is already being mentioned for something greater, as co-ordinator, supplies controller, the sky's the limit. However, you can't forget my dossier. According to my dossier the doors to the most beautiful offices are closed to me, because the Company never, and that means never, forgets. This is something that is particularly curious, when one considers that erasing memories is precisely the business we're in. Be that as it may and for the time being, congratulations, bonuses and good night.

I dream I'm playing poker. I've never played poker, so of course I lose. Your mother manages to get a basketball into the roulette and at the same time she gets all the right numbers.

I wake up thinking about a jacket, not dreaming about it but thinking about it, a blue woollen jacket, hanging from a gold hook in a wooden hut and on the adjacent hook a tie with a pattern of red, yellow and green diamond shapes, very small diamond shapes and some of those rubber straps with hooks that are used to tie down things on car roof-racks. I don't think that either the jacket or the tie belong to me. It's probably just a photograph. I've never had a tie. At least I can't picture myself with one.

It's four in the morning.

Poor Otto. Some shoes!

The sun rises and so I'm out for a walk to buy something and I buy myself a metallic blue shirt. Don't wrap it up, I'll wear it, I put my old t-shirt in a paper bag and only when I'm taking it off do I realise that it's got something written on it and what is written is: THINK ABOUT ME, and underneath it there's a photograph of a beach although there's no-one on the beach. It's so senseless that for an instant I think it must be true that it's the devil who throws the dice and then of course no sooner than I get out of the shop I put the bag with the t-shirt in a dustbin and swear never to put anything on without reading it first.

I eat some ranchero-style eggs and I regret it at once and I order a coffee but I don't drink it and I ask for a beer and naturally the waiter brings me a Mexican beer. I leave it next to the coffee and this time I ask for a German beer. Everything's fine. I drink it slowly and outside there's a terrific wind blowing from god knows where and a man passes in front of the window holding his hat on with both hands and a woman clinging onto a child who really looks as though he's going to fly off. On the other side of the road there's a girl watching how all and sundry are taking off, with a serious expression, as if the wind was nothing to do with her. I also drink down the Mexican beer, that's already warm.

I've been there less than half an hour and I'm already dancing with a mulatta woman in one of those dark dives where women dance very close to you and rub themselves up against you and you pay again each time a new song starts up.

A very nice short and chubby mulatta woman called Maria tells me to go with her to the private room and I refuse because I've got the feeling that I've been there before, not in that exact same place but in a very similar place or perhaps it was there after all. Maria is insistent but I prefer to carry on dancing despite my feeling and immediately verifying that I'm an atrocious dancer. In order to persuade me, Maria promises not to break my heart and faced with that offer I have no alternative but to go upstairs with her and while I'm going up I wave goodbye to those who are down below and I realise that I'm drunk and I also realise that I'm wearing a marvellous blue shirt that I don't remember having bought.

'What are we talking about then?'

When I wake up I see poor Otto with his hideous shoes sitting on a chair at the end of the bed and of course Maria is no longer there and I have the impression that Otto has been talking to himself for some considerable time.

'We're talking about strange people who have never wanted us to be here anyway and we're talking about men who are far, very far from home and on this point you can only be in agreement with me since you're also a son of Old Europe.'

I can only agree with him as to that point even if his Europe and mine are probably different Europes. Let me sit up, friend Otto, and then please let me get dressed, since our brief commercial transaction has not prepared either of us for such intimacy. Having said that I put my trousers on and my wonderful shirt and my boots and one second after doing it I feel that I'm a wretch for having had doubts about poor Maria.

'And if you help me I'll be able to return home and be the same man as I was before being what I am now.'

Good old Otto is now standing next to the door and as I watch him I can't say what he is now but I fear that we're dealing with something even worse than what he was before, so that I begin to put two and two together and while I follow him along the corridor to another of the little private rooms I have the suspicion that, what's more, the certainty that what I'm going to find on the other side of the door is a poor Mexican girl dead.

I'm sure that it was something like this that got me out of Rio. How sadly the wind blows in the distant land of the foreigner. Poor Otto. A sober German architect and a crazy Sunday killer. That's the way things are. Don't cry, my friend. Be brave. Let's not lose our nerve. There springs into my mind, without it having the slightest possible connection with this case, the image of a very handsome, well-built Cuban boy, making a V for victory sign with his fingers. But to return to Otto. Somehow or other, things will return to normal. Courage. Some small and forgotten scenes, like the one involving the Cuban boy, now appear to me.

Or something written on the wall next to the lavatory door: DEAD CHICKENS' HEADS.

Other scenes on the other hand never return to me.

Getting back to the matter in hand, it must be made clear that in desperate situations benefits, as is natural, multiply. A fine man like Otto cannot go back to Munich with something like that in his head and we're no longer talking about partying with his colleagues or about a special lady friend who is left behind in Tijuana waiting for letters that never arrive, we're talkng about blood on the carpet and not allowing the children to see the shadow of the monster in daddy Otto's far away look. The price of forgetting the horror is a very high price, sufficiently high to cheer up both the Company and the agent, and here enter into play what the Company calls invisible bonuses. That's why Otto follows me to the hotel and waits very calmly while I go up to my room and then come down. After a more than satisfactory deal Otto takes away with him enough chemical to forget the last three weeks. Naturally, when he comes out of the bathroom he doesn't even know me and naturally he doesn't even greet me.

Off goes Otto, ever so happy.

Goodbye to you.

I go out into the garden and sit down next to the swimming pool and it's so late that there's nobody left there.

A quick dip in the early hours. The pool's still empty and the water's freezing. An old acquaintance, whom I've forgotten all about of course, insists on joining me for breakfast. I can't see why he should but I don't manage to put him off. He speaks to me about things that seem vaguely familiar to me, things in fact that would seem vaguely familiar to anyone. Isn't it disgusting the way in which people jump out of the past and sit down at your table and have breakfast at your side, as if the fact of having exchanged a few words with you in a bar two thousand years ago gave them some right? Isn't that trust that people show towards the past ridiculous, as if the past were any more certain than the present or the future? While I'm drinking an orange juice, he comes and goes, pouncing upon the hotel buffet, filling plates with absurd things like beetroot salads and crab savouries. He says that he's pleased to see me, but it's obvious that he doesn't mean what he says. People speak without thinking, especially when they're eating. He tells me that he's here on business. He's not so stupid as not to realise that I've no idea who he is, but he's not prepared to humiliate himself by repeating his name. Some people believe that you should protect your name and face as if they were treasures. The man takes his leave but, before going he grabs the end of a croissant from amongst the debris of his breakfast and asks me for news of you. Naturally I tell him that you're dead and he doesn't dare ask anything else. He leaves the piece of croissant on the table, as a sign of respect I suppose, and goes off with that look on his face that people assume who think that death, or the mere mention of death, at once make us a bit more important. In any case, this encounter has a depressing effect upon me so that when I get back to my room, I take a bottle of champagne out of the minibar and take a couple of white lights, happy amphetamine derivatives, as smooth as a stroll through the park once you get over a slight initial tension. There's an e-mail from the Company, with a new list of sales. There's at least one difficulty concerning LTM, long-term memory eroder, something for which I'm not prepared. The orders I place can spend a week knocking around the processing centre so that I send a message back by return straight to the heart of the monster, distribution and supplies. It seems that they've been changing personnel and that not everyone yet knows what their job's about. They apologise for this, of course, and promise to deliver the merchandise to me as soon as possible, which won't be before tomorrow at the soonest.

The sheets are blue, horizontal blue stripes on white, while in contrast the pillow is orange. Outside there is just a small palm tree against a yellow wall on which AIR, WATER is written. There must have been something else there but the rest of the letters have fallen off. Naturally there's a woman in my bed and I can't remember her name. She's wearing a t-shirt like the ones that students put on to sleep but she's not a student, she's at least fifty. The body of a fifty-year-old woman takes its own decisions, behind each movement there's a print, a line on the skin or a mark. Her body has its own memory. Fortunately this particular woman's body takes all the right decisions. On her t-shirt there's printed the photo of a dead Mexican female singer. Under the photo is her date of birth and also the date of her death. A Mexican singer dead by the time she was twenty-eight. May god have mercy on her soul.

On the TV there's a man crying next to a collapsed building. When I come out of the shower the woman has already gone.

On the TV there's a preacher talking in an empty church. One of those one-man sects which are so fashionable on the West Coast. For some reason that escapes me, people living near the beach need to renew their faith more often than people living inland. Next to the bed there is a closed bible and an open bottle of wine. The owner of the one-man sect says: Nothing of what I may say can help you.

I check through the bill for the room on the TV screen and I come across an alarming number of phone-calls abroad. I don't recognise the numbers. Some people fuck others so that they can make free phone-calls. Fortunately, the Company pays for calls without asking any questions. I dialled one of the numbers and there was no reply. Then I dialled another one and a child who was half-asleep answered. I don't know what time it is in Buenos Aires. I told the boy to go back to sleep but it seems the boy's no longer sleepy. He tells me that his dad is going to take him to the football today, to watch Boca Juniors play in the Bombonera, no less, and that it's his first visit to the stadium and that he's so nervous that he's hardly slept all night and that there's nobody in the house at present and that his dog is ill and that he'd speak a lot longer with me if he had time, but that he's still got lots of things to do like watering the lawn and writing an e-mail to a friend who's on holiday in Rosario. Before hanging up I asked him his mother's name and he told me that she's called Vinn Lee.

It seems strange that people who hardly matter to you should mean such a lot for other people, like the name of a winning horse in the hands of another punter, at the end of a race.

There's a small quantity of cocaine on the table and a couple of phials of GPP. I snorted the coke and put the phials away in my suitcase. I got a beer out of the minibar. Then I checked through the messages from the Company. A heap of orders, almost all from Tucson, and a circular about the latest advances of our brilliant chemists. The efficiency of the new downers has been tested successfully amongst blind groups of volunteers. By the end of the year they promise to have overcome the resistance of even the most wayward neurotransmitter. Nothing that you want to remember will be erased. The same old promise. In the meantime we'll carry on burning the haystack to find the needle. They don't tell us that, of course, but it's something that any burnt-out agent knows. With the same certainty with which a dentist knows that everything that isn't going to hurt ends up hurting.

While I have little cookies for breakfast, an immigration patrol helicopter lands in the car park of a 7–11 and three agents in cheap suits start loading the Mexicans on board. I show my ID to one of the agents and then order an orange juice. As I noticed that the man was staring at my cookies I offered him one and he took it while looking around him as if he was accepting a bribe. Then he told me: We've painted a real thick line over there but these people just don't seem to see it. I've deported some of these ones twice in the same day.

When my orange juice arrived the helicopter was already airborne. The Mexicans are pressed against the windows like a crowd of kids with their noses pressed against the window of an empty toy shop.

At three-thirty I closed a deal with the owner of a Japanese car dealership. He's got a leg made of graphite and wants to forget that before he had a healthy one there instead. It's much better if you don't know what you've lost. That's what he told me. He showed me a photo of his wife although of course I hadn't asked to see it. People have got this annoying habit of showing you their things with the same stupid glee with which conjurors pull from their hats rabbits that no-one wants to see. My friend also told me that he lost his leg in a car crash, not in one of his cars of course, you can't even mislay a telephone number in one of these cars. They're perfect machines. I felt obliged to tell him that I can't drive, so that the man would stop making such an effort. A salesman is always a salesman and a salesman without a leg is still a whole salesman. Forgive me but it's in the blood. He said this without much conviction because we both know that whatever it is that's in blood there can't be any of that in it. Then he told me that he buried his leg after suffering rejection following an attempt to graft it back on. He can't understand how you can reject a leg that belongs to you. Well, anyway, he buried his leg and he also wants to forget where it's buried. You can't imagine how stupid you feel burying a leg.

I don't know anything about it naturally, but I can just imagine.

*   *   *

In a French café, in what would be the centre of Tucson if
Tucson had a centre, an Afro-American woman of about
thirty asks me if I want to get it on with her. The café
is not really French, I mean that there's nothing French
except for the name of some dishes on the menu and a
neon Eiffel Tower on the outside. We had a beer before
leaving. The café's surrounded by a huge golf course filled
with old people and an army of Mexican caddies loaded
down with those ridiculous bags filled with clubs. There are
two or three million old people in Arizona, they come here
from all the states in the union attracted by the climate and
the marvellous availability of organs for transplant and false
teeth on the other side of the Mexican border. The woman's
not nervous, when all's said and done fucking strangers is
what everyone is doing these days. Before we go out the
woman asks me if I mind if she brings a friend along.
There immediately appears an Arab dressed in overalls. I
don't know if I fancy doing it with a guy wearing overalls
like that and I tell my friend that I don't fancy doing it with
a guy wearing overalls and she says that he's just going to
watch. My friend also tells me that the guy gives her a
hundred and fifty dollars if she lets him watch her fuck a
white man. The guy works in a tyre factory in the outskirts
of Tucson. He's just a production line worker, to judge by
his appearance, a hundred and fifty dollars must be a whole
lot of money for him. A whole lot of tyres.

When we go out into the car park, behind the café, I'm
sincerely delighted when I realise that I've got a hard-on. My
friend leads the way, looking for a secluded place between
the parked trucks, with me following her and the Arab
bringing up the rear. None of us say a word. As if we
were going to disinter dead cats. My friend's got a great
arse and beautiful tits. Speaking personally I have to admit

that at such moments, fucking strangers, you always wished you had a bigger cock. For the same reason for which on arriving at a party you're always sorry that you hadn't bought a better present. As soon as we reached the back of the car park, between an ice-cream van and one of those MPVs which are so popular even if nobody has enough children to fill them, right there, the girl kneels down on the ground, takes my cock out and starts to suck it with that enthusiasm which can only be produced by girls who are not particularly attractive. The Arab watches very excitedly and as I notice that he's right up against my arse, I tell him to go around the other side. My friend leans onto the MPV and after a few manoeuvres I manage to get it into her from behind. Naturally the Arab has already undone the front of his overalls and has a fine black thing in his hand. While the guy jerks off, on the other side of the car park fence two little old men appear with their golf clubs and their caps and those ridiculous trousers that seem essential if you're going to push the little ball as far as the hole effectively. Naturally my friend thinks about giving up but since the Arab says that if we stop now there'll be no money, we decide to carry on, so I carry on giving it to her while the golfers get out their none too erect cocks and begin to work up an erection with determination and patience. In next to no time the two old men have become three and shortly afterwards seven. My friend starts to get angry and the Arab blames the racket being made by the old men who are preventing him from concentrating it seems. As he sees that I'm losing heart, the Arab offers me another fifty dollars, to which one of the old men, who's about to come, adds a further twenty. In the end we all come. Not all of us, obviously. The Arab, three or four of the old men and a Mexican caddy come. The woman quite naturally doesn't come and nor do I of course. Of the two hundred and twenty dollars, I get fifty, although the fact is that you don't do these things for money. The Arab fastens his overalls. The old men pick up their golf clubs and the woman puts on lipstick using the wing mirror of the ice-cream van. Before he leaves the Mexican caddy give me a cigarette.

I smoke it thinking about the old days before the virus and how things have changed.

When I finish my cigarette there is nobody left in the car park.

For someone who can't even drive, a car park is a very sad place.

A Belgian salesman is found dead in his hotel room, his veins open over a road map of Arizona, naturally no note, no sign, no message. The TV is on, the bed turned down, a sample book of plastic fabrics used in the manufacture of heavy duty overcoats like the ones used in abattoirs, nothing else.

I get up contentedly, ready to work, I look through the newspapers, I take a shower, I get dressed and before going out I see the news on the TV about the dead Belgian salesman. The police think that it's a suicide. In fact they were sure about this. The police know that people commit suicide in hotel bedrooms. First there's a shot of the room, but the dead man is no longer there, just the map and the blood can be seen, then there's a shot of the outside of the hotel and I realise that it's the building on the other side of the street. I look out from my window and see the police cars and the press around the main door. There are a dozen onlookers gathered around the swimming pool.

In the afternoon I close a deal with a couple in one of the housing developments with bungalows next to Highway

16. The road linking Tucson with San Diego. The woman is blonde and shy and the man is dark and a bit more sure of himself, even so you can tell that they've never bought chemical before and they don't really know the effect that it can have and it turns out that they're both afraid of forgetting their children's names because their children are at a summer camp and are only seven and twelve years old and one is a slim boy and the other is a shy girl like her mother and they love them both a lot and they naturally want to be capable of recognising them when they get back home.

There's nothing to worry about, so I tell them that there's nothing to worry about and they both settle back into their armchairs, relieved, and then they offer me a beer that I accept and I have a swig looking out of the corner of my eye at the bungalow, trying to figure out what the hell has got into this couple this summer to make them need to forget before the kids return from their camp and things get back to normal.

Once I've concluded the deal, the man walks back with me to the little garden gate and the woman stays at the window looking out but without looking at either her husband or me, without looking at either the lawn nor the small inflatable pool, looking at the road opposite the house along which no-one is coming at present, thank god.

As I get into my taxi the man says:

Don't you go jumping to any conclusions.

Then he turns and looks at his wife in the window as if he feared that he had already said too much.

Let me tell you how I see things. At night Phoenix is a world apart. The Cuban transvestites throng the area around the zoo to the north of Tempe Park. Tall women drugged up to the eyeballs on horse tranquillizers, as attractive as film actresses after a car crash, who'll give you a blow job next to a bear cage for the price of a hamburger. They wear synthetic fur coats over their naked bodies and keep the local boys away by throwing things. The local boys fight among themselves to do it free of charge in cars while their mothers and sisters fuck tourists on the other side of Salt River, in the motels of Broadway. Amphetamines of all colours as you go down Central Avenue, black flames from back street Indian laboratories driving the football fans wild, mounted police, police on foot, police patrolling in the sky, lighting up the streets with the blue light of their helicopters, the undercarriage of planes scraping the communications tower, Japanese karaoke bars filled with armed Colombians, churches filled with drunken preachers and violent followers and, of course, a whole lot of peaceful people sleeping in their white houses in Paradise Valley.

A trouble-free sale near the airport and I'm in Tempe looking for something clean to help down two phials of LTC that have had a hold on me since yesterday like someone at the bottom of some stairs with the last two steps missing, stairs incapable of touching the floor. I drink a beer in a Mexican taco restaurant. On TV there's a man looking at a flaming cross. Out in the street there's a rent boy with a red silk jacket with a dragon embroidered on the back. That's the way I see it. If I can leave all of this some day, the sales, the chemical, the amphetamines and morphine, the childish stimulants, the random fuck, the noise of helicopters, if some day I manage to leave all this behind and get together a small family in one of those white houses in the valley or far from here, in Old Europe or wherever; if some day I manage it, it'll probably be already too late, because there's something inside me that drags itself out, like the hand of a man sleeping in a boat that slips down until it touches the water.

I buy a handful of pills from a Mexican wearing a suit and tie who sells bibles from a street stall. Then I take a taxi to the hospital and pick up a bag of euphoria downers and anti-depressants. The security guards go down to the car park every night to raise a bit extra to bring their wages up. Night sales are made more exciting by the ambulance sirens.

There are so many people in the street that it seems like a holiday, but it isn't one. Anyway, holidays and bombs come to mean the same in a foreign country, that's to say, nothing.

We stop for a moment in a supermarket that's open all night but once inside I decide not to buy anything. I just stand still between the rows of packets of food before going back to the taxi. Some things frighten me like memories but I can't tell what's on the other side. I experience the fear of someone who receives an empty envelope or a phone call in the middle of the night from someone who doesn't say anything at the other end.

Back at the Holiday Inn I check my e-mails, I fill in my latest company reports and place a couple of orders with head office. Wonderful reports, great sales, congratulations. Naturally I ask how long it will be before another agent comes to cover the Mexican border. They promise an immediate reply. This is too big a state to have to go all the way down to Nogales every other day. Apparently, the guy they had working in the north of Mexico turned up dead in the Sonora Desert. They say that memory vigilantes cut his throat but there's no way of establishing this. People love those stories but nobody has yet been able to prove that that gang of fanatics is more dangerous than members of the convention of abducted ones.

The abducted ones meet in Phoenix once a year to exchange details about their experiences on board extra-terrestrial spaceships. What they call 'first intelligence'.

I take a small bottle of champagne out of the minibar and sit down on the balcony to watch the planes.

On nights like this you always wonder how much you've forgotten and how much of all this you're going to remember in the future. Afterwards the antidepressants block all those cursed neurotransmitters and you don't wonder about anything at all any more.

I've always been ill, says the man sitting next to the window, and on the other side of the window there are other ill people going past in wheelchairs or walking slowly with or without the help of sticks.

I can't remember the names of the illnesses, but I remember the pain. Like someone who has lost his house and still has the key.

The man is an old insurance salesman. The home is full of old people and nurses but in all other respects it seems like a cheerful luxury hotel. There's a huge number of sanatoriums like this around Tucson. The climate is pleasant all year round and old people are more concerned about climate than the rest of us.

'I wouldn't be here if I didn't have a good insurance. This place costs a fortune.'

The man isn't rich. What he has ordered is just enough for him to forget a bad dream. Of course I don't usually handle such small orders but the old man was recommended by the Company and besides I was in the area and anyway there is something in hospitals that always cheers up my day. It must be the silence and the cleanness. You can think in a sanitorium. That is if you have to think about something.

'People become attached to their illnesses,' says the old insurance salesman, who has a trolley with an oxygen bottle by his side.

Behind him, beyond the sick people, is the swimming pool.

'It's closed. When they built this it was going to be a hotel, but it was too far from the city, so they decided to convert it into a sanatorium. Someone has decided that we don't need a swimming pool.'

'Everyone needs a swimming pool.'

'That's what I think, but they don't seem to agree.'

Then the man is silent for quite a time. We are sitting facing each other. Between us there is a low glass-topped table with two green cocktails on it. He asked for them, although he has hardly touched his. I, on the other hand, have drunk all of mine.

'This is an easy life,' says the man in the end.

Pain is a full-time occupation, you can give yourself over to it without feeling at all guilty. That's all that you've got to do. Pursue the pain that travels along the nerves to the brain. Isolate it there and keep a watch out for any movement. Pursue the effects of the tranquillizers as well, like the rain. See what it carries off in its path and what remains.

In his room my friend has a dozen monitors. On all the monitors there are horses, horse races. Hundreds of horses running around his bed. On the desk, a small computer and a bottle of tequila.

'From here I control the bets, all these old people love losing money. I work with old people in Sun City and also with the Snowbirds of Quartzsite.'

I sit down on the bed and watch the horses. Quartzsite and Sun City are the two largest old peoples' communities in the country. The Snowbirds are an organized group of old people who live in caravans and spend every winter in the desert next to the State of California.

'Don't get involved in all that boy, when you don't bet all horses look the same.'

While saying this he goes over to the drawer of his bedside table and takes out a handful of pills.

'Instant sunshine. Antidepressants. The best of the new ones. Take as many as you want. They're not like the cheap and cheerful ones that the secretaries in California take. With these ones you can stay in the bath when the water has gone and god knows there's nothing sadder than that.'

I take two of them and keep the rest.

Naturally we drink a couple of tequilas. The old man tells me something about a woman who died many years ago. He talks about her as if she were still somewhere, at the end of a very long rope, as if he could feel every little movement at the end of the rope. As if you had gone right into a cave and the other person were waiting outside.

It's already night. I should have left ages ago but I'm still sitting on the bed. The old man's in the bathroom, so I'm alone surrounded by horses. For some reason, when you sit in an armchair in an office, on the other side of the desk, or in the seat of a bus driver, or when you simply try on a policeman's cap or hold a butcher's knife, you feel for a second as if you were that person, as if you could be that other person for a whole lifetime. That's how I feel, sitting on the bed, thinking what kind of life this is. When the old man comes out of the bathroom, the bed, the room, everything round about, becomes his once again.

'They've put me on one of those procaine treatments. They say that the memory of pain causes traumas in the body. They inject you all over with those phials of procaine in an attempt to release the demons from you. They inject you in each of your scars, in all of the blemishes, it is presumed that your skin is also capable of losing its memory.'

We drink another couple of tequilas while a horse called Castro beats the favourite by a head at the Santa Monica race course. At sixty to one.

'Shit, I hate surprises. There's always one or other of those old men who bets on sure losers. Some people are capable of betting on a horse with three legs.'

Afterwards the retired insurance salesman shows me to the front door of the home, a black metal gate with lances and shields, worthy of an old film star. As I get into the taxi the man waves goodbye.

'How's your old man?' asks the taxi driver. Presuming that the man was my father.

Better, much better.

The instant sunshine begins to take effect, the saddest letters never reach their destination. That's how antidepressants work. Absentminded postmen who forget to deliver bad news. The neurones turn into little houses surrounded by fences with green gardens and untouched mailboxes.

We get onto Highway 10 and join the Sunday traffic tailback with absolute obedience. Of course I'm in no hurry. In front of the San Javier Reservation there is an upturned lorry. On the ground, at the feet of a huge neon sign with horns advertising the Best Western chain, there's a man covered with a blanket. The wind stirs the blanket. I see the dead man's hand appear and disappear a dozen times.

When the taxi-driver looks in his rear-view mirror all he sees is a satisfied man, the possessor of a perfect smile.

Your mother says that I'm good at this business. She also says that nobody knows for certain where you've got to. You might be in Tokyo but equally you might not be. Your mother always wins, however amazing that might seem to you. She knows something about roulette that others don't.

Incidentally, for the last few days there's been no business and an urgent message by mail from the Company. Suspicion about what they call clear, that is blank days, with no communications, nothing recorded, absolutely nothing. Days that slip away from me like maggots from inside a shoebox filled with holes.

I spend the afternoon drinking mescal. Everything's dark outside, although not the whole time. From time to time, the flash lights of UFO hunters light up the desert.

'How's your wife?'

'I haven't got a wife.'

'Of course you've got one. Or at least you had one. A lovely girl. Wasn't it in Phoenix where you were dancing around the swimming pool, at that party, at the house of a Mexican film producer?'

'I don't dance.'

'Well, she certainly danced. She danced barefoot around the pool. There were naked people everywhere. We were high on amphetamines and TT and French wine. There was also a mariachi and even a tiger strolling amongst the people like a shy guest. You don't forget a party like that.'

'She's dead.'

'Dead?'

'Yes, dead. She doesn't dance any more. She doesn't do anything any more. She's dead.'

'My God! She was a wonderful girl.'

'Yes. That's what they say.'

'Dead. God, can you fucking believe it?'

'Yes, it's fucking hard to believe it but you can't do anything else.'

'The lord always carries off the best.'

'That's what they say. Now, if you don't mind, I've got to leave Phoenix before the offices close, afterwards the traffic gets impossible.'

'Forgive me. I just couldn't imagine, I mean, how could I have thought . . . ? You must have had a dreadful time.'

'Yes a dreadful time, a really dreadful time, but that's the way things go. She's in heaven now and as you know people don't come back from there. Anyway, if you can pay up, I'll be able to leave Phoenix and begin to think about something else.'

My client who is, in all other respects, a very well-mannered business man, hands me an envelope with the money and says goodbye six or seven times while I'm waiting for a car at the door of his office.

When we finally reach Highway 17, it's already too late. There's a long line of stationary cars returning to their little houses in the outskirts after a hard day's work. We're all tired. Some know why and others of us are incapable of remembering.

Bad news from the state penitentiary. Nothing new, in any case.

In the state penitentiary, at six o'clock, they tie a guy to a bed looking incongruously like a cross and they administer six lethal injections to him. Enough poison to kill a man six times over. Naturally ice-creams, flowers, packets of cereals, children, mothers, cars on the freeway, parabolic dishes, good mornings, good nights, breakdowns, fridges, embraces and fines, everything, absolutely everything else carries on just the same as ever. Everything has the same shape and someone sits down to wait at the door of a multiplex cinema and then much later he gets up angrily because the person he was waiting for hasn't shown up.

As strange as it may seem, there are people who are completely incapable of going into the cinema alone.

I reach Winslow at six o'clock and have a beer in a smart Spanish saloon. A restaurant furnished with those sturdy turned chairs that one finds in steakhouses in Segovia. All the waiters are Mexican.

Afterwards I go out for a walk. It's not yet dark but all the streetlights are already on. They say that in the early days of the electric chair, the lights of the city use to flicker for a second during executions. It seems right, even if it were just for a moment that everybody was forced to think about what was going on inside.

It's not the first time that I've done business near the gaol, I also think that on some occasion I've done business inside it although of course there's no way of being sure about this.

Today they've killed a vacuum cleaner salesman who raped and strangled three women. He took photographs of the whole affair with a digital camera and then made them available through the internet to half the world. The operation turned out to be a success, at least half a million people accessed his web page. The state prosecutor aims to prosecute each and every one of them as accomplices in the murder.

It's really nice to watch dusk falling over the red Arizona desert.

At seven o'clock on the dot I have an appointment with a small, nervous guy, who turns out to be one of the official state witnesses. One of those attornies who is paid to attend executions and to record carefully who says what, how some look at the floor and others, in contrast, look at the dead man's eyes and how some cry, while others applaud with satisfaction. On arriving, I saw from the taxi more than a hundred people waiting in the park. There is a backlog of

executions. The number of appeals has been reduced by a
half in Arizona and even less. The machine can't keep up
with it.

The man, my client, has witnessed ninety-three executions.
He doesn't want to keep them forever because he's frightened
that so much misfortune might end up by driving him crazy,
so that while the sun is setting over Winslow Penitentiary, my
friend shakes off the memory with the marvellous chemical,
which is equally unaware of the living as it is of the dead.

'How did it go today?'

'Fine, just like it normally does actually, because they're
frying so many people that it's all become monotonous,
the protest groups, the victims' relatives, the attornies, the
media, it's all the same now. Death is our business.'

So my friend wants to forget all about it, because it's nearly
the weekend and death is affecting his sleep and, of course his
sex life is no longer what it was and, after death row, sex is
the only pastime in the district. More coupling goes on here
than in the rest of the state. Naturally chemical is strictly
prohibited from death row. They don't want a murderer
sitting in a cell with his head empty. It wouldn't be right
for him. It wouldn't be right for his victims. Crimes must
be remembered.

'You have to forget everything,' says my friend, who has
ordered a milkshake big enough to hide the body of a dog in.
'Everyday. The days before and the days after. Five o'clock
and seven o'clock, all hours, but especially six o'clock.'

Why always at six o'clock?

'I don't know. I suppose that everything has got to have
an order.'

First he finishes his milkshake. Then we have a beer. It's
already dark. In the park the trees sway and the people
mill about. Some leave and others have only just arrived.

Some carry bibles, others placards written by hand with the handwriting of a halfwit. One of the placards says:

HURT THEM.

The Promise Keepers sing songs. The Promise Keepers aren't fanatics, they're whites who believe. They hold aloft crosses and flags. They hold children in their arms. They're smiling. They're ready. Nobody knows for exactly what. Their feet are fixed in tradition, their eyes on the future.

The song of the Promise Keepers also says:

IT'S NOT REVENGE, IT'S JUSTICE.

We drink beer and eat cakes. My slim friend is getting impatient. His wife is called Sonia. His wife is Mexican. His wife is waiting for him at home with dinner prepared. So I hand over to him what he wants and I collect my money.

'Anyway, they don't need me any more. They've been broadcasting executions on TV for two years now. They have thirty million witnesses.'

My friend is completely right about that. Yet he carries on looking at me.

'It's an honest job and well paid. We've got two children.'

'Congratulations. And now if you don't mind I'm in a hurry, my bus is leaving in under an hour.'

We stand up at the same time. He hasn't told me the names of his children and quite honestly I'm delighted because I couldn't care less about the names of people's children.

While I'm waiting for a taxi a group of protesters passes by. ENEMIES OF DEATH. That's what they've got on their t-shirts.

The gaol is lit up, like a football stadium. Helicopters are going up and down and making passes over the area. The TV crews finish packing up their equipment and leave. When their lights are turned off, once again you can see the light of the candles. The noise of the rotor blades still masks the muttering of the people who are praying.

An hour later I get onto the bus on my way to the desert. It's after eight o'clock. Most certainly my friend will have already sat down to have dinner, as happy as a shoe salesman.

As I pass through the reservations the Indian children wave at me.

Three hours to Tucson. A plane flies over the bus and lands on the sand. On Fridays the airport gets congested and the planes land where they can. Of course they wake up the Indians and the coyotes.

The wonderful world of foot fetishists turns out to be even more fabulous than you can imagine, and while I suck both big toes at once of a smiling Colombian girl who can't have had more than thirteen candles on her cake at her last birthday, I can't stop wondering what kind of person would arrange to meet you in a place like this and what kind of memories such a person is trying to erase. In any case, if this strange job has taught me something, it is that you shouldn't go around judging other people's motives if you don't want to end up caught in the same traps. What's more, you have to admit that you can think really well with a mulatta's feet in your mouth and that all of a sudden even one's darkest recesses are revealed with the clearness with which flowers can be seen lit up by just the light of a swimming pool in the middle of the desert.

My client, who turns out to be a European woman, almost certainly Italian, tells me that to spend afternoons peering into these little glass cubicles in which girls are stretched out naked, leaving just their feet within reach of the fetishists, has provided her with moments of amazing illumination and that those are of course the moments that she now has to forget at any cost.

I decide in the end not to take advantage of her desperate integrity and I sell her a standard packet at the official price, for which she shows me her gratitude by introducing me to a very sweet Korean girl with tiny feet like lemon ice-lollies.

'On more than one occasion I've flown here from Paris to kiss these feet,' my client says before leaving for god knows where.

I spend the rest of the day there completely enthralled. The girls move their feet towards the tongues of the fetishists through small openings in the glass cubicles, and we fetishists keep the respectful silence that fills confessionals, while we give ourselves over to the fervour of true religions.

When I leave the place, when it's already dark, I'm gripped by the same sense of shame that always catches you on leaving a church and of course the same feeling of confusion.

Amen to that, anyway.

And just when it seemed that the Arizona sun was beginning to melt the snow in the mountains of Sierra Vista and the River Rico was irrigating enthusiastically the plantations of sunflowers in the outskirts of Santa Cruz, the unpleasant affair of the murdered Mexican whore appears repeatedly over the floral tablecloths in the diners, over the blue sur- face of the swimming pools, over the metallic paintwork of the cadillacs and of course the party is spoilt and I can't sleep.

The bus from Nogales is late on account of another air crash. A passenger plane has come down in the middle of Highway 19 this morning. All north–south traffic is blocked. The usual scenes of desolation on the news broadcasts and

I look at the road as you look at things that had meaning a minute before but which no longer have it. Like an empty bottle or a torn up ticket. Helicopters flying overhead all morning, taking the place of the bus service. I've let two go because I'm not in a hurry and I don't want to fly over a row of dead bodies spread out all over the motorway. So I sit down in the International Pancake Store and drink a beer and wait surrounded by syrup and jam, restless like someone who after hearing an impact against his car is incapable of going to look for the dead animal. This is a strange job. Photos of huge pancakes covered in cream and chocolate decorating the walls and hundreds of terribly obese men and women in front of hundreds of pancakes. Chairs and tables painted pink, walls and ceiling painted sky blue, plastic flowers in the plantpots, an old lady en route for Sun City hides a dog in her bag, there's a mentally retarded person threatening a waitress with a plastic spoon, there are at least two old men with just one arm and the water fountain on the way in has dried up.

God doesn't know that this exists.

A waiter comes over and says, 'My name is Rosa but I'm not Mexican.' Then adds, 'You shouldn't eat this shit, people go crazy eating cookies. Too much sugar in the blood. Those who aren't blind are mad.'

Rosa, who in all other respects is a sturdy man of about forty, with tattooed arms, invites me to go out to the car park, behind the empire of the pancake, opposite the old colonel's fried chicken empire, then he takes off his apron and cap and jumps into an old truck, prepares two lines of coke on the leather seat and rolls up a one dollar bill. Then he shows me the photo of two children sitting on folding plastic chairs next to a cactus. I don't know what to say. Then he says, 'You don't need to say anything.' He closes

up the truck, puts on his apron and cap and goes back to
work. A security guard drags out the mentally retarded man
still armed with his plastic spoon. Rosa's cocaine is good.
The International Pancake Store shines like a pile of sugar.
The man with the spoon cries sitting on the ground in the
car park. Now of course I need more cocaine. A single line
is virtually no use. It leaves you like a Christ held up by only
one nail.

Incidentally one of the children in the photograph was
holding a hunting shotgun and the other a dead rabbit.

In Kaibab, near the Grand Canyon in Colorado, there's a
valley where the mist crawls around at ground level and
it's a quick, freezing mist, and it's so strange that you can't
do anything but stop the car and walk from one side to
the other, and although it's the big hole that attracts the
tourists, it's this strange valley that frightens you in an
unforgettable way.

The driver stays in the car, with the heating on and the
radio off. While I walk around the valley you can't hear
anything except for that white mist crawling along the
ground like an army of dwarf ghosts.

What about my teeth? Fine thanks, and I quite naturally
refuse to smile because dentists wait for other people's smiles
as anxiously as a money lender casts an eye over the amount
owing in your bank account.

While half the retired people in America cross the border
in order to treat themselves to a cheap and decent treatment
in Mexico, my friend the dentist drinks French wine in the
royal suite of the most ancient and venerable of the mountain
retreats on this side of the world, built of oak by French
colonists right on the edge of the Canyon, so elegant you
forget you're in Arizona. My friend tells me that Mexican

dentists are reducing the prices by putting in ridiculously white horses' teeth.

'A set of teeth is not like a fridge door. That's something that people never understand fully,' says my friend, who is up to his neck in the jacuzzi with a glass of wine in his hand, looking at the snow on the trees and the vast black hole under the trees.

After making the delivery, for the whole of the trip back to Phoenix, the white mist in the Kaibab Valley is the only thing that worries me and when I reach the reservation of the Hualapai Indians for the next deal, I am still worrying about the same thing. For some reason it doesn't seem impossible that this mist will stay with me for ever. The oldest of the Indians tells me the absurd story about the forest fire more than thirty years ago. I lost everything in that fire, says the old man, 'and as far as I'm concerned it's as if that fire were still burning. That's why I need you, because an extinguished fire can go on burning you throughout your life.'

After finishing with the Indians, my car takes me to the airport in the Golden Valley and, while I wait for the plane to take off, I imagine myself for a moment as the possessor of a different life. I imagine a house near a city but even so far enough away and nobody in the garden and nothing that is worth forgetting nor anything that deserves to be remembered.

Dawn breaks in Tijuana and I'm alone and the carpet of the room is blue and the curtains yellow and I have to be tested again and this time, as is to be expected, I test positive although I don't really know why and of course that's also only natural, because it's only after forgetting that you're completely innocent and, for that very reason, definitely at fault.

I've got to wait for news from the Company. In the meantime I stroll for the first time through the streets of Tijuana and for the first time as always happens I get lost.

Something strange over the last few days. I'm awake all night long. Palpitations, of course, and every step inside the room is the first and only one and the first beer from the minibar inevitably leads to all the other beers and the small bottles of whisky and gin and all the rest and by the time I finally receive the message from the Company, it's already the sixth day and the days have passed, three weeks, and naturally I'm suspended once again.

This morning a very nice agent took away my case and all my records. His words were: I understand and they also understand, in their own way. Then he spoke to me about a German hotel builder and a dead Mexican woman. But none of that means anything to me. He asks me if I'd be prepared to accept a place in Brazil and I tell him that I'd prefer not to but that of course, if there's no other option, then go ahead. There's always another option. That's what he says. For the time being they recommend that I rest, before thinking about a new posting. Great. Bye, bye, friend. When he said friend it seemed that he really meant it. Everything is possible now. I spent the rest of the day in my room and all night on the street.

I know it's not the first time that I've been suspended. There are some things that can't be forgotten, like the noise of planes or cold on your hands.

News. They considered admitting me to hospital and then they considered sending me back home. But apparently they still haven't decided anything definitive. I gradually feel better. Quickly, in fact. Better in the morning and still better in the afternoon. Two more days in Tijuana. Yesterday

Mexico beat Brazil in the America Cup. People are happy.
A national holiday. I kissed a girl in the street. Flags, music
and tequila. At the swimming pool there was a strange man
with some ridiculous shoes, like golf shoes but without the
spikes, and the waiter brought me a daiquiri, courtesy of
the hotel.

When the sky went dark and although it was only caused
by clouds, I had the feeling that everything was finishing
and the feeling of having felt the same thing a million times
before.

It also rains in Tijuana and when it rains in Tijuana you're
well advised to look for something to do. For that reason,
when a fat Mexican dressed in a white t-shirt and shorts
in an old black car asks me if I want to go for a drive with
him, I agree. When we get onto the state highway, the same
one that goes to Mexico City, the Mexican begins to touch
me through my trousers and I let myself come. Then I ask
him to put the radio on and they play a song that I don't
know, but even so I start to hum it, because it's something
by the Fabulosos Potros and all their songs are the same.
The highway goes as far as Mexico City but we're not going
as far as that. Twenty kilometres from Tijuana we stop at a
development of prefabricated houses. It's still raining when
we go in and while the guy is undressing I take a beer out
of the fridge and I wait next to the window watching how
the water flows under the house which is held up by wooden
pillars like a fat insect with slender legs. Round about the
houses, which are all identical, there are rose bushes. On the
other side of the highway there's a gas station but it's raining
so much that it can hardly be seen. What you can see are the
trucks coming in and out. Huge trucks of the type that ride
the Panamerican Highway.

The Mexican is wearing one of those self-chastisement corsets held in position by two large crossbows covered with very fine spikes, as sharp as needles, which stick into the skin. The corset has a screw that allows you to control the depth to which the spikes are stuck in. The Mexican is still not bleeding. The spikes stick into his chest, back, and groin, around his testicles. The Mexican watches me and plays with himself and I watch him, sitting next to the window.

The Panamerican Highway travels the continent from Chile right up to Canada. The trucks are as big as petrol tankers. Some have got their own surveillance helicopters. Nobody who's not crazy ventures onto the Panamerican these days. The trucks flatten everything. Private traffic is banned ever since a bus filled with missionaries crashed into a convoy of milk tankers. They say that the preachers floated in the milk like logs in the river.

The Mexican tightens the screw and the spikes go in another millimetre, small drops of blood begin to appear from under some of the tips. Then he asks me to kiss him, but I don't move from my seat. There's a song that's called 'My Stupid Heart' that says:

There's a line between love and fascination.

When I leave the house it's already stopped raining.

In the morning, back in the swimming pool, everything looks new, as if the life of a million insects was beginning this very day. A Mexican policeman asks me about a German hotel builder. Some days are like that. Of course I don't know what he's talking about and so I ask for a piña colada, although I know that I don't like them and I ask for another for the policeman, although he refuses it of course.

'We have to ask.'

'Ask away then.'

'The waiters say that they saw the Germans in this area. They say that they spoke to another European.'

'I agree that I'm European, but the fact is that I speak to so many people that it's impossible to remember.'

Then the policeman shows me a photograph and it's the photo of a Mexican girl.

'I don't know who she is.'

She's an attractive girl with very big tits. She's wearing a t-shirt with the face of Brigitte Bardot on it.

'I certainly know *her*.'

The policeman smiles.

'I suppose that if you'd seen her you would remember. You don't forget a girl like her.'

Of course I can't agree with him on this point.

'Believe me, everything gets forgotten.'

Afterwards the policeman leaves, so I put the piña colada to one side and I ask for a beer.

At that moment I remember a song that Astrud Gilberto used to sing in a duet with her son Marcello who was seven.

You needn't have been so handsome, I'd have loved you just the same.

Memory is like the most stupid dog, you throw it a stick and it brings you any old thing.

News from home.

Distraught on account of the death of my sister. A woman whom I don't remember. My mother, whom I certainly do remember, travelled from Caracas to Madrid to attend the funeral. My mother returned to Venezuela, with her family, after divorcing my father. My father is a magnificent fisherman and a broken man. A tired man as he says. My

mother was the ringmistress at a circus. A friend of the
lion tamers and the knife thrower. Everyone asked after me
at the funeral. I don't know who is referred to when they
say everyone. Near Madrid my father has a small country
cottage next to a river. He catches sizeable eels. My mother
grew up in Caracas. Her happy life in the Tropics did not fit
in with her sad, dry life in Madrid. My mother was a good
dancer, tango, bolero, joropo. She came and went with the
circus. Then the circus reached the end of the road and I
think she did as well, at the same time. I can't remember
my sister, yet I wonder what it is that draws people to the
barrel of a shotgun but which keeps the rest of us away from
it. The Company, for its part, threatens to send me back to
recreational drugs. To go back to the kids, to discotheques,
is probably the blackest of futures. I should tell them to get
lost but my situation, after the recent suspensions, is critical.
That's the word that they use. They need someone in Berlin
and my critical situation does not allow me any choice. I'm
an agent under suspicion. A salesman about to throw away
all that he's achieved. Of course it's all up to me and of
course they're taking into account my effectiveness and my
worth. Apart from which there is my hard work and good
luck. The message ends with that. So I put TV on, search
for the music channel and take a beer from the minibar.
For some reason I look at my hands for a time and then
I go over to the window and watch the helicopters flying
past. Next to my bed there's a photograph of a family at
a baptism. The woman holds the child next to the font.
It's probably the strangest photo that I've ever seen in a
hotel room. Apart from that I feel fine, slightly worried at
the prospect of going back to stimulants and endless disco
music, crazy teenagers and clumsy drunken little fascists. I'm
as tired as my father. As if the tiredness were a hereditary

illness. I carry on drinking until dawn, then I turn off the
TV and fall asleep.

My father told me that at times he has to wait for hours,
down by the river, until finally some stranger passes by to
whom he can show his wonderful eels.

No treading beyond the line.

I remember having read that on the wing of an aeroplane.
Little else. I remember a photo of a child sitting next to his
father on some tree trunks. Of course I only imagine that
the man is my father just as I imagined him then.

A girl comes over to me in a bar, a Mexican girl. It turns
out that she lives in San Diego and that she's only on her
way through to settle a bit of business. That's the word
that she used. I didn't ask her anything but she insists on
explaining everything to me. A brother who's an astronaut,
a mother who doesn't trust space, a one-eyed dog, a baby
on the way and a boyfriend sliced up by an industrial fan.
In short, one of those ludicrous stories that makes people's
lives so entertaining.

We carry on talking and drinking for a long time and then
we go to my hotel and we swim in the pool. She is wearing a
very small, sky blue swimsuit and swims well. We go up to
my room and she undresses and we try to do it, but I can't
get a hard-on. She sucks my cock and it seems that it's going
to work out but in the end it doesn't and she sits on the bed
and smokes a cigarette.

'Did I tell you that my brother's an astronaut?'

Yes, you told me that.

'The first authentically Mexican astronaut. That's quite
something.'

Then she gets dressed and leaves. As soon as she goes
through the door I open the window and throw the ashes

out and wash the ashtray in the bathroom. I lie down and go to sleep and hear with amazing clearness the bells of hell and when I finally wake up I've got the feeling that ten years have passed, but it's only two hours and someone's knocking at the door.

BLUE NEEDLES

Here I am in Bangkok, sitting on the terrace of the Oriental Hotel watching the boats pass along the Chao Praya, the river that skirts the ancient part of the city, when two guys in white suits and oxygen masks approach in one of those elongated wooden boats, reach the landing stage, jump ashore and before I've got time to invite them they are already sitting at my table talking about money. People are very nervous here and almost everyone wears those masks because of the build-up of carbon dioxide and they all want to get back even before they've got anywhere. Of course I tell them to relax a bit and to have a couple of whiskies which of course are on me. One of them asks for a coconut milk, the biggest of them so I imagine that he's the bodyguard, and the other man, a Thai brought up in Switzerland, young but experienced, asks for a French wine, he changes tack, apologises and leaves the mask next to the cylinder that is hanging on one side of the case of his laptop. Great, we talk a bit about the heat, the river level, apparently it has risen more than was forecast during the last monsoons and finally we talk about money. He knows that the chemical I deal in is good, so he accepts the Company's normal price, to which a substantial reduction has to be applied on account of the size of the purchase. My friend represents a powerful financial group, important people who don't go out at three in the morning, to roam the sex shows of Patpong, looking for late night dross. Of course I understand. I arrange to meet him at twelve o'clock in the flower market. Why the flower market? Because it's a beautiful place. My friend laughs and then says to me, just before leaving, that he misses Switzerland, as if that had something to do with me or as if it were possible to miss Switzerland. When the bill arrives they're both in their boat with their masks and white suits on the way to some other business. I see them change boat opposite Chinatown, they get into one of those luxury launches that look as though they're made of mahogany and probably are. I pay for my beer and the coconut juice and the French wine. There are six storey buildings in Bangkok that don't cost as much as a glass of French wine on the terrace of the Oriental Hotel. The waitress smiles at me. Not all women in Asia look you in the eyes but Thai women do. The smile of a Thai woman makes you feel better at once. Like the end of the rains or the beginning of summer.

At the hotel I collect an e-mail message.

COME BACK.
K.L.Krumper.

I don't recognise the name. This happens quite frequently. The wrong messages or the correct messages that go to the wrong person or simply incomplete messages from people whom you can't remember.

Back in the street after a shower, I take a *tuk-tuk* and go to an air-conditioned cinema. The film had already been going for some time, the guy at my side tells me in English: 'Many have already died'. When it finishes I go for a walk through enormous shopping malls full of students dressed in uniforms. Where in another city there would be one person, in Bangkok there are six, we walk so closely together along the street that we all seem like friends. The enlargement of the monorail system is going ahead, which means that above the track that is above the dual carriageway that flies over the street, there will be a fourth level. Looking from down below, the sky is further and further away.

I've reached the flower market early because there's no other place like it in the world and because I know a guy here who will give me a bit of old opium in exchange for a small amount of memory eraser. The Company has us by the balls but there's always a way of scraping something out of the flask. Metaphorically speaking. Flowers for the dead and calm opium smiles for the living. If the world blows up some day, the Bangkok flower market will doubtless have some of the best rubble. In one of those brief opium sleeps that seem like a whole life enclosed in a jewel case, I've seen a child sitting next to a chewing gum machine in the bus station of a city that could be Tokyo. I'm not sure about the city and I'm particularly not sure about the child. When my elegant Thai gentleman finally arrives, my head has already cleared and at the same time I'm surprisingly calm. We're sitting in a small café, small means a folding table and two beach chairs set up in the street, surrounded by flowers and motorbikes and *tuk-tuks* and now by bodyguards as well since my friend has brought two new fridges in addition to the one I already knew and he introduced me to them all, to be sure, as if we were going to play a closely contested match. He gives me the money and I hand him a rectangular black Adidas bag, the size of a small forearm or a large cock. The man puts it away without even looking inside because he's a gentleman. We ask for tea. I let him tell me something about his business dealings, something that

seems boring to both of us, then I have the feeling that he
wants to tell me something else and perhaps drink beer and
relax and remove the mask and even his shoes and, who
knows, probably to sing old songs, because they no longer
write many songs these days, so I suggest to him that we
get rid of the heavies, and that we go to walk around the
karaoke bars of Sukhumvit. He apologises for the presence
of the heavies, and then dismisses them one by one with the
same tact with which he had introduced them to me. We
leave the market walking past ten or twelve million funeral
wreaths as well as bouquets and flowers as offerings to the
gods and the garlands, floral capes and decorations that Thai
boxers put on before and after each fight.

'My name is Feunang.'

No sooner than he says his name Feunang gets into a huge
white limousine. I get in after him and, I don't know why,
I have the impression that he doesn't want to hear mine.

We go up and down through Sukhumvit, going past the
karaoke bars and the sad porno shows, Pussy Smoking,
Pussy Ping Pong, banana throwing and a very amusing fat
girl who writes WELCOME with her pussy on a blackboard
(Pussy Writing).

We decide to go into one of the two hundred go-go bars in
Nana Plaza, the girls on the street try to grab hold of Feunang
but Feunang walks among them like a ghost. There are not
many people in the dance hall, so that almost all of the girls
dance around our table, Filipino, Thai and Vietnamese girls,
all of them far too pretty and all of them a very long way
from home. Feunang has asked for a bottle of Cliquot.
We drink champagne in silence. Feunang is sad, I'm happy
because I presume that he's going to pay for it and because I
hadn't drunk champagne for ages. Of course there's no way
of knowing how long, the days disappear, entirely swallowed

up by memory eraser. At times just the feeling of having been, of having drunk or of having seen remains. Like a constant *déjà vu*. But let's return to Feunang because Feunang has problems, his own problems, and as I watch his pale face, strangely pale for a Thai, and his long, elegant hands, I have the feeling that I'll probably end the night in his bed and also the feeling that I'll probably enjoy it.

We might have been together before.

'I don't think so,' says Feunang.

Although it's impossible to be sure about this.

I wake up in a huge, white bed, with a canopy and a mosquito net, in a large room, that's also white, with a glass wall through which you can see all of Bangkok or a lot of Bangkok at least, on the top floor of Gem Towers, the highest tower in the gem market.

K.L.Krumper.

The name comes into my head.

COME BACK.

The message also comes into my head. Then they both vanish just as easily. Feunang is out, in another room. He's naked and is talking to his mother. When I go over to the door he invites me to go in.

'Come on, in here, she may want to meet you.'

Great. I'm going to put my trousers on, you don't go to meet anyone's mother with your balls hanging out, apart from which there's just one problem. Feunang's mother is dead.

'He's slept with me, mum. He's a good boy. You can always tell that from the eyes. Come over here. Don't be frightened.'

I'm not frightened but I certainly am shocked. I had heard about programmes of reincarnation, but I don't think that I had ever seen one before. Reincarnation programmes are prepared using millions of pieces of information and guide-lines of behaviour from a living person. When someone fears his death, we all fear it I suppose, but when someone fears his death and has money to pay for one of these programmes, he undergoes endless recordings of memory and patterns of behaviour, notes, diaries, graphological tests, neuronal examinations, photographs, analyses, recollections, home movies, anything. With all that material a programme is created that can take the place of the loved one after death. Like one of those chess machines that put paid to the Russian champions. A reincarnation programme creates natural human reactions based on instincts, memories, genetic data, in short a real hell of a subject but it ends up something like life after death, not for those who have gone, the programme doesn't give a damn about them, but for those who are left behind.

A way of not losing loved ones or, in the case of many firms, a way of still having access to the brilliant decisions of irreplaceable brains.

They say that some great corporations are still run by financiers who died years ago and that more than one president seeks advice from the reincarnation programme of an illustrious predecessor. I've also heard that a dead ballet dancer directs the Paris Opera theatre. Of course it's illegal and of course there's no way of finding out. Legally only a close relation, the person who originally asked for the programme, can access it by means of confirming their identity by their iris print. And of course legally I would be selling controlled doses of memory reducers instead of tearing their memories out of them by sheer force.

Getting back to Feunang's mother, the poor woman is placed in a small black and white monitor, like those 7–11 security monitors.

'It's just a reference image,' says Feunang's mother, who despite being dead is a lovely woman.

'A lovely image however one looks at it, a lovely woman I mean.'

'Thanks.'

Feunang's mother smiles and Feunang smiles as well.

Feunang's mother says:

'So you've slept together.'

First I look at Feunang but as he seems to give his approval, it's me who replies.

'Well yes, it looks like it.'

Then Feunang's mother says:

'Feunang has a lovely body.'

She couldn't have said a truer word. Both mother and son are very proud. They look like each other and they are both very good looking. She's almost as young as him.

'When she died, she was the age that I am now, thirty-two. I was fifteen at the time. We prepared the programme together. She knew she was going to die. I knew it as well.'

It surprises me that he should speak in this way in front of his mother. She seems used to it but even so she is sad. They're both sad.

She is better at hiding things, like all mothers.

After a moment's silence mothers always emerge intact.

'Come on, get back to what you're doing. Boys must be together.'

Feunang is still sad, he has not made up his mind to leave.

'Off with you, foolish boy, go with your friend. Leave me alone once and for all, I've got a lot to think about . . . At times you boys don't understand anything.'

When we go back to the bedroom I ask Feunang if she knows what she is.

Feunang looks surprised.

'Of course she does, she knows that she's my mother.'

I leave Feunang alone with his sorrow and his mother and move across the flat on the way to the lift. As it's in complete darkness I trip over a couple of times until a girl, from the other side of the lounge, puts on the light. It's Feunang's sister, as attractive as him, just like their mother.

'I'm Feunang's sister.'

'I'm his friend.'

'I know who you are. I heard you and I saw you together. I watched you doing it. I also know that you're not his friend, I know that you're the person who has come to tear mum out of his memory.'

I only sell chemical, what each person gets out from within him isn't my business. So I look at her with a serious expression and I tell her exactly that.

'Don't get angry. It's about time it happened. He has spent his whole life clinging to her. That machine is killing him. That machine subdues sorrow as if it were an insect stuck to the wall with a pin through it.'

'Don't you talk to your mother?'

'No; I don't talk to the programme, I prefer to let death do its job.'

Afterwards she goes with me to the lift and we wait together in silence, until it comes.

Then she just says:

'Goodbye and good luck.'

After looking through the window and seeing the fair and the singers, just below the hotel, everything else disappears. Of course the window is open, which makes the temperature in the room quite pleasant despite the humidity. The rest of the hotel is obviously freezing. The corridor is freezing, the lift is freezing, the huge lobby is freezing. On reaching the street the temperature is pleasant again. Despite the humidity.

The fair is set up in an open area opposite the hotel. A site between the big buildings, the hotels and the shopping malls. Almost certainly a construction project halted for lack of funds, because the work site has had a fence put around it and there are building materials, abandoned some time ago, next to the entrance. The fair has only got some old dodgem cars and a row of machines. Video games, video photographs, video messages, video readings of the future. Children queue up to leave recorded messages. Many of them are messages of love. Your picture and voice are recorded there and anyone can choose them later from the menu. The confectioner's daughter is the prettiest girl in Sukhamvit Street. I saw you next to the flyover when you were waiting for the school bus. Things like that. The children leave messages for each other and laugh like crazy.

Behind the machines is the door to the auditorium. Two trucks facing each other and a curtain form the doorway. The auditorium is just the same open ground, with a stage at the back and a pile of plastic chairs facing the stage. After I pay, a child gives me a chair while a girl who's not much older offers me a cold beer. I take both things and sit down in the back row. The singers are all men and they all share the same orchestra. Six musicians up amidst a set made of cardboard, cut out and painted, which represents the sea. The waves of the sea. Between the set and the singer are the dancers. Ten or twelve girls wearing ridiculous, shiny costumes that are too big and too narrow for them, as if the shortest girls were wearing the costumes for the tallest ones and the thin ones the costumes for the fat ones. Each singer sings one, two or three songs, depending upon the response of the audience. The dancers are not always the

same. There are two groups who take it in turns. While some
of them dance, the others change their costumes. The clothes
are also repeated every two or three numbers. The audience
doesn't merely applaud or ignore the singer. If the subject of
the song or the interpretation are successful, the singer moves
to the edge of the stage, then the girls in the first rows get up
and go and hang garlands around his neck. A good singer
can end up with thirty or forty garlands around his neck. At
times you can't even see his face, hidden behind the flowers,
even so the guys carry on singing as if nothing had happened.
Naturally, while I'm amazed by the singers, the flowers and
the dancing girls, I go off to get some beer and drink a couple
of phials of LMB. Despite the noise of the traffic around the
orchestra, the noise of the orchestra on the stage and the
noise of the children in the fair, the LMB keeps me calm,
substantially stable, in a state of moderate happiness and
minimal anxiety. Anchored to the ground. Like a deep sea
diver with lead boots walking along the sea bed.

When I get bored with the faces of all the dancing girls and
the songs of all the singers, I leave the small enclosure surrounded by trucks. On the other side, the rows of machines
are now almost deserted. I go up to one of the video booths
and cast an eye over the menu of messages. Of course there's
one of mine. I select my photo on the screen and at once
the recording comes up. It was dated about a month ago.
I'm on the screen, looking without saying anything. Behind
me there's a girl but I can't swear that she's with me. I'm
certainly on my own. Anyway the girl has got her back to
us. I've got my sunglasses on and it's daytime. A sunny day.
I don't recognise my shirt but I'm wearing the jacket in my
suitcase, in my room. A blue jacket with a zip. The jacket of
a postman or an electrician. A second-hand jacket. I continue
to look at my picture on the screen, but my image on the

screen doesn't say anything. It stays there, in silence, until its time runs out. My time on the other hand still hasn't run out. I can select another message, so I go back to the menu and choose the message that comes straight after. The girl who was behind me in the previous recording appears on the screen. Naturally the girl is a stranger. Now and at the time. She leaves a message in thai and blows a kiss. Neither she nor the kiss has anything to do with me.

I leave the fair thinking about how long I've been in Bangkok, without knowing how long that can be. Worried by the possibility of having suffered a recent erosion of memory and perhaps even a suspension.

I take a *tuk-tuk* to go downtown but I'm caught in traffic as soon as we emerge onto Koncheming Avenue. The traffic in Bangkok is most probably the worst in the world. An hour and two hundred metres later I leave the *tuk-tuk* and walk down to the river. There's no other way of getting about in Bangkok in rush hour and here rush hour lasts from six in the evening until two in the morning. While I'm waiting for a launch, beneath the lights of the helicopters that light up the river, I see large wooden barges pass by with whole families of fishermen on their way to the midnight market. The calm has disappeared. My image in the video booth has unsettled me enough to drive me into taking another two phials.

When the boat arrives I'm feeling better, so I tell the skipper to take me for a trip along the river. We go up as far as the holy city, going past the terrace of the Oriental Hotel. There are a million tourists having dinner on either side of the river. Great activity at the Sofitel heliport. Also dozens of planes circling the skies waiting for a free runway in the airport. There's still a window lit up on the top floor of Gem Towers. The highest building of the gemstones market. The dreadful music of the hotel bands sounding everywhere and behind the terraces and the skyscrapers, the light of a fire. Rakamui hospital enveloped in flames.

I ask the man if he knows anything.

'They've evacuated everyone but they haven't been able to control the fire. It's been burning for hours. There's going to be nothing left.'

We get back to the hotel along the network of canals. The LMB keeps me happily isolated from people so it would not make sense to end up in one of the prostitute bars in Pat-pong. Any contact is now an undesirable contact. When I open my door, the TV is naturally switched on. The image of the hospital in flames seems to keep the room hot.

I take a beer from the minibar and then another one. I allow sleep to slip in slowly behind the final stages of the LMB. Of course it's the hot air that's coming in through the open window that keeps the room at a pleasant temperature.

I fall asleep calmly watching the building shrouded in flames.

I spend the morning at the tennis club. Doing business with a group of English surgeons. Three of them. I don't know if three's a group. Anyway they talk and behave like a group. The daughter of one of them has tried to kill herself. I can't quite work out whose daughter it is because all three talk at the same time and they're worked up and they explain some things to me three times and other things not at all. It's a beautiful day. All the courts are occupied. The noise of the balls and the shouts of the players make me ill. Physically ill. I don't like tennis. I don't like tennis players. It annoys me to find yellow balls inside those marvellous long tubes that could be used for almost anything else.

The surgeon's daughter appeared very early in the morning floating in the swimming pool. Fortunately when they got her out she was still alive. Which I am sincerely delighted about. The girl wasn't getting on well at school but that doesn't explain it all, there's also the change of continent, new friends, Thai food, perhaps, they're not certain about this, there's an older man, a Westerner of course, involved in the affair. Involved and affair are precisely the words that they used. At all events the chemical isn't for her but for her mother. The surgeon's wife. It was she who discovered her daughter's body floating in the blue water of the pool. Naturally she thought that she was dead. For a start they've emptied the pool but that's not enough, because the good woman continues to gaze at the water, which is no longer there, as if it was and as if her daughter's body was still floating on it.

The doctors give me a sealed envelope. I put it away without looking at it. Then they thank me a dozen times. They're dressed for tennis and each of them clutches his racket and the rackets move when they speak like the legs of a stupid animal.

Before leaving I ask them about the hospital. They tell me that apparently it was deliberate, although at once they add that for the moment that's just a rumour. They also tell me that the fire started in the neurology department, and that they have been waiting for a new posting for two weeks.

Two weeks seem a long time to me. What I mean is two weeks haven't passed for me. Worry adds to the effect of the noise made by the tennis balls and I'm soon sure that I can't bear it, so I sit down on a bench in the sun, facing the courts. Watching all these people dressed in white serving and returning, hitting and missing yellow balls, I feel that my blood is evaporating at the same time as two rays of light, solid like two forks, pierce my eyes right through to the brain and still further until they emerge through the nape of my neck and naturally I pass out.

The palm trees, the players, the lines painted on the courts, they all suddenly vanish.

As often happens in such cases, the wretched noise is the last thing to disappear.

It's six o'clock at Bangkok airport and everyone is devastated by the tragedy. It's the fourth plane to crash into the river in less than three weeks. There is talk of a stricter control of helicopter traffic. The immediate effect is that all the flights are behind schedule. The small capsules in the airport hotel can't accommodate so many people. Tourists grow desperate in endless queues. Thanks to my company card I manage to get a capsule in the VIP area. There's a woman lying on the ground, crying. A woman who's lost someone in the accident. Naturally the airport emergency services try to do something for her, but there's doubtless nothing that can be done because the good lady remains clinging onto the floor. I have already seen this before, after an air accident people literally embrace the floor in order to weep for their loss. A more than reasonable reaction. A bad atmosphere in the VIP lounge. So I have a couple of beers and go off to sleep. I dream that I am sitting in a bar happily drinking a shot of bourbon and a dark beer. A guy beside me gets to his feet, goes towards the jukebox, determined yet unsteady and puts on an Irish song. One of those sad songs that sound fine when you're drinking alone in a bar and you've nothing to do and nowhere to go in the immediate future. At ten o'clock I'm woken up by a nice Thai girl on the screen suspended from the ceiling of my capsule. She tells me that my flight is ready to board and that the air traffic is speeding up. She also tells me that there's a typhoon over Malaysia, but that apparently the weather in Vietnam is great. I leave my capsule and go along ten corridors until

I reach the boarding gate. In the plane a man tries to buy something from me for a child. I refuse him for more than one reason. Firstly, there's evidently the normal prohibition preventing sale on flights. In addition to this, and of much greater importance, the protection of the neurones of minors has become the only unbreakable law. At least in companies working within the law. Particularly since the scandal of the sleeping children of Ko Samui. Hundreds of children found in the brothels on the coast whose memory is burnt up on a daily basis in order to preserve the sexual innocence required by refined European sex tourists.

After the Thai has offered me a lot of money which I naturally refuse, I feel obliged to report the matter, but in the end I decide not to do it because the guy persuades me that the boy is his son and that he just wants to free him of an excessive love for his labrador that had been run over by a *tuk-tuk*.

A dog that meant the world to him.

That's what his father says and the fact is that I look at the child and he's as sad as anything. He can't take his eyes off the window. There's an aeroplane so near to ours that we can see the passengers' faces as clearly as they can ours.

The child says:

'I want all planes to crash.'

Then he closes his eyes, as you do when you're waiting for a wish to come true.

When he opens them the other plane has disappeared.

Three hours later we land at Ho Chi Minh airport. As stupid as it may seem, when the plane comes to a halt on the runway I feel strangely happy. For one moment it seemed perfectly possible that such a small child could bring down such a big aeroplane.

*   *   *

Tarmac machines obstructing the clouds.

They are re-surfacing the road between Hoi An and Hué, on the Vietnam coast. The woman who is at my side is Vietnamese, the man is Uruguayan, they all call him Darwin. The driver is a Vietnamese raised in the United States. The car is big and black. German, I think. We're all kissing each other. The driver isn't, of course, just the woman and Darwin and a girl of about fifteen whom I thought was his daughter but apparently isn't. I can't remember how it started. Darwin is an amazingly good chemist who deals in TT and staples and all kinds of euphorias and downers, also Czech red sky which has not been available since the fire in Prague. The driver looks in the rear view mirror from time to time and says: '*Oh Boy!*', but at once he turns his eyes back to the road because the bends follow the edge of the cliffs and, as if this weren't enough, there are tarring trucks in the way of the clouds.

There's an airship in the sky.

Darwin's wife does up her shirt, looks out of the window and points at the sky, where there is indeed an airship flying over Hoi An Bay level with China Beach.

'They're coming for you, Darwin.'

The girl gets dressed as well, Darwin and I remain naked. I'm not certain that I understand what's happening. Darwin hands me my trousers.

'Get dressed. I think that we've finished with all that.'

Then he offers me a glass of champagne and a couple of tiny green pills.

'They're very smooth but quick.'

Sure enough, within ten seconds of taking them I feel my body as if it were inside a Father Christmas costume. Hot, happy and relaxed.

'My wife thinks that everything that flies is coming after

us. I left the laboratories six years ago. Now I concentrate on recreation. Little aids to help balance our days.'

'It's very strange to find a chemist like you on the street.'

'He's not on the street.'

It's his wife who answers. The airship has turned off from the route we're following.

'I'm sorry to have jumped down your throat. Since he's left the laboratory they've been on his tracks. He's too good to be allowed to go.'

His wife is ten years older than Darwin, she's a strong woman. Whoever pursues them is not going to have it all his own way.

'We can try it again later.'

The girl smiles. Darwin smiles. I smile as well inside my imaginary Father Christmas costume.

A really good chemist. Of the type you don't see nowadays. The laboratories end up losing all the best ones with their controls and their greed and their drugs for teenagers. Too quick and too easy.

'The best chemistry was carried out in the AIDS years, now they spend their days fucking, it's cheaper and more fun. They have those limited effect stimulants and those blue phials that are like sweets. The only interesting thing is what you carry. Those hunters of mnemonic imprints, but they work too quickly, they're burning up neurones indiscriminately. It isn't as easy as they want you to believe. The limits of memory are vague. Don't forget that, if you can help it.'

On the other side of the clouds the jungle stretches as far as Hué. When we pass in front of the huts on the side of the mountain we see little rooms just lit up by the blue light of television sets. It's already dark. The girl and the woman sleep in each other's arms on the back seat. Darwin works on his laptop, the driver sings quietly to himself. As strange as it may seem in all the rooms, in all the huts, the television is tuned into the same channel. The monitor in the car doesn't work so I don't know which channel that is. A news programme. For one second on all the TV screens there appears the frozen image of a Western woman. For some reason a frozen image always makes you think about someone who has disappeared or who has died.

A photograph of that woman lights up the jungle for a moment and then disappears.

Swimming in the pool of the Hotel Rex, an amazing building that served as a headquarters for American officers during the war and that is now filled with foreigners and North Vietnamese business men. Each time I take my head out of the water I hear that fantastic music, almost certainly mambo. There are people dancing around the pool. Magnificent French women and fat German women. Drinks are being poured out to the rhythm of the music. I'm out of the water now, in my bathrobe, when a woman asks the waiter at the top of her voice what the title of the song is and the waiter replies, also at the top of his voice, that it's *Cha cha cha du loup!*

Which doubtless means cha cha cha of the wolf.

When the white lights start to bring me down, I put my hand in my bathrobe and take out a couple of yellow pills, simply beds on which to rest the body after a good shake-up. The white lights have become so popular in Vietnam that tourists on the beaches of Bangkok come down here to fill their heads with happiness. White lights originated in Cambodian laboratories but now the production and particularly the sales are basically a Vietnamese business. Of course there is white light in Europe and America, but of course it's not the same. To get drugs out of here is as difficult as pissing on Ho Chi Minh's grave and it could be even more dangerous. Less than a week ago they shot three Dutch kids who were in possession of two soup tins full of phials. I saw it on TV this very morning. I've also seen the funeral of a Japanese sumo wrestler who committed suicide out of love and a hundred stupid containers of plutonium floating in space, but that's of no importance now. I put my hand into the pocket of my bathrobe and swallow down two yellow pills. It's beginning to get dark. The last bather gets out of the pool and shortly afterwards the water is still.

In the room a Vietnamese girl tells me from the TV monitor that I have six calls and as there are so many it surprises me but then they all turn out to be from the same person. I arrange a meeting with my impatient friend.

I drink a miniature of whisky from the minibar and then a beer. The wake left by the white light has dispersed. I lie down on the bed. I leave a handful of yellow pills on the bedside table. The yellow pills have a limited effect but are more than pleasant on top of sleep.

Just one e-mail message:

COME BACK.
K.L.Krumper.

It begins in the morning. With the image of a man sitting at a table in a café in Berlin. He looks like a memory but he must be something else. Probably a vision. A man without memory constantly sees images of the future. The nostalgia disappears and in its place a million riddles are installed. New loves, new cities, new rivers, new bridges. Probably tomorrow. The man sitting at a table in a café in Berlin asks for the bill, pays for two beers and leaves. He's about to take an overcoat from a coat rack next to the door but finally realises that the coat isn't his. When he goes out into the street he feels the cold of January on his face and then straight away the rain. He doesn't remember having imagined the same cold and the same rain but there's no way of knowing this. On passing in front of a shop window he stops to look at a wedding dress and without giving it any thought he crosses the street, between cars, and goes over to a tobacconist's. At the tobacconist's he naturally buys a stamp.

Afterwards he looks for a postbox and posts a postcard there. On the postcard, overleaf from a brief text, hand-written, there is a photograph of Las Vegas. Of the Flamingo Hotel in Las Vegas. It's a letter that he wrote a long time ago although he doesn't remember having done it. All that the postcard says is: 'I'm thinking about you all of the time.'

Back in the hotel, the room is too hot so he opens the windows and tries to sleep. It's still raining. It's after two o'clock in the morning. On the table he's got an airline ticket and a passport. On TV there's a girl singing, an Asian girl dressed in silver. With a silvery dress. For some reason the picture and the sound of the TV don't match. The picture belongs to one channel and the sound to another. What he hears is the voice of a man reciting in German the results of the Bundesliga. At three o'clock he's still awake and he knows that it's three o'clock because there's an alarm clock next to his bed. He hears something in the room next door, a woman talking quietly, probably praying. The woman is talking in French and he doesn't understand French. It's at that moment, as he is trying to follow the prayer in a foreign language, when he real-ises that the waiter of the café called him by his name as he was leaving and that disturbs him so much that he forgets about everything else and just begins to think about that.

He's still thinking about his name uttered by a stranger when dawn breaks.

District 25.

Nothing to do for the rest of the day.

After concluding a quick transaction with a local politician, I tell the taxi driver to drive around for a while, because the weather's fine and because the traffic in the hills is light and the houses have huge swimming pools filled with lovely girls. Naturally there are dogs and wire fences as well and armed guards with baseball caps pulled down to their eyebrows. Vietnamese millionaires don't hide their treasures, they protect them with the help of private armies, made up mostly by former mercenaries from Laos. People capable of eating members of their own families. Life in the hills of Saigon is a party without gatecrashers. The new shopping malls of Cholon, the foreign banks of District 1, the spectacular refurbishment of Tan Son Nhat international airport, all the prosperity of the new Ho Chi Minh, emerge from these pools. From the green water of the rivers in which this nation lives submerged, only rice emerges. It's from the blue water of these pools from where the new wealth of the new Vietnam emerges. And it's these pools to which it returns.

A strange pain in my back, a familiar pain however. A pain that's not new. For a second I close my eyes, or that's what I think, although I then realise that my eyes are still open and it's the world, all around, which has gone. A momentary disconnection. Small flashes of darkness. Undoubtedly a neuronal problem. Just one second. I ask the taxi driver to turn down the music of his monitor and naturally the taxi driver takes no notice of me.

The war veterans sing songs of love.

That's what the taxi driver tells me.

One of those horrible groups of octogenarian singers sitting in wheelchairs.

You can't fight against them. The debt owing to the old heroes still hasn't been paid. When the brave child soldiers of the Cu Chi tunnels sing, foreigners have no right to express any opinion about it. And so show respect and please leave the TV as it is. The music comes out of the open taxi windows, crosses the peaceful groves and finds its way into parties. There of course it collides with the violent organ music that has just arrived from the clubs of Tokyo. The war veterans' love songs disintegrate over the rose bushes and of course there's no-one who can prevent that.

Incidentally, it doesn't escape my notice that over these districts the planes gain more altitude, respecting the sleep of the important people I presume, and even helicopters do strange turns and sophisticated loops to avoid the paper serviettes from taking off in the porches, and the tea services from vibrating and the ladies from having their hairdos spoilt. Of course it could also be the case that the brightness of the sun reflected in the swimming pools distracts the pilots. Whatever the reason, the dogs show their gratitude for the outline of the helicopters in the sky by wagging their tails and howling, beside themselves with joy.

At the house of my friend the politician, a most well-mannered Filipino servant served me four martinis while I was waiting for his boss, sitting next to the pool in which there were unfortunately no girls nor anyone else. Just a tiny little gardener who was taking samples from the plants and putting them into plastic bags as if he were a mad scientist or one of those detectives in films who attempt to seize a criminal by gathering hairs from the carpet. When my client finally arrived, I couldn't keep my mind on what he was saying, on account of the heat or the martinis or probably because sunny days prevent me from paying attention to real things. However, I couldn't help hearing the word *luck* at least twice in the course of our brief conversation. I wonder what the hell he could be talking about.

Luck is a word that the owner of such a large garden should never use. Luck is a word that should be reserved for those who are still waiting.

I ask the taxi driver to stop the car opposite a white house that's full of ridiculous stairways and towers, a house that looks as though it was built by a six-year-old architect. There are loads of people in the garden. Businessmen with rolled-up sleeves and ties still in place and girls wearing bikinis around the pool. The girls go up and down from the diving board. Some jump off very confidently and others pretend that they're frightened to seem more charming. The businessmen drink and put their hands in the water and splash the girls and it all looks like a playpen full of idiots. We men, all of us, always make an effort to go down really well with whores, as if beyond the commercial exchange there was also a bit of fascinating seduction and even festive joy, hidden somewhere or other. It's as sad as getting all excited about a rigged fight, as ridiculous as shooting at a dead duck. That was what was going through my mind when for some reason the taxi-driver decided on his own initiative that he'd had enough, he started up the car and said to me without looking at me:

'Where to, now?'

Naturally I had no idea what answer to give to him.

*   *   *

The child's sitting near the window. Keeping an eye on the staircase that goes up between the palm trees to the first floor. The ground floor rooms are so near to the pool that, at times, the water splashes the curtains because the window is open, because apparently the air conditioning has broken down, because the motel owner has probably spent the maintenance money on whores. That's what Hai tells me as she gets a bible out from under the bed. Hai is a happy, small, slim, ugly girl who deals in coke and who has three or four children who help her out, keeping a watch on the door, the stairs, the corridor and the swimming pool, because the motel owner besides spending everything on whores has the funny little habit of taking wadges of coke and money, in return for his silence. Naturally Hai has tried to kill him on at least one occasion by pushing him over the banisters but this guy, a muscular old man, a former cyclo operator, had fallen into the pool and had got out of it roaring with laughter as if nothing had happened.

'His silence isn't worth a shit,' says Hai while she is shaking the bible so that the paper wrappings drop out.

'He'd never bring the police here. He's got the place full of whores.'

The child laughs each time that his mother mentions the whores. Hai quite naturally gets angry.

'Keep a look out and stop laughing, this is business. My kids occupy their minds with absolutely anything. They laugh at anything at all, just like idiots.'

Hai opens one of the wrappers, she replaces the other two in the bible and puts it away again under the bed. Then she puts quite a heap of coke on the glass top of the bedside table.

'Take a look at this and see its quality.'

I move the little heap over to the edge of the glass pushing it with my little finger. Then I bend down to inhale it. The boy looks at me very closely.

'Yes, it's very good stuff.'

When I walk past the pool I see the rest of the children having a great time with their sophisticated supervision system. There's one of them up a palm tree. He bends down when the helicopters fly overhead and yet stretches out his arms trying to touch the planes. They're all too far away.

District 6 is not a good place to go for a stroll but you don't come across anything worthwhile in the centre. A spot of good cocaine always tenses up the bones in your back and arouses your feelings, terrible come-downs of course, nothing to do with chemical for kids, smooth and pleasant for downtown clubs. All the same as I flag down a cyclo, although a taxi would suit me better, but it's all the same, while I stop a cyclo because it's too hot to wait in the sun, I can't help feeling faith in old substances being reborn in me with the enthusiasm of the start of the summer.

I'm thinking about the week's appointments. Almost all of them in the city, although one of them at least near the River Perfume on the outskirts of Hué, the city that divides the country in half, the zone that suffered most in all the wars. I am thinking about my visits to the forbidden city of Hué, of which hardly anything remains, and about how you sit down gazing at an empty site covered with grass imagining a temple or the wonderful library burnt down by the French. At once over the image of the huge invisible city there appears something else: the image of a woman and a man lying on a sofa under a green light in a hotel room. The man lying on top of her, with his head between her legs so that I can't tell who he is, and she's smiling at the camera. One of those photos done using the automatic shutter release giving an exaggerated importance to someone's life. Greeting the future. A time machine that only works in one direction. Of course there's no connection between the cocaine and the images. The cocaine's only effect is to ensure that the image does not focus, that it jumps and finally disappears.

It takes the cyclo almost half an hour to reach District 2.

I get out of it opposite the Continental, I ask for a beer and go straight to the bathroom. I take a heap of it between my fingers and I push it directly into my nose. I get out of the bath as if I were going to take a corner kick. With just as much desire but it's not the desire to do anything, just that vague and nervous enthusiasm that cocaine gives you. I drink my beer greeting the foreign colony that's already there waiting for the evening dance.

The waiter, who's apparently an old acquaintance, looks anxiously around him, the band hasn't turned up and there's now a crowd of people around the dance floor.

Overdone the cocaine, badly stabilised by the staples, with undercurrents of TT and pushed over the top by the venomous Vietnamese rice wine.

I spend the evening smiling and clenching my teeth in turn, looking at the girls on the dance floor, incapable of undertaking any action. Shattered by neuronal flashes, uncontrolled and naturally unwanted, uncoordinated speech whatever the language and finally an absurd fight because of an already forgotten acquaintance who insists on collecting a debt of which I have no record and which of course doesn't appear in my records. Erosions of memory have created this chaotic situation in which debtors and creditors chase their tails like lizards, incapable of discovering any trace of their debts. After a couple of shoves and a punch in the air, my friend decides that he's not sure enough of his case and in the face of my more than credible ignorance of the matter, decides to leave me alone and goes off with a group of happy Vietnamese who have already been working a table full of solitary Danish widows for a long time. I ask for a bottle of champagne to celebrate it, since two good sales that very morning have given me a passport to having a whale of a time backed up by a wadge of little banknotes in my pockets. And they said that disco music had died, if that's not Donna Summer's 'Love to love you baby' that's playing, let god come down from the heavens and saw off my legs.

Before closing my eyes, perhaps for ever, I check today's date in my electronic organiser.

Ho Chi Minh. The twelfth of September. The third year of the new millennium.

They're crazy, these strange old French women who allow the years to pass them while they're thinking about better times and hating themselves for it. As if growing old were a matter of principles. They wear black and dance on the terraces. We're in the Continental and the Frenchwoman tells me a story that's at least a hundred years old. A story unknown in this country. That's what she says. Apparently we've already worked together but there's no way of telling. An American who's always wandering around here with his shirt open like stage curtains through which an important actor was going to appear, invites the woman to dance and they dance. And they dance so well that for a moment everybody stops to watch and I feel strangely proud, perhaps because when the song ends the woman returns to my table and smiles at me and they all realise that clearly she's with me.

We carry on drinking in the lounge of the Continental until a stupid agent of the Vietnamese Secret Service comes up to our table and tells me to watch out. I do not know what the hell he's talking about. He's probably confusing me with a salesman of tablets, because the French woman and I have been incessantly swallowing down yellow pills, which when all's said and done are the least stupid of all the amphetamines of the latest generation, easy to use, quick, direct, spirited and crazy like flares.

Before I can explain myself the agent jumps over to another table in order to carry on bothering the local dealers. But my friend has already taken fright, so she suggests that I should visit her mansion tomorrow and she promises to send me her well-shaven chauffeur at twelve noon so that we can conclude a deal at our leisure. Naturally I agree to this and a short time later she leaves as well, walking straight across the dance floor like a queen through the ruins of her palace. An elegant woman and undoubtedly a profitable deal.

Before turning in I go to the swimming pool in the Rex. There's no-one there so I swim naked. Afterwards, in my room, I stay up watching the news for a long time. It turns out that a Mexican astronaut has died in a flight simulator. This piece of news gets to me in a way that I can't understand. Of course they've got a video of the cockpit of the flight simulator enveloped in flames. The Mexican astronaut can be seen coming out and burning on the ground like a match. When I finally get to sleep I'm certain that I'm going to dream of the astronaut but instead of that I dream of two naked women and a whole lot of strange animals, zebras with the heads of elks and tiny elephants which sleep next to a circus.

The man drives an old Russian car towards the outskirts of Ho Chi Minh. The girls are coming out of the factories with their lovely blue uniforms, smiling like girls coming

out of school. Surrounded by bicycles we move slowly
along the national highway. Stalls selling food all along the
road and a band of musicians celebrating some Cao Daist
festival, passing noisily in front of one of the new English
petrol stations. The love that these people have for music is
absurd. The Cao Daists have recovered from the sad days of
the war, have assembled more than three million followers
over recent years and have a magnificent army hidden in
the jungle, gaining ground in the opium trade, because the
Cambodians have not been able to skillfully wage a civil
war that's already been going on for a century. Worse luck
for them. And it's a beautiful afternoon and the guy who's
driving, a fat Vietnamese, quite an uncommon occurrence
indeed, tells me that we're there. An hour later we reach
the ferry that crosses the Mekong in the direction of Tien
Li. On the ferry I get out of the car to see the water and
have a breath of air and greet the children who exchange
sweets for ballpoint pens.

The driver asks me what I think of the river, so I tell
him honestly that the Mekong is my favourite river and the
driver is as delighted as the owner of a garden would be.

Shortly afterwards, in one of the former French plantations, the woman, my customer, tells me that she's already
forgotten all the other rivers but that she still remembers
the Seine, and so we talk about the Seine for some time.
About the bridges and the walks next to the water and I
soon realise that there's nothing sadder than talking about
a river that you can't see. We drink tea and French wine, but
we hardly eat anything. The woman invites me to spend the
night there.

The woman is about sixty and when she undresses next
to me, I feel like someone who goes into a ruined church to
pray. Her body could have been all right a couple of decades

ago but there's now no way of telling. We kiss each other
naked but we don't fuck. When she goes to sleep I collect
my money and leave.

   Not just the rivers but everything, absolutely everything,
has to be forgotten.

There's always something that leads people to consider
themselves as being fortunate. My friend is a businessman
from Kyoto who got into the last carriage of the last train
that left Kobe station before the sarin gas bomb exploded,
and for that reason thinks that life is smiling upon him
and even calls him by his name. Understandably there's
the unpleasant matter connected with child prostitution in
South-West Thailand that he is more than ready to forget.
My friend says that those children are devils, that their
bodies are those of devils and that their eyes are those of
devils. The children dance and drink and cut themselves with
razor blades and kiss each other and piss on top of each other
and my friend is no longer sure if it wouldn't have been better
if he hadn't taken the train in Kope station, because the mad
children of Thailand are ruining him and he spends his whole
life trapped between the music of the clubs and the ludicrous
dances of the boys wearing only American underpants when
they're not completely naked. My friend believes that this is
no way of living and he might be right, so I give him what
he's ordered and leave the small French restaurant, beside
the port, without finishing my dinner, because at times other
people's stories clutter up my head after leaving theirs. All
too frequently people feel it necessary that things should
not be lost altogether, like someone who wants to get rid
of something but who doesn't dare to burn it and leaves it
in the street for someone else to pick it up.

   So I start to walk calmly along Ham Nghi Boulevard

trying not to pick up anything of what other people don't want, thinking about the following day's deliveries, paying no attention to the watch vendors who start out from the market and carry on down to the seafront in pursuit of tourists. The watches in their suitcases show all the times in the world because there are not two of them that tell the same time, not two of them that have the same day of the month.

The local newspapers highlight the affair of the three Russian businessmen found dead in a room in a Hanoi hotel in what has been regarded as a ritual suicide. Three men dressed in lounge suits sitting around a table holding hands and with their veins cut open. It's not the first case like this. Apparently a hundred and forty have died in a similar fashion so far this year. All of them businessmen. Always in hotel rooms.

I spend the night overcome by the state of euphoria produced by the local chemical, Laos white flames bringing with them small momentary depressions. Midgets with daggers hidden behind the big top of a circus and a German girl whom I apparently met in Berlin asks me what I'm doing here and I honestly don't know what to answer her and then we go to have a tequila on the terrace of the Rex and we dance around cardboard cut-out bears and we're so drunk that, despite their amazing patience, our Vietnamese friends have no alternative but to kick us out of the hotel, so we end up down by the river buying old-style cut cocaine at the door of the floating hotel, counting the planes that appear and disappear into the jungle like trained dogs.

Monica, who's a nice German girl on a business trip, shows me her tits and they're lovely tits and she swears that they're hers and then she sucks me until I come in her mouth and she swallows half of it and spits the rest out and apologises to me like someone who leaves just a bit of what has been put on their plate. Then we kiss a lot because I think that it's right to kiss a woman who has just given you a blow job or any woman in fact or any man who spends enough time with you.

Monica tells me a lot of things about Berlin, but they're generally things that are of no interest to me. She tells me that the police have cleaned up the station near the Zoo like a kitchen floor is cleaned up after a murder and that the Turks have established themselves at the old North Station and that from there they have organised armed defence against the new groups of the old far right.

Berlin, like so many other things, is something that I know but also something that I have forgotten.

The ups and downs caused by cocaine alarm us because we don't achieve any coordination and when I'm going to offer her a light she's no longer got a cigarette in her hand.

Monica puts her feet in the river and the current is so strong that I have to hold her so that the river doesn't carry her off and in the river, halfway across the delta, there's an illuminated tower and two helicopters on the tower with the blue lights used for night flights lit up and Monica allows the water to take one of her shoes and carry it off and a bit more cocaine allows us to keep our wits about us a bit more for a moment and then become despondent and bewildered once again.

The people of this land have an excessive faith in the river, in the water of all rivers.

And it's all so beautiful. The boys, the girls, the stalls selling bananas, tea, beer and Halong Bay with its three thousand islands and its millions of mountains sunk beneath the sea

like the badly concealed tail of a dragon, it's all so beautiful
and yet it's all of absolutely no use.

I leave the hotel in a happy mood, almost running, almost
singing, and after a short time out in the street the heat
overcomes me and I begin to sweat and choke and finally
I collapse.

I wake up in a Red Cross post next to the beach, tended by
a Vietnamese nurse resembling a bride. Not any old bride but
one bride in particular. A girl who was celebrating her wedding
dressed in blue on the terrace of the Huong Giang Hotel in
Hué. Vietnamese brides don't get married in white, they get
married in blue or green or yellow or any colour they fancy.
And what does it matter if everything comes to an end and you
walk around and go up and down and look at the sky to see if
the bad weather's abating, children sitting at the table obedient
as ducks and days spent waiting to fall on them like murderers
in a ditch. The mother waiting. The father waiting. Nobody
comes back along the path next to the river. The Palace of Hué
in flames, set alight by French soldiers. Unexploded bombs in
the lounges of houses, broken bicycles in the garage and open
pianos in the lounges of sunken boats.

And it rains and gets late and all the sadness of the world
doesn't change anything.

I wake up in a Red Cross post next to the beach tended
by a Vietnamese nurse who looks like a bride. She tells
me in English that I have just suffered an epileptic fit.
The word epilepsy doesn't mean anything to me. But I
recognise the pain in my back, the flash of black light
and also the sensation of waking up in another place, in
another life. I've probably always been epileptic. There's
no way of telling. The Red Cross post is only a canvas
tent and the canvas is open so that from my stretcher I

can see the sea and the Halong Mountains. There's a stage
on the sand facing the sea surrounded by people, and on
the stage there's a very small girl singing in Japanese. The
girl's dress is soaking wet, they're all soaking wet. So are
the audience and the sand. I ask the nurse how long I've
been unconscious. She doesn't know for certain, perhaps
for ten minutes. Ten minutes more than long enough for
a monsoon to flood a city and then to disappear. The girl
isn't wearing shoes.

'The festival's on.'

At first I don't know what she's talking about. You emerge
from an epileptic fit as you emerge from a car accident.
Everything that's normal surprises you and you only accept
the extraordinary.

'It's the festival celebrations in Halong Bay. Groups are
coming from all over the country and also some Japanese
bands from Okinawa.'

I ask the nurse if they've found a case. She says that they
haven't. I didn't even have a passport on me. Then she tells
me to rest.

She also tells me that it's Sunday although I didn't ask her
which day it was.

'On Sundays a lot of people always come to the beach but
nothing ever happens. I've been here for three months and
you're my first patient. Are you on holiday?'

'I don't know. I don't think so. I had a case.'

'Nobody has taken anything from you here. They're all
honest people, fishermen. The pirates are on the other side of
the bay, beyond the mountains. The pirates no longer come
down to the port.'

I can't tell if she means what she's saying. I ask her if she
means it and she says that she does.

Then I ask her if she's married.

She also replies in the affirmative.

When I got back to the hotel I found the case next to my bed.

The room's freezing, of course. On account of the absurd air-conditioning that you find in the Tropics. Five degrees, even less, so cold that a hake would keep perfectly fresh on top of the television set for six or seven years.

A new message from Krumper, the same text.

COME BACK.

That's all.

The image of a woman dressed in yellow with her hair in curious plaits twisted in a spiral has installed itself in my head after the epileptic fit with the arrogance of someone who squats in an empty flat. Tokyo could be the city in view behind the woman, they could be the lights of Shinjuku.

There's also a message from the Company. Two appointments missed in recent days. Two lost sales. No explanation. Waiting for a reply.

I immediately send them a reply and of course I include my medical certificate. There's no immediate reply. Now it's me who's waiting.

Shinjuku, in the centre of Tokyo, illuminated buildings and a woman looking the other way, not towards me but behind me.

Then the lights of Shinjuku start to go out.

Next other images appear like an old TV set which takes some time to sharpen the contours of things again when it's turned on.

Things have now got their shape back and of course the woman has gone.

*   *   *

It's raining hard and it's raining lightly, this way and that way and vertically, with an absurd perfection, in short, except for upwards, it rains in every imaginable way. The Company has forced me to undergo a thorough neurological examination. Apparently the graphs that they've plotted of my epileptic fits are often closely related to the rerouting of consignments for my own use. I've tested negative in the two most recent control checks, but that of course doesn't mean anything. They're also concerned about my health or so they say. I read the sentence twice, as if it were written in Sanskrit. The Company is only worried about itself. They've already lost more than one agent with a significant consignment. The Company just wants to be certain of carrying on burning up peoples' memories all by itself. It doesn't want free agents carrying around chemical taken out of their own stores.

The main thing is that I'm going back to Bangkok for a thorough neurological examination and they've cut off my merchandise and all my orders until they can see if I'm in a fit condition. I'm not suspended but put 'on hold'. I'm a man 'on hold' walking around the streets of Bangkok with an appointment in his pocket for three days' time with an eminent neurologist in the Asia section of the Company. Wonderful. And so let's go to the cinema and to drink and dance until everything's cleared up and they give me back my little case and they leave me alone once and for all.

Incidentally, there's an e-mail message from a certain K.L. Krumper, whom I don't believe that I've ever heard of. The message says:

COME BACK.

Indeed, that's all that the message says.

I have a swim in the Sofitel's indoor pool. When I'm under the water I don't think about anything. Perhaps just a bit about a certain Krumper and his strange message. When I get out, through the transparent dome I can see boats going along the river. The very long launches and jet skis and ten or twelve helicopters. A guy next to me, a huge Dutchman called Gliuvan or something like it, tells me that he still remembers when Bangkok was just one storey high, before the monorail and before the six overhead motorways, before the shopping malls intersected by glass corridors, even before air-conditioning.

He tells me all this without any regret, then dives into the water and swims to one side and then back, then the same over again, until he gets out breathing heavily and grabs his kimono and waves goodbye to me and walks away.

I stay there thinking about how strange it is to meet someone who still remembers so much.

I spend my second day waiting between the cinema and Thai boxing. I get up late, because in the end yesterday because of one thing and another I couldn't sleep well and I was drinking in Sukhumvit until a Filipino dancer insisted on cutting my index finger with some pruning shears. Undoubtedly, some nights are worse than others. No new e-mail messages for me. Not from Krumper, nor from the Company, nor from anyone. So I leave the hotel and go into a multiplex cinema and first of all I watch *Silver Surfer, the movie* and then a very bad film about people in hospital who cry, one of those American films that they make to see if they can win an Oscar and there's a very famous actor whom I don't remember ever having seen who plays the part of a seventy-year-old man but who in fact is only nineteen. Hollywood stars love taking on these impossible challenges

but then there are very few of them who can manage to
tie up their shoe laces and utter a simple line like 'give me
another beer' without it sounding wooden. I put up with it
for half an hour. Then I go out, I buy a beer in the street, I
hide it in a paper bag, I go back into *Silver Surfer, the movie*
and I watch it all over again. Brilliant. Silver Surfer wanders
through space and has a dreadful time and is as miserable as
hell, but if you try to touch his balls he strikes you with a ray
and knocks you out of the galaxy. When I leave it's already
three o'clock, so I take a *tuk-tuk* and go to Ratchadamnoen
to catch the first fight.

The best fights are those on Thursdays at Ratchadamnoen,
everyone knows that, so when I arrive the stadium is already
packed. I buy a programme at the door and take a ringside
seat. The ringside seats are ten times more expensive but the
good odds are always offered on this side of the wire-mesh
fence. The tourists and the rabble are outside. Rabble is an
absurd word, I know, a military expression from the Boer
War, an expression that is only used by a Dutchman at the
other end of a hunting rifle but one which, anyway, describes
the start of the fight. I bet 100 baht on a small but in form
fighter. Not very muscular. A fine colt. Thai boxers move
like colts. They raise their knees and lower their heads like
thoroughbreds from Jerez. My friend has some problems
that cause the atmosphere to heat up but at the end of the
last round he sends the other lad to the canvas with a hook.
My lad gets up, but he has already received so much that
he straightaway falls down again with a blow of the knee
to his kidneys. I'm still counting my money when the two
fighters for the next bout come out. Two unknowns, I bet
on one of them, the ugliest, and I lose. I don't like the third
bout, there's a fighter who comes out really pumped up,
protected by a former Liverpool policeman who's making

his pile by training fighters and rigging fights. I don't like
dirty play so I go over to the bar for a beer. The crowd
shout enthusiastically when the Englishman's pupil sends
the other poor devil to the floor but it's a film that I've
already seen. I win in the fourth and fifth bouts, I lose in
the sixth and win again in the last one. My man wins on the
decision of the judges. There's naturally a lot of people who
don't agree but that always happens. I collect my money and
leave. My usual bookie isn't at all happy. I don't think that
she'd suffered from such a winning streak for ages. Although
there's no way of telling.

'I thought that you were a man with no luck.'

My bookie, an old woman consumed by the dark atmosphere of Thai boxing, tells me this.

'Luck has nothing to do with it. You've just got to look
them in the eye.'

If that's all there is we might as well keep on dancing.

There are always limousines waiting for the winners on the
way out of the stadium. I get into a white stretch limo so long
it seems the driver will arrive at my destination before me.

The driver asks me if I like the music. Then he puts on
the radio and a Cole Porter song is playing.

If that's all there is we might as well keep on dancing.

As I pass close to the Meuang market, next to the network of canals, I see a man sitting on the ground burning
a letter.

For some reason I fear that even after burning up the
memory, that memory, precisely that one, will be the inde-
structible image. The one that's just before the last one.

The rest of the journey is as absurd as taking a dead child
for a ride on a ferris wheel.

I drink French champagne inside the car, I carry on

listening to songs, I stretch my legs and tread on the flowers. My friend the driver asks me very politely not to screw up his decorations. These people take flowers very seriously and they're quite right. In Bangkok limousines are always covered with flowers, in fact everything in Bangkok is covered with flowers and that of course doesn't improve anything.

The stretch limo leaves me in Sukhumvit and then gradually disappears.

The girls dance to fashionable songs on the plastic catwalks. I have a German beer and then a Japanese one and the fact is that I don't notice any difference. A local friend, whom I hadn't ever seen before, sells me two GPGs. Tiny moments of ecstasy. Canned euphoria. They're not German, far from it. You don't find German chemical on the street. I drink a phial in the bath and come out of it in good shape. Not very good, just all right. Home-made Vietnamese chemical, what we refer to as basketwork. When I say "we" I refer to authorised chemical agents. Legal ones. That's what we're called on the street. God knows we will burn up the earth with ten or twelve official documents and a million rules that the Company stubbornly refuses to recognise.

A Cambodian girl tells me loads of things that I don't understand. Then she insists on taking me to one of the private karaoke bars but as I don't want to die of shame, I ask her Mama Sam permission to take her to my hotel. Mama Sam is the old whore who controls business with the girls. Mama Sam agrees in exchange for an adjustment in the price. The girl collects a strange gold coloured fur coat and says goodbye to her friends as if she were going on holiday to the beach, I say goodbye to everyone as well, smiling and waving like a stupid bullfighter.

There are more lights in Sukhumvit Street than in many

Austrian cities and even so, from behind the cheap happiness of the GPG, I see a million black clouds.

In the *tuk-tuk* on the way back I take the second phial. I shrink back into my seat waiting for the rush. We move forward slowly surrounded by cyclos, by those noisy little motorbikes, by cars, by helicopters, by girls and boys who never sleep. The girl and I, alone, together, perfectly sad.

The girl is called Lin Tho. When the monorail passes, you can just hear the noise of the bridges trembling then, straightaway, everything else can be heard once again.

Lin Tho doesn't speak much. There's no reason for her to do so either. Her enthusiasm is kept for love-making. Lin Tho undoubtedly has a boyfriend in the jungle. Love is what matters, nothing else. Even so, when we reach the hotel, with GPG taking decisions for me, we fuck. Lin Tho is beautiful and has a magnificent body but her mind is in Cambodia, with her arms around a soldier in the opium war.

Half of the Cambodian girls of Patpong and Sukhumvit fuck idiots in order to get their boys out of gaol. The warlords sell their prisoners in order to continue buying jewels from Japanese arsenals. Anyway, the moment that Lin Tho leaves the room I burst into tears. Not because I want to but because Vietnamese GPG is terrible without the descent smoothed out. Home-made chemical is like a DIY chair, the person who makes it enjoys it more than the person who sits in it. For a moment everything's as sad as a circus whose trapeze artists have been hanged. Then, miraculously as we're dealing with basketwork, the pain disappears all of a sudden. Bravo for the amateurs in Saigon. I thought that it would be worse. I've still got six hours before I have to undergo the neurological examination.

I get to sleep straightaway despite the noise of the heli-copters.

There's a woman who must be you. Standing, with a camera hanging from around your neck, amazingly slim. You've got rubber boots on and a long Prince of Wales kilt and a tight black t-shirt and you're smiling, although smiling doesn't seem the right thing to be doing. I can't explain why. Behind you there's a lake or probably a very very calm sea. In one hand you're holding a reed. That makes me think that it's a river trip. Malaysia or Vietnam. Your other hand, the one that's not holding anything, is clenched tight, like a fist that has got something hidden inside it, something that can't be dropped. There's an infinite distance between your fist and your smile. A body overcome by anarchy.

When they talk about you I don't understand what they're talking about.

I'm looking at the roof of the Wat Pho temple, the largest and most ancient of the temples in Bangkok, near the Reclining Buddha. The vast white walls and the wooden roof hold within them, or at least this is what they say, all the wisdom and tradition of Thai medicine and of course the hands of the best masseurs in this part of the world and, although on the outside, the traffic jams and the fumes frighten the children dressed in uniform as they come out of school, here time stops and runs up and down your back like a million happy spiders.

After you have a bath, the old masseuses scrub you from top to toe with heather branches until your skin loses its memory and it's another new skin that takes its place with the promise and joy of someone who, without really knowing how or why, hopes for better times.

Good afternoon, says Feunang's sister, who's lying on an oak table, naked, very near to my oak table and, for a moment, I don't know who she is, nor why she's speaking to me but at once she says: I'm Feunang's sister, and then once we're outside, at the temple door, both dressed of course, with the sun slaying the dragons at the gate of the forbidden city because it's almost dark, she says to me:

'Feunang has died.'

In his room in Gem Towers, above the whole city, she tells me that Feunang decided to take his own life with a massive opium infusion rather than forget the memory of his dead mother, because Feunang's courage in the face of oblivion was less than his courage in the face of memory or the pain of death.

Feunang's sister's bedroom is also white and large and from its window you can see the river and, on the other side of the river, the planes and beyond the planes the jungle of Burma. Feunang's sister is still wearing mourning and she's pretty and she offers me sake and slow-nights, which are the best morphine derivatives in Asia and then of course we fuck.

There's nothing as good as fucking with a sad woman and it's for that reason that, may god forgive me, widows and mothers and sisters of dead men are always far and away the best fucks.

Feunang's sister then sits on the bed, naked, and tells me that her mother's still alive inside the reincarnation programme devised by Feunang.

'She hasn't got much time left. Without the iris print of my brother, the whole programme will disintegrate in less than two week's time.'

Naturally I ask her if the mother knows that her son has died.

'Yes, she certainly does know and she doesn't understand why she's been reborn to see her son die and she also wonders if the other death wasn't best, the first one, the death that overtook her when she at least knew that her loved ones remained here, in a bad state but in one piece.'

When Feunang's mother calls us from the lounge she tells me that her mother, like all mothers, sleeps very little and with the light sleep of hunters and that like all mothers, however quiet you are, she always knows when there are strangers in the house.

She puts on a white silk dressing gown, a dressing gown from Milan, and it's not that I understand that much about dressing gowns it's just that she herself tells me this. I put my trousers on and then we both go into the lounge, which is dark, with just the blue light coming from the monitor.

Feunang's mother greets me and smiles at me and remembers me, because the memory of reincarnation programmes is as good as the memory of their owners and Feunang's dead mother's memory was, it seems, prodigious.

'I remember you and I remember your efforts to free my son from his own memory of me. You can't know how painful it is to me that my poor Feunang will never use the superb chemical that you came here to bring him.'

'Good evening, madam. Rest assured that I also regret it.'

And so we sit down next to her. Next to Feunang's mother. So close to the monitor that I can see her eyes as I've never seen them before and in her eyes there is the grief of a woman who has come back from death to see something that she didn't want to see, in order to have a life that now no longer matters to anyone.

Feunang's sister doesn't look at the monitor as Feunang looked at it and that's something that both women know.

'She never wanted me back. She loved me while I was here, but not later on. She never speaks with me, she just waits for the time to pass and for me to disappear for ever and there's no earthly reason why she should be blamed. A reincarnation programme knows what it is and even so it can't help feeling what it feels, the death of my son puts paid to me for ever and that's the way it should be. Don't get the idea that this bothers me. I learnt to wait for death once and that helps me to wait for it now. It's grief at Feunang's death that has occupied all my time for these last few days, because this is a grief that I hadn't encountered.'

Feunang's mother is only speaking to me because she knows that her daughter isn't listening to her.

Feunang's sister looks at the monitor like someone who looks at a photograph album, like someone who only sees her intact memory of the past.

'Now that you're here I would like you to make sure that she forgets all this. All the deaths as well as this absurd reincarnation. It's all I've got left, my only daughter, and even if she doesn't believe it, I'm still her mother, even inside here.'

Feunang's sister leaves the room.

The image on the monitor watches her leave and then looks at me sitting opposite her and then looks towards the window as if she could see Bangkok on the other side and I wonder if in fact she can see it and at once she tells me that she can't. That she can see no further than the glass of the window.

'I can't see Bangkok from here, I can't see the city as it is now, I can just remember the city as it was before.'

Then she asks me if I'm going to stay long and she asks this with the annoying politeness of a tourist guide.

'No, I'm not.'

'Make the most of your time then,' says Feunang's mother and then closes her eyes, so I ask her if she's tired and she says that she is and then, like a perfect living hostess, she tells me to have something to eat before I go, because boys nowadays scarcely eat anything and she also says: Look after her while you're here and then please leave without making any noise.

Then Feunang's mother goes to sleep because it's late, and when I leave the lounge, Feunang's sister accompanies me to the lift and when the lift arrives, waves goodbye to me, without wishing me good luck.

The good weather ended. The monsoon flattens Bangkok and it's difficult to breathe without an oxygen cylinder and so, contrary to what I usually do, I buy a two hour one in the World Trade Centre in Wireless Road. Bangkok has turned into a shopping mall. The whole of Asia is a huge commercial centre with the nervous life of its rivers swirling all around it. It's just water that saves Asia from total destruction. And then there's the heat and the mosquitoes. To hell with all of it. There's nowhere safe for you to walk. To the barricades.

Life's a shopping mall that only closes once and for ever.

At seven o'clock the results of my tests arrive.

Positive of course and naturally I'm suspended.

I sat down to have dinner next to the holy city. Near the buddha who can't be fully appreciated with a single glance.

When I get back to the hotel, the agent in charge of merchandise was already in my room, waiting.

He's a Westerner. Probably Swedish or Danish, definitely Scandinavian.

Smiling, that's something at least. Scandinavians have the annoying habit of smiling only when there's nothing to smile about.

'Your merchandise has been withdrawn, along with your record book.'

'What happens with the orders that I have already placed?'

'We've already got someone covering the area. Calm down and rest. If you carry on like this you're going to beat the record for suspensions.'

'I think this is the first one.'

'It's always the first one.'

I don't like being in my room with someone I haven't invited, and so I get out my things and call a taxi.

'Where are you off to?'

'The airport.'

'And where are you going then?'

'Don't know. Wherever the planes are bound for. I'm sorry but I don't like your job and if I don't like your job, I probably don't like you either.'

'Don't worry I don't like yours either. I was in chemicals for three years, Eastern Europe, then I asked to be transferred to administration.'

'Nobody asks to be transferred to admin.'

'I did.'

'Why?'

'Don't know, I suppose because I'm fond of memory.'

The Company must definitely be run by an imbecile. You don't employ Jews to work in a sausage factory.

'How many chances have I got left?'

'You've failed too many control tests and you screwed it up in Arizona, on the other hand you've shifted a lot of goods, you're a quick operator and you know the area, besides which you have to realise that they're not exactly falling over each other to come to Indo-China, so they're prepared to give you a couple more chances. This is just the word on the corridor. But you know how things go.'

Indeed, we all know how things go: The door says what the corridor knows.

The door is what we agents call the command group. When the door opens, the decision is already on the street. If someone mentions to you that you're dead on the corridor you can look for another job, because the door will announce a suspension in under a week. The corridor is as sure fire as a horse race with just one horse in it.

'So I'm still alive on the corridor.'

'It looks like it.'

When I leave the room my Danish friend stays there sitting on the bed with his tremendous smile hanging from his face, like a dead mouse in a cat's mouth.

And the songs say that after the rain comes the sun and then the rain again. It's not true. After the rain comes more rain and on the monorail on the way to the airport I can't take my mind off the empty time that stretches ahead of me and the strange list of suspensions attributed to me and the stupid Danish agent and his stupid love of memory.

When you sweep away the dead leaves from the garden, it's the garden that matters.

It's so hot that you'd swear that it's August but it's November. The room has a wooden floor and the walls are papered. Papered from top to bottom. Green and blue wallpaper. Thick blue stripes and thin green lines. Nothing new. The hotel is literally built over the water of the large lake in Hanoi. The swimming pool is suspended two metres above the surface of the lake. Water on top of water. An absurdly rational hotel. The kind of future that was imagined in the past. That perfect future that never actually turns out. Everyone knows me. I've stayed here before and yet nothing seems familiar to me. Nor is there anything surprising either. In the pool there are just five Japanese men sitting in a row of white deckchairs under artificial palm trees. Businessmen.

Naturally there is a background of that trivial music that you hear everywhere, in planes, lifts, waiting-rooms. A music that seems imaginary.

The days are at times so sad that it's simply not worth doing anything. It's not worthwhile running, nor waiting, nor keeping watch. Days that are so sad that there's no point in making the slightest effort, nor the slightest movement. You've got to let days like that slip by, like night trains. Despite everything, I dive head first into the pool and swim for quite a while and, every time that I come up for air, I see five Japanese men and two palm trees, one on either side of the pool, and the grey water of the lake and the dark sky over the lake.

When I get out, a waiter offers me a drink and I ask for a tequila and then I sit down to wait in my deckchair, on the other side of the pool, just opposite my five Japanese men. I drink my tequila while they drink their strange mixtures. Five against one.

Whatever the game is, at this moment it seems an impossible one for me to win.

Your mother deals the cards in a private room next to the dining room. I can't see her but I know that she's there. I watch downcast gamblers leaving in the course of dinner. All of them Japanese. Not the same ones from the pool, other different ones. It isn't strange, Hanoi is full of Japanese men on business trips. One of them, an older man overwhelmed by an earlier piece of bad luck before this one, tells me that your mother's gambling hard and that she's winning.

'I know.'

'How do you know?'

'She always wins.'

'Don't you gamble?'

'I don't know how.'

'You don't know how to gamble?'

'I don't know how to lose.'

The man sits down beside me. First he asks:

'Do you mind if I join you?'

I don't reply and then he makes up his mind and sits down beside me.

'She's a terrible woman.'

'I'm only too well aware of that.'

'Do you know her very well?'

'I think I do, but I don't really know why.'

The man asks for a beer for himself and another one for me. We drink in silence for quite a while. The dining room is gradually emptying and my Japanese friend and I carry on drinking beer, one after another, until they stack up to a fair amount of beer. Then he says something in Japanese. Something that I don't understand.

'Forgive me but I don't speak Japanese.'

'I have to phone my wife but that good lady won my mobile from me with two pairs. Can I use yours?'

'I'm sorry but I don't go in for those contraptions.'

'My wife loves me, as incredible as that may seem.'

'That's great.'

'These hotels are dangerous. The décor is so normal and at the same time so strange that, when it comes to it, suicide seems the natural solution.'

Then the man gets up and leaves, not without wishing me goodnight first.

'Goodnight, friend. Don't gamble with her.'

'There's no risk of that.'

Next morning. No sooner do I wake up than I find out that man has died. The boy who brings breakfast tells me that they've found his lifeless body in the bath.

Lifeless body seems to me the perfect way of describing all of us.

The empty days come. Days spent alone, without anything to do, sitting in town squares, watching barbers and fortune tellers, masseurs and couples out on their mopeds. Days like this come and there's nothing that you can do with them. They pile up remorselessly. It's a matter of letting these days pass by and then others, until I get back to my activities, record books, orders, visits, encounters, work.

First I tell myself:

Now, work is everything.

And straight afterwards:

It's not enough.

And I've returned to Ho Chi Minh because returning is like covering up your eyes with a blanket, something that doesn't change anything but which, at the same time, is comforting. And for someone who now lives continually abroad, there is no alternative but to return to strange places. Saigon, in this context, is as strange a place as any other.

So here I am on the terrace of the Rex Hotel greeting some strangers when the waiter brings me an impossible cocktail, one of those coloured drinks with sparklers and little parasols that they're so fond of in this part of the world and naturally I refuse it, because, whatever it is that I've gone through, I'm certain that I was never a man capable of drinking such things. But it turns out that it's a gift from the management and there's no worse insult than refusing a gift, and so I keep quiet about it and drink it, although at the same time I do ask for a beer. It's eight o'clock and the terrace of the Rex is already lit up, which means that there are hundreds of coloured light bulbs in the shape of harps and mermaids and the huge crown that dominates the front of the building, rotating in all its splendour. I understand that it's a stupid expression, but I can't see any other way of expressing it, and all the animals made of papier-mâché: elephants, deer, sharks, bears, snakes, looking at their best for the tourist and the professional. Until very recently indeed I included myself in this second category, now, suspended apparently for the umpteenth time, I don't really know into which category I fit. In short, welcome to Saigon anyway and hopefully the bad luck that's following me about will relent once and for all, in bewilderment, in one of these ridiculous turnabouts that life tends to make and that definitely accompany each memory burn-up.

Another beer?

The waiter looks me in the eye as if he was trying to convey to me something that I don't catch at first but which I pick up immediately like a piece of paper that falls from my pocket and which turns out to be a ticket for a football match.

The hours elapse, two, three and four, until it's twelve o'clock and they change the shift on the terrace and the lovely Vietnamese waiter, a boy of about twenty, slim, elegant, dry, which is now unusual in this country only partially reclaimed from the water, as I was saying the lovely waiter and I go together to my room and we do it, beneath the unsettling lights of the Rex's rotating crown, not because I was in desperate need of having sex with him, but apparently because it was a prior arrangement that I had apparently forgotten about and because since the end of the virus, people, here and there and everywhere, are desperate to fuck, in a great rush, I suppose in order to make up for all those years of ridiculous abstinence.

In the morning I'm alone once again.

*   *   *

It's after midday in Ho Chi Minh and there's a congestion of bikes under my window and you can hear the bells, and the fortune-tellers and the masseurs just can't cope in Catinat Street and the revolution is already forgotten, like everything else, despite the video cameras and their stupid way of recording the most trivial gestures, the most vulgar landscapes, the most absurd days. And it's always so sad to be alone.

I spend the afternoon in the pool and on the tenth or thirteenth length, swimming with real passion, I realise that this latest suspension, which I thought was the first, but which of course wasn't, has turned me into an amphibious man, a guy continually beneath the water in front of rows of Japanese lying on rows of deckchairs under coloured sunshades.

In the changing room of the Rex pool, which also happens to be on the terrace, a local salesman, naked, with his swimming trunks in his hand, offers me three TT capsules and of course I buy them from him, because everything's so sad and because I think it's ages since I've taken TT in Asia. For some strange reason some drugs travel better than others. TT's only a slightly euphoric relaxant very similar to pondinil, it's perfectly legal, but a bit more exciting, not just because it's on the black list but because it caresses the bones softly in a way characteristic of derivatives of amphetamines elaborated to supply a sufficient buzz. Innocent velvet for afternoon use. And a boat trip around the delta watching the cargo boats going up and down and the glass bottomed boats full of American tourists and children on the banks throwing coins into the river and praying their wishes in quiet voices.

Suspended and alone. Given over to the brief euphoria of TT like a European adolescent on an end-of-term trip.

Undoubtedly there are drugs for men and drugs for children and the chemical industry is doing everything the wrong
way around and at the same time it's ensuring that each day,
in the strangest way, becomes once again the day it was
meant to be. Like a witch who lies and yet despite this
gets it right, always, however twisted destiny may be, since
a sensation, more than an event or an idea, is absolutely
irrevocable. I suppose then that all these canned sensations,
but none the less real for all that, will always be the destiny
of all of us, although it may also be the case that TT is
wide of the mark, since these and not others are the absurd
and truthful thoughts produced by derivatives. What they
call the shadow of spiders' legs in the laboratories. The
characteristics that eventually mark out a compound as
much or more than their primary effect. The tiny thorns
of chemical happiness.

On closing my eyes, I see a typhoon on the other side of the
window and then a woman sitting at the table, but there's
nothing on the table. Her arms are folded, she's so serious
that she looks funny. The look of someone who at any
moment is going to say: We must speak.

I'm in one of those bars in Dong Khoi, in the centre of Ho
Chi Minh. It's ten o'clock at night. There's nothing on the
other side of the window. The TTs of the previous night have
brought all this cheap grief but I've tried to cheer up with a
bit of grass, a lexatine and six beers. A plane has crashed
into a zoo on the outskirts of Lima, Peru. I saw this on a
news bulletin. The lions ate up almost all of the corpses.

There's a man sitting at the back of the bar with a knife
in his hand. A hunting knife, one of those big ones that are
used for skinning wild boar. I presume that's what they're
used for, I'm no expert. An impressive knife however one

looks at it. At his side there's a woman of about fifty with a body twenty years younger. An impressive body. There aren't many people in the bar. Two Vietnamese wearing suit and tie and a big Hindu with a big bag of cement. The man with the knife has the knife stuck in the table. When he realises that I'm watching, he raises his hand and greets me. Then he calls the waiter. The waiter goes over to him and then he whispers something to him. Then the waiter goes back to the bar.

'The gentleman wants to buy you a glass of champagne.'

I accept the drink and afterwards I naturally go over to his table in order to thank him.

'Sit down, my friend.'

I sit down opposite the man, the woman and the knife.

'Are you alone?'

'Yes.'

'That's a pity. This is a bad place to be alone. In fact all places are. My wife was telling me that if she had to fuck someone in this bar she would start with you.'

'Thanks.'

'We're from the south, you know, from the south of the United States. Good people. I'm a pastor of the Church of the Promise Keepers. Have you heard about us?'

'Yes, I think so, probably in Arizona, although there's no way I can be sure about it.'

'We keep our promises and that's more than can be said about other people nowadays.'

The woman smiles at me. She's wearing a small dress and she's got very large tits.

'First I thought about fucking the Hindu, but I think that it's too hot to handle so much flesh. That's why I thought about you.'

'Much obliged.'

'We can go to our hotel, it's at the end of the street. My husband will wait for us here.'

Naturally I accept her offer. The woman gets up and I get up as well and we cross the bar and then the street.

The man carries on drinking champagne and looking at his knife.

The hotel room's yellow. The walls, the carpet, the quilt on the bed, everything's yellow. The woman tells me to get it out and then she tells me to touch it and while I'm doing that she slips her hand inside her panties and touches herself until, after some time, she comes. To watch a woman coming is like watching an electric train, you can't do anything about it, but it's entertaining. Then she takes her clothes off, gets on the bed on all fours and tells me to put it in and naturally I oblige. A woman like this is undoubtedly the result of a whole series of amazing plastic surgery operations, but that's not to take anything away from her. A body that fights is always better than a body that has given in.

She shouts a lot. In a theatrical way that's a bit embarrassing. My cock, which isn't too big or at least not as big as would be desirable, goes in and out, it slides around and falls out, it dances about inside her like a baby in an inflatable paddling-pool.

When we get back to the bar, the man is still sitting in the same place. The Vietnamese and the big Hindu are no longer there. In their place there are other people. Tourists and watch salesmen, as well as a girl of ten or twelve years of age dancing next to the video machine.

I accompany the woman to her table but I don't sit down.

'Promise Keepers. Our memory is sacred. You can't fulfil what you can't remember. With this very knife I've already killed three of those memory murderers.'

I had heard about these people in Bangkok and possibly before. Murderers of memory murderers. *Promise Keepers*, white American hicks. I didn't know that they would have gone so far.

'I caught a Scandinavian in Bangkok Airport with a suitcase full of it.'

'Full of what?'

'I don't know, there's no way of opening those contraptions without the code. But he had a fair number of sales records in his electronic organiser. What was it like up there?'

The woman says it was fine, although she says this without much enthusiasm. I don't feel offended or anything like that. The woman also says that I hit her, which isn't true. The guy seems satisfied.

'Now, if you don't mind, I prefer you to leave. I have to speak to my wife.'

I'm only too pleased to get away and as I leave, I notice how they look at each other. The man with the knife and his wife. Violent Promise Keepers.

He looks at her, like a man peering into a well and she looks at him, like someone who fell down a well and had now given up all hope.

Love is a million different illnesses.

So I leave the bar on the way back to my hotel, helicopters fly by skimming the aerials. The skies are black. It's hot and it's late. The poor Scandinavian's dead and my suitcase has followed me here in the strangest of ways. Perhaps I can still carry on with the business, after all.

I've spent the morning on the beach, behind Can Gio market. It's not a great beach but there's nothing better near to Saigon. The water's clean and on a clear day you can see the hills of the Vung Tau peninsula. Of course it's not a clear day, so that all that can be seen are the old oil platforms of Vietsovpetro. Old Russian oil platforms abandoned years ago. The Russians left everything behind like someone who leaves their gloves in a café. Just as elegantly. A girl selling pineapples told me that they're thinking of getting them operational again, although she personally doesn't believe that there's any oil left in this area. She doesn't say this just for the sake of saying something, she says it because she's been gathering shells on this beach for a long time. I listened to her assessment carefully. I also bought a pineapple.

The girl stayed next to me for a while. Preparing the pineapple. They cut it up into small pieces. With swift diagonal cuts. Then they give it to you holding it by the leaves. She was a very pretty girl and very useful with a knife. It seemed to me that both things went well together.

I think that I fell asleep on the beach. I was woken by a plane. I naturally felt guilty. All of a sudden. Because you always feel guilty when you fall asleep and when you suddenly wake up you act as if it hadn't happened. As if someone said:

'Did you drop off?'

And, without thinking, you deny it.

Of course there was nobody else about.

At night, later than two o'clock, I'm dancing with a Vietnamese girl educated in Europe who remembers everything and tells me all about it. The green fields in Holland, the black sky in London, the music of the time, the names of all the magazines, a doctorate in dead languages at Cambridge, a stolen bicycle and a boy in Brixton who was madly in love. The girl's name is Hiang but in London they all called her Fu, on account of her looking so much like a very very

famous Japanese actress or other who has made films in
Hollywood and all that kind of thing. Fu is a clever girl
whom some guy has been fucking on the other side of the
world and who's now back home because her parents are
elderly and God alone knows if they'll make it through
the winter. Particularly her mother, a good woman worn
down by giving birth nine times, all of them girls, all of
them scattered throughout the world, two in Australia, a
few more in Paris, one in Rome, two more killed in a
plane crash and the other one, Fu, living in London for
the past two years, sad, wounded but still alive, keen to
forget everything as soon as possible. I feel almost obliged
to tell her that that's precisely the line of business I'm in, but
she fiercely despises chemical alterers of memory, and that
word and no other, I refer to the word 'despises', is the one
she uses. I explain to her that in any case I'm an agent who
has been suspended perhaps even indefinitely.

I hope so, she says, and just at that moment I realise that
I'm not sure that I know what I hope for.

Then I have another TT and we fuck.

Later, I watch dawn breaking lying next to Fu, the Saigon
sky goes blue at the same time as the water in the river
starts to turn red and I imagine, because it's something that
I've already seen before, that it's going to be a horribly
hot day.

It's the same yellow room. The man who takes care of
promises is in the bathroom washing his prick. A prick
that's a bit bigger than mine, covered in veins. I mention it
because on a prick and on hands veins are always attractive,
a prick much darker than the skin of his stomach. His wife
is also lying on the bed, naked, with her legs open and her
eyes closed, like a girl after doing it for the first time lying

on the grass next to the swimming pool. But it certainly wasn't her first time and there's no grass and while I went into her, her husband tried to take me from behind with his cock all covered in veins, but fortunately he didn't have it hard enough, so I felt it slipping out time after time like a distracted worm. In the end he came but in spite of his endeavours he didn't get it in me, and he certainly made a mess. As if he hadn't come for a couple of years. Just imagine. The case, my case, was sure enough just inside the wardrobe. Because these two are too stupid to know how much that chemical is worth or because they trust so much in God that they don't worry too much about anything. I thought about his huge knife a couple of times while we were fucking, but this time, fortunately, the knife didn't appear. When I went past the bathroom door, over the noise of the water coming out of the tap, I thought I heard the guy praying.

These people are like that. They pile up their scars one on top of the other and they don't want to know about chemical. The guy is wearing one of his church t-shirts on which is written: BLESSED GUILT.

He came wearing that t-shirt.

In the corridor a happy Japanese song was playing. All the staff smiled at me and there were lots of them, because in Vietnam there are always lots of people in hotel corridors and though you never know exactly what their job is, they're probably there in case you need them. Charming people anyway.

In the lift I opened the case using my key. Everything was still there.

I thought for a moment about the poor Scandinavian with his throat cut in the toilets at Bangkok Airport. I thought about him as you think about a rabbit hanging from a hook. That's to say, without too much interest. Even with joy, certainly the effect of the staples, that fasten a pleasant sensation of well-being onto any thought. Beautiful lift, lovely day, delightful Vietnamese waiters, splendid carpet. The kind of substance that softens the edges of Sundays and turns them, not into something wonderful but certainly into something that's more bearable. Sweet chemical, in the words of the Classification Committee.

When I reached the hotel reception I fancied a martini so much that I had no alternative but to stop off at the bar. It didn't seem likely that the old keeper of promises would turn up there. Most couples like to kiss and utter sweet nothings to each other after fucking.

Lovely rain from the windows of the bar. The lovely noise of small motorbikes in Le Loi Boulevard. Lovely women hanging about the reception.

Another martini, admittedly downed very quickly, because it's not a good idea to tempt fate either. Especially if the fate in question is brandishing a knife for killing wild boars.

It's only when I look at the bar wall and see a framed photo, the shadow of a tree against the door of the garage of a small white house, one of those classic American houses, I have the feeling that the effect of the staples is beginning to wear off and that everything is gradually returning to normal, that's to say, getting worse.

Without any obvious connection another image comes into my mind. It's a black and white photo. In the photo you can see a woman in the sea, with just her head above the water, her hands over her face, crying or probably wiping the salt out of her eyes.

I drink my second martini and leave the hotel. I walk along slowly, down the boulevard, on the way to the river. Considering seriously my new condition as a free agent.

Considering the opportunity and the risk. Being alert, look-ing around without seeing anything except the same people who fill the centre of Saigon day and night.

Clean, alone, deprived of my recent excess of self-confidence. Abandoned for a moment by the chemical, guided by two martinis and by the light from the boats that comes up the avenue from the river.

Ho Chi Minh isn't the ideal city for an illegal agent. Too much activity. Here they all say more than they know in order to get rid of the police and get the chemical regulators off their backs. The news of the death of the Scandinavian will have put the company on the tracks of the lost material. In that case not a single sale in the area.

Near to the Thai Binh market, I buy two Communist army badges from a girl of ten or twelve years of age. Not because I need them, but because at times it's impossible to say no to such pretty girls. I know that it's ridiculous and no-one who hasn't been faced with one of these lovely girls could understand it, but it's impossible not to think about a life-time at her side. How impossible it is to hear about one hundred thousand and not think, even for one second, about what you would do with one of them.

I sit down at a tea stall that's only ten beach chairs lined up in the street and I drink a tea and then a whole bottle of rice wine. With my case, needless to say, always resting on my knees. More than enough chemical to bury the boulevard, the rain, the children, the road down to the river and the whole river.

Drunk on rice wine. Encouraged by the shameful joy with which a living soldier steals a gold watch from a dead soldier, I see the approach of a better future, based on this lucky turn in the spiral of my own misfortune.

Now that I'm a suspended salesman carrying around unauthorised merchandise, suffering from serious epileptic episodes, without a viable contact in the area, with all the eyes of the Company focused on me, and there are lots of them, undoubtedly, as the main suspect for the death of the courteous and smiling administrative agent. What's there left for me to do around here?

Quite certainly very little indeed.

The barbers carry on working in the street, with their mirrors nailed to trees, and it's as though you're remembering them when you're really watching them. That's the way some things are. They never seem as if they're being seen for the first time. Those barbers with no customer sit in folding chairs in front of their own mirrors. Looking at their own faces. Now a child sits on the pavement next to his little brother and explains things to him, undoubtedly important things, until some tourists pass by next to him and then he jumps to his feet and pulls them by the sleeve in order to take them to the river. There are boats waiting on the river. The boats belonging to the parents, brothers or uncles of the children. The boats that sail up and down the delta, offering wonderful trips along the Red River.

Naturally everything is filled with the tremendous noise of the helicopters, and the towers on which the helicopters land give Saigon, which is still a flat city compared with Kuala Lumpur, Bangkok or Hong Kong, the appearance of an upturned table. They say that the Vietnamese don't like skyscrapers. They say that no Vietnamese can bear sleeping very far from the earth in which his ancestors are buried. That may be true, in any case it's not advisable to jump to too many conclusions about what's going through the minds of these people. Underestimating the Vietnamese has brought the free world many bitter experiences.

The sun is already halfway up the sky. The bell in the French cathedral strikes two o'clock and then all the other hours, one after the other. Evening comes and night falls and I lie still in bed waiting for tomorrow.

There's nothing more to tell.

LEBUH CHULIA AND
INFINITE GOOD FORTUNE

Bangkok.

Two commercial planes have flown over low and close together. The recent increase in plane crashes is mainly down to this crazy behaviour by pilots, who try to make up for the actual lack of air space with imagination and arrogance.

But what would airports be without these little delights.

The next monotrain won't be in for another ten minutes, so I go over to one of the drinks stalls, next to the track, and I ask for a beer. There are about two hundred TV screens the whole length of the platform and there are goldfish on every screen.

I've got a day and a half left in Bangkok before the first flight leaves for Penang, the most beautiful city on the most beautiful island of Georgetown, to the west of Malaysia. Penang is a happy city, full of money, but even in the first years of the millennium much calmer than Kuala Lumpur or Singapore. A good port in which to do business without attracting the attention of the Company, which by this stage must be monitoring the sale of every artificial or natural dose of oblivion. If an old man forgets the name of his children, the Company will want to know how and why, if a whore from Patpong forgets how long she's been doing this and forgets her promise not to kiss the clients, not a single one of them, and forgets the title of her favourite song, the Company wants to know who's behind such oblivion, and if the light of the neon advertising signs opposite the bridges flickers, the Company will want to know what's been forgotten in that instant, when for a second the whole city was only lit up by the black light of the dance halls and the white light in the bedrooms of those who can't sleep or who are frightened even when they're asleep.

I decide, quite rightly, not to spend the night in one of the capsules at the airport, because you can hardly fit your feet into one of those niches and because it's much more stimulating, for body and soul, to go for a walk around the delightful hell that is Khao San Road. I don't have to record my movements now nor justify my expenses. Now I can watch life on the streets and let the e-mail messages pile up like letters at the door of a dead man. Now pleasure is the first and only priority I have. Now I could spend the night dancing and the next night as well, if I wanted to.

But I don't want to.

Now I can forget the image of the woman, your image, every time it appears.

The monorail draws into Bangkok and the people crowd together in the stations and under the stations, waiting to find a space on the platform. I go down the stairs, first to the level of the express service and then to the level of the slow service and down to yet another level until I reach the ground. The stripes of light under the umbrellas light up the faces of the cooks and the customers, on either side of the stalls selling boiled fish. In Khao San Road there are gathered together all the shady drifters in South East Asia waiting for money, cut-price plane tickets to any corner of the planet, visas, the worst of home-made chemical, anything needed to carry on the journey. Khao San Road is the great station for travellers in transit, limbo, the waiting room. No-one wants to stay here for long, and the person who stays here for a long time knows that things aren't going well, although of course he always maintains the hope that everything will improve. Like you wait for the rain to stop. With the same vague hope. Khao San Road is never the end of the journey.

The beer sellers go up and down the avenue with their plastic freezer boxes hanging around their necks. I buy a can of local beer, I take a room in a hotel that's not too dirty, I have a shower, I change clothes and I go down to the alleyways behind the bars filled with foreigners who spend hours watching American films on TV sets hanging from the ceiling by chains. I buy a gram of coke, something resembling DMT, and a little bag of marihuana. Naturally I take two lovely Thai girls up with me to my room. We drink, we smoke, we snort almost all of the coke and a bit of the dreaded DMT. I fuck both of them for all I'm worth. To fuck without love is always an act of despair, especially for a good old Catholic boy. I pay them more than they ask and less than they deserve. With all the chemical that I've got in my case, money is not going to be a problem for quite some time. One of the girls leaves at once, the other one stays with me. It takes me two or three more hours to get off to sleep. I see the dawn break and I watch the carriages of the monorail from the window. For a moment I have the feeling that it's going to be the best week of my life and perhaps even the last.

I fall asleep thinking about the woman who appears in my dreams as well as outside them.

I know things about us and I store up other things that I imagine, as if they were letters signed in blood.

In the end I am ready to forget it all.

I wake up in a suite of the Shangri-la, the best hotel in Penang, the old English capital to the west of the island of Georgetown, with an appalling headache and a magnificent

view over the Malacca Straits. I take two good mornings,
the miracle chemical against hangovers. My headache disappears and the waves in the bay liven up like drunken children.
There's no longer anything that chemical can't hide or
anything that chemical isn't capable of bringing back again.
I'm wearing some delightful leopard skin trousers and there
are at least six good friends, strangers of course, in my room.
Three women, two boys and a Thai transvestite who bears an
extraordinary resemblance to the Princess of Wales. They're
all asleep. There are bottles of Cliquot lying on the floor as
well as on all the tables and on the two trays covered with
food, along with a bicycle. On TV there's a group of fanatics
praying at the gates of Cape Canaveral, on their placards is
written: GOD DOESN'T WANT US UP THERE. The good
mornings have taken away the pain but they haven't brought
anything good. After eating a plateful of cold rice with sweet
and sour prawns, I take a beer out of the minibar and take
a phial of GPG. It takes effect when I'm in the shower. I
dry myself and put back on my leopard skin trousers and a
black Japanese silk shirt. One of the boys has woken up. A
pleasant Malayan who has nothing on except for some Air
Jordan trainers and a garland of flowers. He greets me with
a smile and goes out onto the terrace to watch the waves.
I don't know how long I've been in Penang. The boy has
found a music channel on the TV and dances naked on the
terrace. It's six in the afternoon. I'm in good shape. I move
about inside my own life with the arrogance of a complete
stranger. I can't recognise anything. My room is the room
of a stranger. My friends are the friends of a stranger. The
boy comes back in. He asks me for a gold bracelet that I'm
wearing and that I hadn't seen before. I give it to him. He
thanks me ten or twelve times and hugs me and kisses me
and puts it on without stopping dancing. It's a thick bracelet

like a fat snake. I ask the boy whose bicycle it is and the boy points to one of the sleeping children. A present. Apparently I'm a great guy who goes around giving presents to everyone. We're all very happy. That's what he said. I don't know if 'all' just refers to them. I ask him if I'm happy as well and he says that I'm the happiest, the happy man who makes everyone with him happy. That sounds great. Princess Diana has also woken up. She smiles. And she says something in Thai. The boy with the golden bracelet lies down beside her. She strokes his head as if he were a dog and he licks her toes like a dog. I get out my case which is under the bed, amongst a heap of shoes. There are more shoes than there are people. I look for some shoes of my size. The boy finds a boot with a Cuban heel, a black one, and then searches and searches until he finds another and helps me to put them on. It's a beautiful day. I say goodbye to the boy, the Princess and the sleeping bodies. I'm the happy man who makes those with him happy. I go down to the hotel bar. The Shangri-la has a dozen bars and restaurants, round a huge entrance hall intersected with golden columns. Cooks from Hong Kong. Cooks from Peking. Cooks from Las Vegas who watch as the hamburgers ooze blood. The *crème de la crème*. I opt for the European lounge. There's an old Frenchman sitting at a piano singing an old French song. I ask for a martini. Although they're no longer in fashion, I still like the songs. At first I think that everyone is looking at me, but at once I realise that, in fact, everyone's looking at my trousers. I drink my martini and ask for another. There's nothing better than drinking in a hotel bar, you can also be at ease drinking on planes and in airports and in all the other places without memory.

I take a cyclo at the hotel door and make a leisurely trip over to Chinatown. Of course I still see her face next to the chinese stalls selling fabric and next to the brightly coloured façades covered with dragons and flowers, but it's her face as it appeared in photos. The face of a woman in a photograph is remembered long after you've forgotten her. I remember the sound of the Polaroid and the seconds spent waiting before her image appears on the paper. I can't remember the sound of her voice and I can't remember her. Just the image that appears gradually, until it is fixed once and for all in the photo.

The old Muslim men drive their cyclos at the inconsequential speed of important business. So slow it seems it is the entire city that is being dragged along at their side. Penang is the slowest city in South East Asia. The only one that keeps itself outside the absurd speed of the economic growth that feeds the pride of all the neighbouring cities. The towers rise up slothfully in Penang, without the vanity of the towers in Hong Kong or Singapore. Children stroll along the walkways in the shopping malls with their heads down, dragging their feet, looking at the shop windows out of the corners of their eyes.

Penang has exactly the right speed.

The people in Penang don't follow planes with their eyes and planes land in Penang with the discretion of nocturnal burglars.

Penang is a paradise for slow people.

When the shops close, the night market opens, with the calmness with which you light a candle from the flame of another candle.

There's a band playing in front of the Lebuh Chulia Temple. The music of tin drums. The procession goes through Chinatown in search of ghosts, because these people believe that everyone's got a ghost hidden up their sleeve, and they also believe that the noise of the drums and the procession of standards and flags wakes up the ghosts and makes them emerge and takes them down the street, back to the temple, where they can carry on sleeping without harming anyone.

Penang gathers up its ghosts and deals with them calmly and without fear.

I sit down at a stall next to the harbour. The ferries cross with one another in the bay, the chicken satay sticks and the beer come without being asked for and they're cheap. It's night-time now and there's nothing to worry about.

I've got money in my pocket now. Now I've got a case with enough chemical to make much, much more. Now I can live the days, one after the other, and forget them, one after the other, so that they don't get in the way. Now I know that tomorrow, come what may, nothing will have happened.

After having dinner I walk along the beach, and after walking, I take a cyclo to one of the nightclubs in Lebuh Victoria. On the way there we pass a dozen Australian rugby players, dressed in tracksuits, all the same, with some friendly Nordic girls who smile at us from their cyclos and say things to us that neither I nor the old Hindu driver understand. It could be about love but it could also be because they're looking for the road to the beach. If everything that looks like love really were love, my God, this would be a different and better world and even the darkest nightmares would be followed by unbearably happy days. But, anyway, let's not get off the point, for if it's true that the cathedral bells ring out for joy it's no less true that the same bells, from time to time, are tolled for sorrow. At the entrance to the club there's a huge neon sign with the outline of a naked girl dipping her feet into a glass of champagne. One has to go around continually following signs and most signs are ambiguous but, fortunately, some signs are as clear as this one.

In a dark area of the car park, I take out my little bag of coke and take a line and straight afterwards take a yellow pill in order to ease the first come down. At the door there are loads of Malayan girls queuing up. Of course I don't have to wait, my friends the doormen welcome me with huge smiles, while they move the crowd aside to make room for me at the doorway. All very smooth. There's nothing like jumping the queue of a stupid nightclub in order to make you feel stupidly happy.

I drink a beer and congratulate myself once again on a perfect day. Clean and perfect.

I feel like a murderer after he's burnt his rubber gloves. Convinced that the fingerprints that may be found on my own life will not be mine.

Trance music with DJs recently brought over from London. Trance music is what kids like now. Dreadfully slow dreadfully good mechanical rhythms. They call it trance music because it gently meshes with the derivatives of morphine, like a tired Pied Piper of Hamlyn, dragging behind it sleeping rats.

Sleeping rats with their eyes wide open, because the new chemical keeps continual small flashes of euphoria under the pillow. Much better than the horse tranquillizers, that used to result in children ending up asleep at the wheel and shortly afterwards, all too frequently, dead against the shining advertising hoardings on the motorway, smashed up against the adverts for their favourite films.

A boy from Kuala Lumpur slips me ten blue phials without having to talk me into it. You don't need much imagination to know that the old cocaine will outlast the smooth yellow pills and will re-appear at the very end and then there's nothing better than a couple of blue phials to knock me out, with the smoothness of happy sleeping rats, and from

then on to start again with the happy vertigo produced by the
first lines of coke until I spin round again and rediscover the
fear that is always waiting behind the euphoria, or probably
fuck someone and take advantage of someone else's fear, or
probably drink, or probably ride happily in a cyclo to the
hotel and then sleep, alone or with one of the friends that
I left inside there and who are probably still there waiting,
like a soldier's girlfriend.

Another day on the happy coasts of Malaysia.

Death through repetition.

Chemical reality also has long claws.

In the cheerful nightclubs of Penang the boys dance slowly
to their trance music and the Australian rugby players lift
up the Malayan girls from the floor as if they were glasses
of Bordeaux.

A friend asks me if I want to go up to see his people, so I
go up to the second floor that looks down on the dance floor
and in one of the private rooms I meet up with a whole lot of
Argentinians on a business trip and the Argentinians have a
huge selection on a glass table, coke of course, as well as pills
and phials and blue needles and apparently all that's missing
is my chemical and they all know who I am and what I sell
and they've enough money to buy an island, and for much
less money than they've got, but a great deal however you
look at it. I sell them a fair amount of short term and long
term memory erasers and they ask me about yesterday but
I don't know anything about yesterday and they ask me if I
want something and I grab a supply and a bottle of Moet.

We talk in River Plate Spanish and I don't know what
they are telling me. One of them, who is called Alejandro
and who apparently remembers me sitting in a club in the
centre of Buenos Aires less than ten paces away from no less
a person than Maradona himself, asks after my wife and of

course I tell him that she's died, in an accident, although I'm
sure that it's not true and the man then appears really upset
by this and says to me:

She was a very attractive woman.

And looking down at the floor at the blue carpet under
the glass-topped table I reply:

Yes, yes she was.

Although in fact I don't know what I'm saying.

I've got lost in the hills of Georgetown. I've got tired of the
compulsive euphoria of amphetamines. I've left my hat in
the house of one of the whores. I went to sleep in the
cinema. I made a bet of one hundred dong with a child
on the quayside and I lost them. However many stones I
threw I didn't manage to bring down a single seagull.

He brought down two of them.

I bumped into a woman who claims to be your mother
and who apparently has amazing luck. I allowed myself to
be taken in by a salesman of blue needles and I put up
with all that stupid sadness as best I could. Some Burmese
salesmen invited me to have dinner with them but then one
of them punched me on account of something that I said
and for trying to have it off with his wife in the toilets of
a French restaurant in the city centre. Another one of the
Burmese, one who bore a striking resemblance to someone
whom I have almost completely forgotten, a distant cousin,
took out his knife. He didn't do much with it. He didn't
seem like a man capable of killing another, although you
can never tell about things like that at first sight.

I left without having dessert. I sat down near to a mosque
and listened to the evening prayer. I drank a small bottle
of whisky that I carried about in my boot. I snorted half
a gram of cocaine. I stretched out on the grass in the

park opposite the library, but then straight away I got up and went off.

It started to rain and it rained for quite a while. I watched the rain from the terrace of a café in Lebuh Chulia. When it stopped raining I went back to the Irish bars and had some beer and spoke about football very rapidly with a Liverpool supporter. I took three black stones to bring me down off the coke. After that, I talked much more slowly. I spent a couple of hours calmly and then I came up again while on the dance floor of The Sanctuary, a club for millionaire kids near to the marina. Naturally I wasn't dancing. I was just there, quietly watching the dancing. Just the way I was watching the rain before and the way I was watching the knife even earlier on.

The way you look at things that might or might not kill you.

Friday, I think, and my suite in the Hotel Shangri-la is perfectly tidy, empty and clean. There appears on TV the picture of a Belgian murderer and it's the face of a normal man. Men kill women because they can't bear the real women who live inside the bodies of the women they desire. The Belgian murderer has been put into one of those re-education camps into which many men, actual or potential murderers, are put these days. Men brought up on the old pornography or on the old religions, who go into camps in order to get out the murderer from inside them. Men who murder women. That's what they've got written on their t-shirts. Despite the fact that the results vary from case to case, the re-education camps have shown their effectiveness. There are lots of men who kill women. The papers call it the new virus. International feminism calls it the old enemy.

Next to the bed there's a bottle of champagne inside an electric ice bucket. Cold champagne in the morning and the noise of the Penang traffic coming in through the open terrace door and the sound of the sea coming in through the same door.

Of course I've dreamt about a woman inside a closed car and, of course, all the pain of that dream disappears at once after a tiny quantity of my own chemical.

In the shower I'm visited by one of my old shaking fits. My head bangs against the glass partition after a momentary disconnection. Fortunately I don't fall down and straightaway regain control and feel my neuronal activity recovering like the lights on a Christmas tree after flickering.

I repeat aloud: Tomorrrow wi'lll be annoother day, only to realise that I've still got small problems with my speech. I say it six or seven times until I achieve a normal, non-altered vocalization.

Tomorrow will be another day.

I stay under the hot water until I get over the fright and then I get out of the shower. I look for a bottle of mylo-depressants, I only take one of them and lie down on my bed with my eyes closed until the tension produced by the partial epileptic episode disappears.

My head is once again incapable of bearing all the chemical that my heart needs.

Brilliant party.

A former leader of the Prohibition Party, Asian Section, won over by the Chemical Brotherhood, was about to smash his yacht into one of those hospital boats that operate without a licence in the bay. Cheap plastic surgery for the local transvestites. Implants of dead people's skin on the lips and re-implantation of the silicon bags recovered from the

Catholic cemeteries of Hong Kong. Extremely unpleasant techniques, supposedly given up years ago in the West. When I say that we were on the point of crashing, I mean that I saw the face of one of those monsters on the bridge of the old Russian boat. Fortunately the skipper recovered control at the last moment, avoiding a catastrophe. Then he went down to the lounge, where Japanese executives indulge in uncontrolled sex and karaoke, this latter a lamentable custom from which the Japanese should have freed themselves a decade ago, the skipper came down, according to him, to confess to all of us that the entire manoeuvre had been carefully programmed into the on-board computer in order to liven up the crossing. Very entertaining, yes indeed. Apparently, as he explained to me later, these luxury boats have the same system installed as in the big one-man boats. The latest generation of oil tankers that cross the sea from one side of the planet to the other with a single man on board. A kind of symbolic captain, who has nothing to do but gaze at the sky waiting for the seagulls to arrive. Anyway, my interest in the advances of the naval industry is very limited, so I go out to find something better to do and almost at once I find myself watching how a South African fucks a very famous old astronaut. One of those who returned from space with something very much like a voice, floating in something very similar to a radio wave. Of course I don't waste the opportunity and I ask the guy what the fuck it was that they heard up there and the old astronaut, without stopping his puffing and panting, tells me that it was a voice. He says this twice. It was a voice, my friend, whatever they may say, it was a voice. There's a woman sitting on the floor taking off her false eyelashes while she listens to the owner of the faith refuting the old astronaut's thesis. The owner of the faith is a large Thai who's wearing a t-shirt on which is written OWNER OF THE FAITH. The large Thai says that up there and down here there is only one voice and that that voice doesn't hide and that that voice will send us its angels, who will make us pay for all that we've done, even for everything that we've forgotten. Of course I had the impression that he said this last bit with his eyes on me, although I can't be certain about that either. I suppose that in the end everyone feels like an executioner in the house of a hanged man. Incidentally, I haven't come here to sell anything, I've come because a grateful client, a young Chinese industrialist, has invited me along and because recently I've allowed myself to be taken around like the ashes of a dead man inside an urn.

White flames, exotic drinks, cocaine, GPG, dancing on the deck and full moon.

I must have fallen asleep and the days must have elapsed, but I'm still in the boat, in a cabin the size of a suite with a Japanese girl high on blue needles, silent, gentle and pleasant like a good piece of news at the end of a bad day. Chia, for that's what this attractive girl is called, tells me that her father died in a suite at the Ritz Hotel in Paris, like all those suicides that are talked about in news bulletins, and then recites, one after the other, the long list of misfortunes that always accompany the twisted chemistry blue needles. Slight misfortunes like the shadow of geraniums swayed by the wind against a white wall. Misfortunes in which anyone who is ripped on blue finds a curious satisfaction. Nothing new in any of this. The sweet routine of people addicted to grief. All very boring, if it were not for the fact that my friend Chia is completely naked and hell bent on us spending the rest of the night fucking, drinking champagne and looking at the lights of the

Butterworth Coast, swarming with ferries, hospital boats, floating casinos and arms salesmen.

The quilt on the bed is a mustard colour and the mosquito net and the curtains are red and there are fresh flowers next to the bed. Nothing very nautical. This is something to be grateful for, since for some reason which I can't get my mind around it's very difficult not to feel a dickhead when you're on board a yacht. On the TV there's only one of those photographic channels on which there's a succession of fixed images of trivial objects: lamps, electrical appliances, aerials, chairs, ash trays . . . never people, so that you can watch for hours without any fear.

Chia has just had a bath and the water is still hot. I undress and get into the bath. Chia is crying naked on the bed but it's only that comforting put-on kind of crying. Crocodile tears that accompany the stories that she's making up as we go along; all of them sad, some of them vaguely familiar and others ridiculous. I know that she makes them up because she's told me as much and because almost nobody who can avoid it now has so many tales to tell and it's obvious that Chia isn't a Cambodian whore, but rather a little crown princess.

Then, after a moment, Chia asks me if I'm all right, because I've clearly been in the bath for too long.

Of course I reply that I'm fine, and I raise my glass of champagne although she's not watching, but it's not true because the fact is I can't feel the hot water on my body and that's always a bad sign, neurologically speaking.

Chia carries on making up ridiculous stories and it makes me think that it might be better if these people addicted to grief kept their misfortunes to themselves.

I turn on the hot water tap and choose the temperature and see the steam collecting on the mirror above the wash basin, but I can't feel the heat, nor can I feel the water against my skin.

A moment later Chia asks again: Is everything all right?

And this time I neither raise my champagne glass nor do I lie.

No, I'm afraid it's not.

There's nobody else at the top of the Post Office Tower and you can sit there calmly watching people in the street; Muslims, Catholics and Buddhists moving about around their mosques, churches and temples, as well as the tourists, all around the faithful and the cyclos, moving slowly like exhausted animals. The whole of Penang seems like an invention, something that you imagine from up here. Something that disappears when you just close your eyes.

Undoubtedly my only faith is resistance.

And then I go down to eat at one of the stalls in the Chinese quarter and those chicken satay sticks, with almond sauce, taste wonderful and the beer tastes wonderful and time, the hours that have no importance because there's nothing to do, also taste wonderful. The waiter only brings you the beer and only charges you for the beer and the table. You've got to buy the food at the street stalls. For some reason everything smells bad and tastes good at the same time.

Here the climate is mild and January is a month that's friendly towards plants and people. I ask the waiter if it's going to carry on like this all winter and the waiter looks at the sky, but the sky can't be seen because there are coloured garlands hanging from the cables that cross the street. Then he says that the worst is already over and of course I don't know what he's talking about. Everyone talks about the weather according to what they expect of it, on account of which two people looking at the same sky expect different clouds. Some people see clouds moving in the direction in which they live with annoyance and others just hope that the clouds are here to stay. It's not going to rain much more now says the waiter, and you get the feeling that on rainy days this man derives a strange consolation from the rain.

On the TV, at the back of the bar, on a wooden platform surrounded by flowers, there appears a burning car and next to the car there's an entire family sitting on the ground, next to the road. When you see something burning, you can't help imagining yourself inside it. You can't help feeling at the same time half dead and half alive. Incidentally, this morning I intercepted an e-mail circular from the Company asking the agents in the area about my whereabouts and of course nobody knows where I've got to and they speak of me like someone who has died or someone who has been lost forever. It alarmed me to see a brief note about how worried my family were, because I don't know who they're talking about, or exactly why they're worried. The recent constant erosions of memory move me further and further away from all of them, whoever they are, like a boat that moves so far away from the shore that it's already nearer the other side than it is to home. There's also an e-mail from Krumper. Someone who searches for me without conviction, like someone who shoots into the air. Someone who for some reason, certainly nothing more than the shadow of an intuition, I associate more with my future than with my past.

Apart from this just a tremendous pain in my shoulder clouds the happiness of these days.

Today I caught a guy following me. He followed me from the Kuan Yin Teng temple to the coffee shops in Lebuh Chulia, where the Irish gather to drink beer, and from there to St George's Cemetery. I sat down in front of the tomb of an English sailor called Lambert Hutchins and I stayed there, looking at the gravestone, waiting for the guy to get tired. But the man, a strong smiling Hindu, sat down a short distance from me, opposite the tomb of a woman called Hortense Robbins, and he put his hands together, because that's the way he thinks Christians pray, and he's pretended to pray without the smile leaving his mouth for a moment. Of course I could have said something to him, his silly audacity was frankly irritating, but I preferred not to give him that satisfaction. And so we shared our moments of feigned meditation in total silence. St George's Cemetery has a magnificent view over the northern channel, on the opposite side to the peninsula and out over the green valley that goes down to the sea, and in the air there was naturally the calmness that one associates with cemeteries. Hortense and Lambert have had unexpected visitors this afternoon and Hortense and Lambert must have been sincerely moved by the devotion of two strangers, once they'd got over the initial surprise that must be produced in dead people by the respect of those who are very far from sharing their blood. Nevertheless it was a real pleasure, putting to one side the annoying matter of my being followed, to see yourself surrounded by so many stones and so many names inscribed years ago by people who are also now dead. When those who name dead people have gone, there just remains the calmness of foreign cemeteries, in which nothing appears familiar and nothing frightens you. The heat of the sun on your arms makes you want to have a siesta. Needless to say I went to sleep. Returning to the tiresome matter of my pursuer, it's not right nor decent of me to fall asleep in front of the spy. When I eventually took my leave of Lambert the Hindu followed me, like a discreet friend, as far as the gate

opposite the church, and then, always at a distance of five
or six yards. We went down together to Gat Lebuh Prangin, a
street infested with foreign franchises, shops selling records,
sports clothing, Danish television sets, Italian fashion clothes
and American donuts. In front of a pair of second-hand
Levis my friend displayed the same respect towards me as
at poor Hortense Robbins' tomb which, quite naturally,
didn't seem appropriate to me. It could be concluded that
this poor Hindu had never followed anyone before. Nor can
I remember having been followed, although that of course
doesn't mean anything. The Company must be short-staffed
if it employs smiling beginners to track down their valuable
missing chemical. We may well also be dealing with a Hindu
who's in love. Or a bored Hindu. Or a frightened client. I'm
still turning these various possibilities over in my mind when
I realise that I've been completely clean for over three hours,
the duration of this trivial adventure, and I start to notice
the harsh comedown from the cocaine, once the effect of the
sweet amphetamines has finally vanished. Before reaching
the port I take two white flames and I buy a beer at a stall
in Lebuh Victoria. I'm about to drink to the health of my
faithful stranger but I don't do it because the Hindu is no
longer there.

I look all over and search for him really hard but there's
nothing that can be done because the Hindu, whoever he
was, has already gone away.

So here I am in the basement of the Komtar Centre and the
Komtar Centre is just another of those huge shopping malls,
full of supermarkets and Nike shops, which have turned the
whole world into an idiot's gallery. All the Georgetown buses
leave from the basement of the Komtar and always go down
to the ferry, to cross the strait to the peninsula. Of course

only those who can't help it travel by bus and that's why
bus stations are the saddest places in the world: because all
those who wait and those who get on and off, those who
leave and those who arrive, are totally vanquished, bored,
alone, old, sad and dead.

I'm sitting drinking beer. I'm waiting until I feel strong
enough to get back to the hotel. I'm looking at a Malay
bus driver who is giving me a really enthusiastic blow job
as the dawn breaks.

Good morning.

A rather unpleasant night because of the LSD, something
that I had definitely decided not to take again long before
having forgotten all about it. Acid opens doors and behind
the doors there's nothing. Terrifying almost all of the time
and eventually soothing, because you always return from
a day spent in the company of acid with a small victory
to your credit. Not necessarily a two-headed dragon, but
rather a small headless rabbit. A victory anyway. The man
who goes deep into the jungle and survives always returns
singing a song although, it has to be acknowledged, the
jungle is now burnt, not still in flames, but devastated and
blackened. Anyway, what makes you frightened isn't fire,
but what's left after fire and after fire there's nothing left.
A beer and two GPGs to get the day moving. After LSD, if
you're not careful, there are a succession of ridiculous signs:
smiling supermarket check-out assistants, yellow cars with
devilish number plates, hands with six fingers, absolutely
anything. Everything as credible as a bramble bush burning
in the middle of the desert.

I leave the Shangri-la and put my few possessions in a
taxi heading for the Cathay Hotel. The Shangri-la is too
popular, everyone who imports in this part of Malaysia

passes through it, and I've no intention of seeing my old friends from the Company, who continue to circulate details of me via e-mail, with the infinite faith of mothers who have lost their children. So I move on. Apparently those running the hotel remember all the parties that I forget. The naked transvestites running along the corridor, the women crying next to the swimming pool high on blue needles, the children dancing on the terrace drunk on vodka. Too much noise. Too many complaints. According to the way the hotel employee in charge of public relations explained it, and you can't beat his description, my happiness is too obvious. So, farewell to the Shangri-la then. Farewell to its martinis and its amazing chef from Hong Kong and the marvellous dumplings that he prepared. Farewell to the French pianist and the Bulgarian dancers. Farewell to all that.

Welcome to the Cathay, the old colonial hotel backing onto the bay, the Chelsea of South East Asia, where romantics and armed men sleep. A very old Chinese man wearing a bowling shirt takes me up to one of the rooms on the first floor. He lets me go in first but at once moves ahead to open the shutters of the balcony. The weather is beautiful. I give the old man a good tip and the old man asks me if I want anything else and I ask him for a bottle of whisky and before I realise it the great guy is back with a bottle and two glasses. Naturally I invite him to join me for a drink. He drinks it down in one go, thanks me and leaves.

Then, straight after, everything goes black. And a second later I collapse.

On Tenuck Bennang beach, the boys run near the water's edge and aim blows into the air like miniature boxers and from time to time get involved in half-hearted fights.

Without getting hurt, but going through all the motions of real professionals. These same boys have sold me shells and wooden crosses and cartridge cases hanging from a silk cord, they also asked me what New York is like and Madrid and the rest of the world, and I've tried as best as I could to recapture old images, but not all the images were clear, not all the streets were in the right place, not all the descriptions were exact. I'm naturally scared on realising the chaotic state of my memories and the new silence that has taken the place of many of the noises that I thought it was impossible to forget. The noise of cars in the street or the noise of rain falling on the ground. Two GPGs to by-pass the fear and a cold beer to help me bear the sun and the heat of this ridiculous January.

Then at once I turn my attention to business, because there's a woman on the beach, sitting next to me, who wants to forget a man, a man whom she's already lost, and she can't think what wrong there can be in forgetting something which, when all's said and done, you no longer possess. Apparently, the woman had never forgotten before and those who have never forgotten can't hide the fear that there's something devilish in our chemical memory erosions, however obvious it may be, and that's how I explain it to her, that it's memory, not oblivion, that's the real invention of the devil.

Are you sure? asks the woman, who can't be more than thirty and who's staring at the sand as if in the sand there was written something which only she was capable of reading.

I'm sure.

The woman has a business in the port, next to the ferries, a small stall selling fabric, Japanese silk and embroidered materials, but she doesn't sew, she told me this herself although I had already reached this conclusion as her hands

are clean and white. When she realises that I'm looking at
her hands, she hides them under the sand. The woman then
tells me that she was not born in Penang, but in Kota Belud,
and that she came here with her husband, and that her
husband then left, because things collapse suddenly and
come to an end, and that the man, her husband, left just
like that. Without taking anything from what had been his
home. Without taking his clothes, or his books, or even his
glasses, and that's why she thought at the time that he would
soon come back, but he'd never returned and then she started
thinking what kind of life is led by a man who doesn't want
to take with him anything of what he has possessed, anything
of what was his. Afterwards, of course, she had carried on
living surrounded by all those despised things for so many
years, until today, and now she also wants to leave and forget
everything.

I'm genuinely happy to be able to help her, so I tell her that
she's got nothing to worry about because forgetting is my
business. Then she rescues her hands from the sand and takes
a whole lot of money out of a small embroidered bag.

In the adjoining room they're celebrating Hitler's birthday. Military marches come through the wall and get into
my room. Old Luftwaffe hymns cheer up the afternoon,
hot, but otherwise beautiful. My high spirited neighbour,
who isn't German or anything like it, but rather a confused
Burmese, puts his head around my balcony, which is close
enough to his, and gives me a kind invitation to come to his
party. As he himself said, the happiness of your neighbours
is always annoying unless you share it. Won over by his
words and with the natural curiosity of someone who's
never attended a birthday party for Hitler, I go out into
the beautiful corridor of the Cathay, a magnificent hotel;
wooden floors, white walls with blue edging and genuine

Art Deco furniture, I go out into the passage, as I was saying, and walk barefoot, just a few steps, to the door of the room next door. My Burmese friend has two Eastern couples in there as well as his wife, an American whose face is flushed due to the champagne and the glory of old German victories. The walls are naturally covered with swastikas and military flags, beside the bed an illustrated edition of *Mein Kampf* serves as a bible.

Champagne? asks the Burmese Nazi.

Yes please.

Then the American woman, who turns out to be from San Francisco, hands me a dressing-table mirror with quite a heap of cocaine on it. I feel obliged to offer them in exchange some pills but they decline them enthusiastically.

Not those drugs, says the girl from San Francisco, false empathy is the most dishonest of emotions.

Great. I put my pills away and to the sound of a beautiful tune of the Wehrmacht I cross the room to the terrace and look down at the garage of the Cathay.

Everything's peaceful, the drivers of the cyclos under the shade of a tree waiting for the hotel guests and further away people coming back from Chayamangkalaran Wat, the temple of the blue dragons and the gigantic reclining Buddha. Everything's in order out there and inside these crazy Nazis do nothing but sing and march up and down and consume champagne and cocaine.

I say goodbye to the six lunatics most politely and one of them, a Thai woman dressed like an astronaut's wife, insists on going with me to the corridor, and when I go into my room to put on my boots, I've still got her behind me, and then into the bargain she insists on kissing me, so we kiss, we kiss for a long time, although it doesn't seem long to her since when we split up she blames me for something, but as she does this in Thai I don't know what it's all about, and of course I don't pay too much attention to her.

A cyclo is waiting for me at the door of the Cathay. You can get around so well in these contraptions that you feel like touring the whole world in one of them. When the old Hindu asks me where we're going, I'm naturally far less ambitious.

To the Komtar Centre.

In the baths at the Komtar I have a rapid and shameful encounter with a muscular boy from Brunei. Then, straightaway (and this is the good thing about shopping malls, that you can do everything there) I go up to the art galleries on the top floor and stay there for quite some time watching one of those guys who inoculate themselves with sophisticated viruses designed by daring genetic engineers and who then exhibit the surprising results on their own skin. The man is standing, naked, against a white wall on which is written the name of the virus: ZERO.

They've called it zero because it's capable of reducing a guy to the size of a donut in a couple of weeks. Not at all nice by any stretch of the imagination. These new suicides make you long for the old masochists, with weights hanging from their penises and their nipples pierced with nails. So that's that! Everything moves forward. It's a sign of the times.

Now I come to think of it, I ate a hamburger, something that I don't usually do, and I bought a whole lot of useless things: trainers, pipe-smoking accessories and some wonderful sunglasses. I threw it all away, except for the sunglasses, because I hate walking around carrying bags.

I'd already been sitting in a ridiculous Mexican cantina for some time, drinking mescal, when I realised that I was high on roses, a light, pleasant, gentle, ridiculous substance that's produced a lot in the Nordic countries and that brings with it all this prolonged and vague happiness that makes one waste time, six or seven hours, in the shopping mall or any other place, without the slightest shadow of anxieties appearing. Undoubtedly an immature drug, probably an accidental discovery in the development of a more interesting, more energetic compound, something that's certainly not my kind of thing but which for some reason that I cannot remember I must have taken, although I don't remember when or where.

The half-life of roses, that's to say the time that the compound takes to disappear in the blood, is so long that it gives you time to forget why or with whom you've taken it. All you've got to do then is wait until the fair closes. Unfortunately, the neuronal decay caused by this invention is terrifying. The pointless happiness that it provides demands a disproportionate effort. Something like a paper boat that needs a hurricane in order to go round and round the bath tub.

Anyway, there's nothing else I can do for the time being, so I ask for another mescal, I smile as nicely as I can at a Malay in an unconvincing Emiliano Zapata costume and I start to ponder as to whether Hitler was indeed born in January.

The last time I wake up in Malaysia I see a boy dressed in jeans and a white t-shirt standing on a chair looking out of the window, from between the strips of one of those blinds made of white vertical strips. When he realises I'm looking at him, he gives me a quick explanation.

'If I don't get up here I can't see the sea.'

Then he gets down from the chair. He's no more than twenty, with very short black hair, he speaks Castilian with a Portuguese accent. He's nice and he's my friend. I know this because he tells me.

'I'm your friend. We were talking for a long time in the rock garden. There were also two Filipino girls. They left before you had your seizure. We didn't fuck, you and me I mean. Nothing like that.'

Of course I'm naked, at the foot of the bed there's a wonderful grey linen suit and a wonderful white silk shirt.

'And what about the Filipino girls?'

'Ah yes, the Filipino girls . . . I mean we sure threw them out.'

As he says this his eyes light up.

'I'm delighted.'

The room's cold, the window's shut. All the heat's outside. The Filipino girls were wearing French hats. I do remember that. Hats that were made in France. They were so very proud of their little hats.

I don't remember having fucked them, any of them at all. I only remember their hats.

The name of the hotel is written on the sheets.

Paradise Bed and Breakfast.

'Where's breakfast?'

'I've eaten it all myself . . . I'm sorry . . . it didn't look as if you were going to wake up. I've got a bit of coffee left but it's cold.'

'I never drink coffee. It's not good for you. How long have I been asleep?'

'A day and a half.'

'That's not too long.'

'It's not too long in Malaysia.'

'And what about in Lisbon?'

'I'm not from Lisbon, I'm from Madeira,' says the boy with the pride with which people leave one place to go and live in another. Lisbon's nevertheless a wonderful city, slow, a city that's always got its eyes fixed on somewhere else. Like a child watching from the bridge of a ship. Like someone holding a closed letter before posting it, something that's still here and which is already far away. Madeira is a small island in the Atlantic. I can't remember having been there but that, as always, doesn't mean a thing.

I certainly feel the pain in my back, but now it's a bigger pain, as if some mad doctor had ripped out my spinal column and had put a broomstick in its place. The room is white and only has a bed, a table and the chair onto which my friend from Madeira climbs to look at the sea.

'Where's the TV?'

'I swapped it for ten phials of GPG with a Chinaman.'

'Have you got any left?'

'You've got a bit of everything in your case.'

My case is beside the bed. On seeing it I feel like someone emerging from an absurd dream with a piece of gold in his hand. There's enough chemical in the case to make the Pope forget where he works and samples of all the best products made in that part of the world, and even something that had come straight from the chemists of Shinjuku, pills for Japanese models and their poet boyfriends. It's common knowledge that all these beautiful girls have gone in for poetry now.

'I've hardly taken any of it,' says my friend, although I don't understand why a guy who lets me have his bed and looks after me like a mother was not going to be able to take all that he wanted.

Two good mornings and a GPG don't improve anything. Almost all the pains stay put, like the defence in an Italian football team.

My friend passes a bottle of champagne over to me but the

champagne is already warm and it's not French and I think that that's what finally puts paid to me, because when I try to thank him I'm seized by a distressing attack of aphasia and what I say, apparently, cannot be understood.

Nor can what I say next.

In Lisbon, from the monastery, you can see the rooftops of the old city that descend towards the port in a disorderly way, as if some houses were giving way to others, although it's obvious that the houses have always been where they are. But for some reason, in Lisbon, you have thoughts that have no meaning later on, once you're away from Lisbon.

This is the situation: I can think about Lisbon but, if I try to say the word Lisbon, I don't manage to say anything.

Aphasia is the name that they've given to the oblivion that obliterates words. It's as amusing as trying to read a letter of farewell written by a monkey. After that happens there's not much that you can do.

Simply close your eyes and wait for better times.

BETTER TIMES

They're not ghosts because ghosts don't wear boots or leave footprints in the snow.

I'm sitting up in bed, waiting. Happy people from the north cross the road under my window. Happy people from the north of Europe. Coats firmly closed, heads lowered.

Now a bus passes by with an advert for beer stuck on its side. German beer. The text of the advert is also in German.

They're not ghosts, they're Germans.

The window's shut. I don't listen to what they're saying. Nor do I listen to the noise of the cars, nor the sound of footsteps in the snow. I'm sitting up in bed waiting to hear something. Still incapable of saying anything.

The room's empty. I don't recognise the room and I don't recognise what I've got inside me. I don't know which chemical it is, probably neutral sand. The restful chemical of sleep. The noise of rest. My ears are buzzing and my legs hurt. My cheeks are burning and my hands are sweating. I'm here and I'm in many other places. Like the lost suitcases of a traveller on their way to a different country.

Of course I've eaten, with something of an appetite, and I've even said th... th... thanks to the nurse, admittedly after a bit of an effort, but thanks nevertheless.

It starts to rain and then, all at once, I fall asleep. When I wake up, it's already dark and there's no point in being awake. There are no books in the room. There's no TV set. There's nothing. A doctor came in at nine o'clock. I asked him why the room's empty and he explained to me in a very kind way that it's still early to accumulate information and that I only got my speech back six days ago.

Six days out of how many days?

Six days out of an awful lot of days.

I naturally don't remember this place, not the window, nor the street, nor the walls, nor the bus, however much the doctor insists that the bus is always the same one. But apparently that's normal. The doctor says I can't retain anything. The doctor says that for the time being my brain is a colander, an open net through which all the fish slip, of whatever size, without a single one being trapped there.

Good night.

Goooood Nighhht, doctor.

A net with a hole as big as a German bus.

The white room is in the dark. My hands are cold. Just my hands. There's nobody in the street. The light from a video phone booth lights up the road. Not all of the road, just a couple of metres around the phone booth, beyond that the road disappears.

First I think of a number:

Seven.

Next I think of the same number again:

Three.

Then I fall asleep.

Good morning nurse.

And the woman is sincerely happy for me, so much so it seems as if she'd never been greeted before, and that might be true, because people are very ill-mannered. It's not that it's a particularly good morning and it might even rain although equally it might not, because you can never tell when you're dealing with the weather.

In the re-implantation room I watch cartoons. There's a rabbit playing the piano dressed in tails. As she sees I'm laughing, the doctor asks me if I like it. I tell her that I do, because it's quite a funny rabbit, with a foul temper, but funny. Then the doctor asks me if I know what the rabbit's called and I reply to her sincerely that I'd never seen that rabbit before in my whole life and then she tells me that the rabbit's called Bugs Bunny, which from my point of view is as good a name as any other for a rabbit.

Back to my room for lunch. Through the window I see a German bus passing by with an advert for beer stuck on its side.

The nurse takes away the lunch tray.

It's not raining.

It must be Autumn. My body's fine apart from a slight pain in my chest that's probably just fear, but the fact is when I look at the walls I don't know which walls they are. No needles, please, I hate needles. I'm a cowardly drug addict. Capable of causing myself any kind of irreparable harm, but fearful of any intermediate harm. I can't grasp a simple idea and leave it alone until night comes. I have to be continually thinking up new pieces of idiocy. How much longer is this going to last? What a strange situation this is. What colour was the ambulance that brought me here? What were the streets like?

When you see an ambulance go by you can never imagine yourself inside it. When you're in it you can also imagine that you're outside it. Ambulances always go around empty. You're somewhere else, in the same way that you're in your car when it leaves the road and turns over and you don't feel the pain of the blows, nor do you recognise the fire that destroys your own house. How incredibly tedious illness is and how obsessed you become with your head at the same time. Like debts. How terrifying to be in the corridor and how terrifying to hear the voices of the others and yet straight away what indifference. Come in nurse. No; I'm not doing anything important. So I swallow my pills and gradually become sleepy. There's nothing to worry about. I've got to rest then from keeping a close watch on myself. If you don't mind I'd prefer if you didn't leave me yet. So the nurse stays with me for a while and you feel better, much better, when someone watches you and also watches the things that you're watching. Your own room. Your terror at imagined things disappears, your terror at imminent catastrophes. I'm still awake. I want to get my mind back. To build something that doesn't collapse from one moment to the next. What destruction my friend what destruction. I still feel the strange chemical running through my body like an army of armed orang-utans. So many stories threatening to appear and then escaping like children who ring your doorbell and run off and hide. What dreadful mornings. What dreadful nights. God is a dwarf with a knife hidden in some corner of my head. God is a dead nurse lying next to me. Don't go to sleep, nurse. Not before I do, at any rate. Where's my mother? Why isn't there anyone with me? How sad. How ridiculous. How idiotic. Dying must be like this. Very much like this. Something that only matters to you. I'd give my arm for a beer. Tell me the end of the joke, nurse, and then you can go. And didn't we run along the beach like everyone? And didn't we paddle in the water? Well then, why has all this happened now? And didn't we do it the best we could? Why so much punishment then? I'm not getting angry with you, nurse, it's not that. It's because my head's hurting and I'm frightened and I don't understand. What a disaster. And to think that I was with people, drinking, listening to ridiculous stories, having a really great time, walking around airports, buying magazines, looking at flight times on electronic screens and now what? Don't answer me if you don't know. Well I've certainly got around, I've travelled all over the world. That's why they give you a passport. Don't worry nurse, I'm calm and, as soon as I can, I'll go to sleep, but it's just that for every light bulb that goes out inside my head another one lights up.

They've given me twenty minutes to get ready. I showered calmly. Nothing hurts me. They've taken me to the rest room. That's all that I need now. They massaged my back. They gave me two pills. The room is tiny. There's just a masseur and a gentleman who must be a doctor.

'You a doctor?'

Yes, he is. Because he nodded his head very seriously as doctors do. And where does this good mood come from? Undoubtedly an effect of the medication. And where's all the fear?

'Do you remember the fear?' says my friend the doctor.

'I do, yes I do remember the fear, because fear's like cold. Once you've had it, it never goes away completely.'

'How come I'm in such a deplorable condition?'

'You've done yourself a lot of harm. You've bombarded yourself with everything possible.'

'That's probably true. By the way, what a good massage. Shiatsu?'

'Yes sir, Shiatsu.'

The masseur said this because, when all's said and done, massage is his business. How pleasant that someone should take the trouble to caress you. What great hands this man has got.

'Will you give me my head back?'

'We'll do everything possible,' says my friend the doctor and then he says goodbye and leaves. What an unsympathetic man. What lack of concern. His head lowered, his eyes almost closed. Anyone would say that I've come here to cause him problems. You make me better my friend and cut out the nonsense.

A nice stroll between the trees to work up an appetite. That's what they've told me. So I stroll about. I look at the trees, tall and strong, I don't really know what kind of trees they can be. I ask the nurse who's walking beside me, like a silent friend, but he doesn't know either and the fact is that we all wander around the world without paying attention to the important things in it. I also look up at the sky, it smells of water, as if it were going to rain. It's a bit cold, but not unpleasant, as they've put on me a wonderful quilted jacket. Warmth on my body and cold on my face, like travelling in an open top car with the heating on, like swearing with your fingers crossed, like stabbing a tiger with a wooden spoon. Anyway, I lose track of my thoughts and I don't know what I'm saying to myself. Long before we reach the road, at the end of the grove of trees, the nurse tells me that we've got to go back. The cars move along the road slowly. I stand there watching the cars for quite a time. Many of them have children in them who are going back from school. The nurse tells me not to watch anything too closely. That it's not good for me. I don't know what kind of science this is. We haven't moved more than a hundred yards from the building. What a bloody awful walk.

I ask the nurse if he knows the names of the trees but the man doesn't answer me.

Now I'm sitting in front of a good steak with mashed potatoes. I naturally ask for a beer and they naturally don't give me one. That's obviously how it all started, says the nurse. With a beer.

Obviously. Let's get on with the meal then. Without beer, it's not the end of the world either.

Now I'm lying on my bed. Leave the window open, please. I like the air to come in. There's no problem, says the nurse, and then she asks me what sort of day I've had.

Well I don't really know what to say to you, my friend, I suppose it was all right, all muddled up with this stupid happiness that's not going to be of any good to us.

A man's carrying a plastic bag full of empty bottles. The bag has a broken handle and the bottles fall out and roll down the street until one of them bumps into a telephone box and breaks. The other ones have come to a halt in the snow next to the ditch. A plane crosses the sky. I can't see it, I can just hear the noise it makes. The man on the road then looks up and probably sees the plane, because for a moment he forgets all about the empty bottles and follows something, almost certainly the plane, with his eyes. Then he finishes gathering them up and moves off.

The nurse came into the room to bring me a little plastic cup with three pills in it. I took the pills out. I filled the cup with the water from a plastic bottle that's next to my bed. I swallowed the pills.

The nurse asked me about the name of a rabbit.

It's not raining.

*   *   *

I dreamt of a bronze panther on a black building next to a factory on the other side of a river.

The doctor is particularly interested that I'm capable of remembering this dream, considering that I'm not capable of remembering what I ate that morning by the time night comes, nor what I saw from my window yesterday.

It's always the same bus, says the doctor. Then the bus stops next to a video phone booth, not because it has a scheduled stop there, but because the traffic forces it to, because there's a long queue of cars that are stationary for a second and then slowly move off again.

Every day I see the bus for the first time.

The doctor then asks me about the city in my dream.

I don't know its name.

Then I ask him about the city that I can see from the window.

Berlin.

On the large screen in the re-implantation room there's a family sitting around a table. The doctor changes channel with the remote control. Now there's a car race. One of the cars crashes against the barrier but the driver emerges unscathed. He takes his helmet off and throws it to the ground. The doctor asks me what colour the car is. A red Ferrari. Then he changes the channel again and a black man appears eating his dinner. You can see the face of this man, who talks and puts the fork in his mouth and talks and eats without stopping, all at the same time. Laughter can be heard over his voice. The doctor asks me about the man's family, but I don't know anything about this until a wider shot appears and the whole family can be seen having dinner next to the man around a table. The doctor changes channel. There's a documentary. Giant turtles swimming among the coral reefs. I tell the doctor that I wouldn't mind being there right now. The doctor then asks me if I like the sea and I tell him I do. Then he switches off the TV set and asks me what colour the car was.

Which car?

Next he asks me what the turtle was like.

I don't know what to say. The doctor then asks me if I'm tired and I reply that I'm not, despite the fact that it's already dark and nothing can now be seen through the window.

The process can last for months. That's what the doctor says. And apparently these people are expert at all sorts of memory disorders.

'Did you know that Ronald Reagan, in his later years, was incapable of remembering his presidency?'

'I don't know who Ronald Reagan is.'

'A President of the United States. The one who had been an actor before.'

'In which films?'

'I don't think that I've seen any of them. At least I can't remember any of them.'

'Poor man, he forgets that he's President while others forget his films.'

'That's just an example for you to see that there's not a single imprint, however big or insignificant it might be, that can't be erased. You shouldn't feel guilty for having burnt out yours, but you must help us to recover them, if you really want to re-establish a minimum of harmony in your mental processes. Now then, we know it's not an easy task. The difficulties of this undertaking are linked to the characteristics of the brain itself; ten or twelve thousand million neurones and their multiple structures represent a dynamic system, whose enormous complexity is greater than that of the most advanced computers. To analyses based on synapsis and on a molecular level, we would have to add at least those factors affecting the functioning of the polysynaptic and polyneuronic configurations. An act of memory implies the reconstruction of certain constellations of synapsis and neurones out of all the possible existing constellations. Neurophysiologically speaking, the act of evocation consists in looking for, reconstructing and recognising a specific constellation acquired in a previous situation. As you can deduce from all of this, you're dealing with something slightly more complicated than finding a missing sock in the dirty linen basket.'

'Thanks. That's made me feel better.'

Today there's a man sitting next to me on a red metal and leather chair. The window's closed. I mean that there's a window but it's closed with the blind lowered. I asked the man sitting in the red chair if the blind works, and if you can see something from here, and he says that you can, that the blind works perfectly well and that on the other side of course there's the road and further away the city. The man has explained to me very carefully that my case presents fascinating variants of Korsakoff's Psychosis.

Fascinating is the word that he used, a word that I on the other hand would never use. Korsakoff's Psychosis, also known as Korsakoff's Syndrome, is caused by a degenerative polyneuritis and presents the following clinical profile: patients affected by this keep their capacity to summon up in perfect disorder old memories, acquired long before the beginning of the illness, they're able to adapt to the present circumstances to the extent to which they are familiar to them, to respond adequately to a question that's put to them, to repeat correctly a phrase, a series of figures or words but, after a short lapse in time, often just seconds, they don't manage to evoke any more the objects, events or people that they have just noticed or the actions that they have just carried out.

The whole business is of the deepest interest to me. Behind me, on the other hand, there's a window, but it's closed, the blind, lowered.

Beside my bed there's a man sitting on a red metal and leather chair.

I ask the man if he thinks the blind works and the man tells me that the blind works perfectly about which, needless to say, I'm absolutely delighted because when you're stuck in a hospital there's nothing quite like an open window and a city in the distance. Indeed, the man turns out to be a doctor, a neurologist, a nice guy anyway. The doctor asks me if I had seen him before and I ask him:

'Before? When?'

'Before . . . just now.'

'Before, just now, I was looking at the window and wondering if there was a city on the other side.'

'Berlin.'

'What?'

'Berlin's the city on the other side.'

'I was thinking about Berlin before without knowing it and then, on turning my head, I saw you in that chair.'

Then the doctor raised the blind and went away.

It's raining today. Nobody has come to see me today.

On the screen in the re-implantation room, the photograph of a man sitting on a pile of logs next to a child brought me the memory of that same image. Not the memory of that man and that child, but the memory of that same photograph. Perhaps the man without memory is capable of seeing images of the future. In the same way that blind people develop an extraordinary hearing and lesbians have those fiendish tongues and prisoners make friends of mice and astronauts are capable of catching bubbles of milk in the air as if they were peanuts. In short, necessity certainly forces you to do extraordinary things.

The man and the child in the photograph seem to be father and son, without there being anything to allow me to establish that relationship with any certainty. In the same way that the image of a woman by herself, wearing a red coat crossing the road at traffic lights in an unknown city makes me think of a deserted woman, probably a widow, when she could equally be a woman in love, a woman who's on her way to meet her lover in a hotel room, or a woman who, quite simply, is on her way home from work.

The image of a man at the door of a hospital leads me to think of a sick man rather than of a cured man.

On seeing the photograph of a train I think of an outward journey and not of a return journey.

On looking at the frozen and smiling image of a soldier, I think of someone who has died.

The photographs on the screen follow each other with an awkward and at times painful slowness. The doctor tells me that the frequency of images will speed up with time. That the content of your own images will be more and more subjective as they have more material to work on and as my resistance allows it. For the time being this is all I've got. The gestures and faces of a crowd of strangers entrusted with drawing out carefully my very own memories. Hunters in the forest following the tracks of unknown animals.

Good luck to everyone concerned.

*   *   *

It's ten in the morning and it's a beautiful morning. When
the nurse asks me if I remember any dream I reply to her:
Nevada, the Nevada Desert and on the other side of the desert
Las Vegas, the Luxor Pyramid and the lights of the Flamingo,
also the giants above the buildings in the Gran Via in Madrid,
the phoenix and the angel over the Circulo de Bellas Artes.

She notes down my dreams with close attention, as if she
were going to do something with them. Then she goes away
and comes back with breakfast. She's a tall, severe, fastidious
woman. She's a woman who for some reason spends her life
surrounded by people who have lost their way. I ask her
about her family and she tells me she's got two children. I
ask her about her husband and she tells me she hasn't got
one. I ask her about her work and she tells me that seeing us
getting better is her greatest reward. I ask her if she thinks
I'm getting better quick enough and she laughs and tells me
that I am. She also tells me not to worry, that at present, time
is of no meaning to me, that one day is just the same to me as
any other day and that in next to no time I'll be completely
recovered and I'll have a clear mind with my thoughts in
order and I'll remember each moment as a Jewish accountant
remembers each figure, with just the same fervour.

I get showered, I put on the clean clothes that the nurse has
left next to my bed. I jerk off thinking about the contorted
body of a female world body-building champion – a strange
woman whom I saw on TV – God knows when, God knows
where. Then I get undressed, I get showered and then I put
on the clothes that are on my bed.

The doctor has asked me about my dreams but I can't
remember my dreams, so I don't know what to say to him.
The doctor then tells me about my dreams as they appear in
the notes that the nurse has taken down this very morning.
I don't know which notes he's talking about, I don't know

which nurse he's talking about. Nevada and Madrid. That's what your dreams were about. Las Vegas, the Luxor and the Flamingo. That could be true. That's what I tell the doctor and it could be true, because I remember having been there, although I don't remember having dreamt it. The doctor says that things elude me and that each new impression takes the place of a previous impression. With the same absurd precision with which a wave wipes the sand clean after another wave. The doctor says that some of my memories prior to the great collapse are still there, others aren't. Naturally I ask the doctor what kind of principle governs the wiping out of mnenomic imprints. The doctor tells me that the incomplete episodes are the ones that are hardest to erase. These are the ones that cling on, even when almost everything else has gone. The doctor tells me that they call that the Zeigarnik Effect. The doctor tells me that the subjects in the Zeigarnik Experiment had to carry out a series of 18 to 21 consecutive tasks of a diverse type; puzzles, arithmetic problems, manual tasks and that half of these activities were interrupted before the subjects had the chance to complete them and that it was precisely the interrupted tasks that the subjects summoned up afterwards most strongly, while the other ones often got lost without leaving any trace in the memory. The doctor says that the Zeigarnik Effect is based on the will to complete things. The doctor says that the evocation of the interrupted tasks is without any doubt better than that of the completed tasks.

The doctor says that residual tensions help memory retention.

The doctor doesn't know it, but it now seems certain that it's because of the Zeigarnik Effect that, despite everything, I still remember your name.

*   *   *

How well dressed the doctors are with their smart suits under their white coats and what an expression of calm hope. Of faith. On the other hand, how little faith is displayed by the patients. What ridiculous pyjamas, what hideous sports clothes, what hats, how ungainly, what low morale, how much time I spend walking in the gardens, how much I talk for the sake of talking, how much silence as well, and how annoying both things are. How little sun, how much rain, how short the days and how strangely short the nights as well.

You'll know that more than one person here has gone out of his mind because of a sudden unrestricted improvement.

No, I didn't know that. But now that you mention it, it doesn't seem so strange to me. Having said that, I go off to look for the ball, because this brief conversation is taking place while I'm playing football with a Croat who's incapable of hitting a tractor with a beach ball, so that however careful I am in my passes to him, this guy returns them to me with wild kicks that sometimes fall in the flowerbed and at other times hit the yellow panels that cover almost all of the outside of the building.

Once inside, the Croat says goodbye and walks off breathing heavily with his ball under his arm. An uncontrolled improvement means that the order of all the buried things traps you once again. What happiness, what sadness, what an avalanche of unnecessary feelings, what an assault upon calmness, what a dreadful defeat. Anyway, each one to his own. At about six, just before dinner, a girl from Brixton, whom I don't believe I've ever seen here before, invites me up to her bedroom, and we're soon fucking with genuine enthusiasm, at least as far as I'm concerned, because she's a wonderful girl with a lovely body that smells incredibly good, the same way as some of the things that I've forgotten undoubtedly smelt. A wonderful black girl destroyed by the endless chemical of London clubs. After fucking I fall asleep and when I wake up, she's dressed, sitting at the foot of the bed, reading one of those fantastic English magazines that reinvent the world every fortnight.

She tells me she had a boyfriend who lived with the heart of a monkey for six years, until a passenger plane fell right on top of his little house in Chelsea, only two blocks away from the stadium.

Then, at once, I hear the supper trolleys rolling along the corridor.

The photographs taken near the Saigon River now appear like extraordinarily slow polaroids that are finally outlined on the white paper, years after having been taken. As if an absurd delay had occurred between the stride and the footmarks.

The doctor, who's a man of my age, happy and noisy, a man who likes making light of things, tells me not to be in a hurry or to be frightened, that memory hides things but that things often remain there, somewhere, and then he talks to me about his wife and tells me that his wife has hidden a diary for years, a diary in which she has written down everything since she was a child, and that she hides each one of these little books so that he can't see them, but that these books are somewhere around and that, sooner or later, he will find them. The doctor says that everything that is hidden is waiting, quite literally, to be found. On the other side of the window a woman can be seen inside a video phone booth. After talking for quite some time, the woman hangs up and remains inside the box until everything that she has said and everything that she has heard find their place and then she leaves it and crosses the road barely looking at the cars, as if what was at the other end of the telephone line was infinitely more dangerous.

'And how is it, Doctor, that when I see your face I can't remember it and yet when you're in front of me I'm certain that I'll be able to remember you all day, until . . .'

'Until you look at the flowers.'

The flowers, yellow ones, tulips if I'm not mistaken, are in a glass vase next to the bed and when I look at the flowers the doctor may well disappear but when I turn round he's still there.

'Retroactive and proactive interference.'

'That sounds all right.'

'One memory replaces another. Like when we try to think of a tune and another older or more recent one interposes itself.'

I once saw a couple, both naked, talking in front of a window in a building opposite my own where I lived. Behind them there was an enormous fish tank with a blue light in it. Red carpet. The TV was on. A man and a woman talking naked in front of the window. I wonder which other memory will have been replaced by this one. Of course I don't tell the doctor anything about this. So the doctor gets bored and impatient.

'Will you come back tomorrow?'

'Yes I will.'

'Will I remember you then?'

'I don't think so.'

'Before I forget you, can you tell me why some images return without being sought and others seem to have disappeared for ever?'

'Quite honestly, I can't. It could be that by means of a process of inhibition, of an emotional origin, you're repressing a memory linked to a negative emotion, but it could equally be because a filtration process is giving priority to specific information relegating the rest of your memories to a waiting situation. In both cases almost everything that you don't manage to see isn't lost for ever.'

'Tell me something else, Doctor, am I a good patient?'

'No; you're not, I believe that you hide things that you haven't yet lost.'

With this, my friend the good doctor ups and leaves, not without first having said goodbye with that sense of mischief that distinguishes doctors from the rest of human beings.

'Now, if you wish, you can look at the flowers.'

The flowers are yellow, undoubtedly tulips.

And then the sun comes out and in the distance the city seems like Berlin and it's stopped raining, although if you look at the clouds, it doesn't look as if this non-rainy state is going to last and the cars on the road are wise enough not to drive too fast, because the tarmac is still wet after a recent rainfall which I can no longer remember.

The nurse comes into the re-implantation room happily singing a German song and on the big screen, by contrast, there's a Japanese garden. The Japanese Garden in Brooklyn to be more exact. It's not that I know so much about gardens, it's because it's made very plain by a notice stuck in next to a small stream surrounded by flat stones. The nurse thinks it's a splendid garden and so do I, so we talk for a while about the curious Japanese tradition of making strange silent gardens in which flowers are hidden away and the stones turn their back on you and we also talk about how beautiful these gardens are despite this and about how little they've got to

do with us, with all of us or with all of them, because these
Japanese gardens have the capacity to ignore passers-by, a
very Japanese virtue, in any case. Then the nurse leaves the
re-implantation room singing an absurd German song.

Under the water looking at the glass screens at the bottom
of the swimming-pool and on the screens naturally images
of flowers swaying in the wind and also flowers motionless
in glass vases. I'm sure that I've seen one of these decorated
pools before, although naturally I don't remember where.
I'm not alone, far from it, there's a person in each lane.
Next to me a lady wearing a yellow swimsuit swimming
with a very fluent style and much quicker than you could
imagine. In the next lane a boy of fifteen or sixteen. Beside
him an Oriental girl. I watch their bodies as I swim and
I watch the flowers at the bottom and for a moment I'm
at ease. Afterwards, as I raise my head out of the water,
I experience a return of the dizziness caused through not
knowing how long I've been in this place, nor where I was
before coming here. The fear of a relay runner to whom
no-one has handed a baton. In the changing room I talk
to a patient who seems to know me well, although I don't
manage to locate his face, nor anything that he says, among
my disordered memories. He also seems used to that. Every
day we have to make friends again, he says with a smile and
conveying that he does not mind too much it being like this.
Naturally I apologise for having forgotten him so quickly,
but the man smiles and tells me all over again his life story,
which consists of at least ten chapters, of which the most
interesting bit turns out to be about a daughter who's a local
ice-skating champion and about an attempted suicide, hers,
in a Hamburg hotel. When I ask him about his work, he tells
me that he works for the European Space Agency and that he

has been very close to the top in the organisation of Project
Ambar. An important project that, according to what he tells
me, smashed the record for time spent in orbit thanks to a
Hungarian astronaut who spent five years alone in a small
station before taking the decision to cut off his own oxygen
supply, thus becoming the first space suicide. My friend also
tells me that the death of this man, whom he hardly knew,
almost forced him and six others to leave the project. Then,
he takes off his wet swimsuit, gets into the shower, comes out
of the shower, dries himself, gets dressed, combs his hair and
leaves, not before wishing me all the very best for this new
day, which in any case I'll end up forgetting. Five years alone
in space is a long time, even for a Hungarian. I'm standing
naked in the changing-room. There are other men going in
and out of the showers. I, on the other hand, decide not to
get showered. The smell of chlorine might help me later on
to remember the flowers in the monitors at the bottom of
the swimming pool.

The doctor has taught me a song. The song goes: *I'll wait
for you for a thousand summers*. It's a good song. I've tried
really hard not to forget it. Later, the doctor gave me a list
of numbers. When he asks me about the song all I've got left
are the numbers 7, 10, 43, 5, 12.

The doctor asks me to look through the window but
the window's closed, the blind's down. Now he asks me
about the numbers, but I don't know what numbers he's
talking about. The doctor says that any impression, however
insignificant it might appear, replaces the previous one. The
doctor says that my brain has suffered too many chemical
attacks, but that gradually the wood is being replanted.
When the doctor leaves, I remain there looking at the blind
lowered over the window trying to imagine what's on the
other side. In the end I press the button that raises the blind

and I see the road, a city in the distance, cars, a video phone booth. I close my eyes and lie back on my bed. I don't manage to remember any of the numbers, but after quite a time I'm sure that the song said:

I'll wait for you for a thousand summers.

A man beats me at chess and is really delighted. I tell him that I've certainly never known how to play chess, but this doesn't seem to matter to the man.

'That's what all those who lose here say.'

'Think what you like.'

I get up feeling angry and walk around the games room. A woman is playing one of those virtual reality love games. Virtual reality romances are tremendously popular, you have to choose a character and handle a situation in the most successful way in line with some predetermined character traits. One comment out of place and you're screwed up. *Game over.* Infinitely more complicated than killing Martians. And then, would you believe it, some guy comes over and asks me if I owe him money? There's always one clever dick who tries to profit from another's misfortune. Almost nobody here remembers anything, so it's easy to persuade anyone about anything. No, I don't think that I owe you anything.

'Forgive me, I was almost certain that I had lent you a hundred marks less that a week ago.'

'A week ago I was the same person that I am now and I wouldn't ask you for a hundred marks not even to save myself from the gallows.'

So the guy moves off muttering to himself, something that is a very unattractive habit anyway, and I'm left there looking at the trees on the other side of the large windows, listening to the insignificant canned music. Isn't this obsession with chasing you around everywhere with music absurd? It's as if they were throwing soup over you when you're not hungry. Now some twins go by talking about a Christmas present and one of them is sure it was a bicycle while the other honestly believes it was a quartz watch.

Meanwhile, at the back of the room, an old man has just remembered his dog's name.

That I'm lost seems obvious, because the days are piling up, and here the nurse, who's certainly very nice, and the doctor begin to lose their patience, although naturally they conceal this effectively while they cast sidelong glances at me and jot things down in their little notebooks and talk with their colleagues and see the rest of those suffering from memory loss and come in and go out and come in again and the red roses at the bottom of the swimming pool surprise me this morning with the same violence with which they surprised me yesterday and the day before yesterday and all the other days.

It's also obvious that nobody really knows what to do with me, because when I ask the doctor how I'm going to recover from this, he says looking at the floor: 'We'll see about that in due course.' As a diagnosis this was on the cryptic side.

The doctor explained to me with great patience that I alone had caused all the neuronal damage with which we were faced, prompted by the very unreasonable behaviour of someone who throws the engine overboard in order to travel more rapidly. He used this exact image of the boat and the engine and another including a baseball bat, two kilos of strawberries and the name in French of a twelve-stringed instrument, although this image eludes me however much I have tried to grasp it with the same attention and the same faith with which you listen to a penance being given.

And now two friends come in from the adjoining room and sing and dance on the beds and the moment they enter

it strikes me that they're twins and that they're wearing the
same pyjamas and for an instant I have the feeling that we're
all the same. It's also true that a second later this same idea
leaves my head as happily as it had come. My two friends are
definitely identical, but I of course am completely different.
Without that making any of us better than the others.

My friends ask me how I'm feeling today, and I tell them
that I feel fine, which is almost true.

I ask them what I was like yesterday and they tell me that
yesterday we shouted from the window until someone in a
car looked up at us and that then we waved at him as if he
was a friend who was coming to visit us but that in the end
the man looked away and his car passed by.

When the nurse comes in the brothers go away and then
the nurse tells me that only one of the twins remembers, and
that the other one has forgotten everything and also tells me
that the doctors find this case incredibly interesting because,
apparently, when one brother looks at the other, he sees the
reflection of what he is now and of all that he has been, yet
the sick brother only sees a strange man with the same face
as him.

Of course I'll forget both of them as soon as they turn on
the bedside light, even before this, after I've followed with
my eyes the cable on the wall quite attentively enough.

Other people's problems, even their faces, were probably
something I was trying to forget right from the start. Cars,
houses, windows with lights on and footprints in the sand,
lost gloves, open address books and closed doors in hotel
corridors.

Behind the soft drink vending machine there's a woman
hidden. God alone knows why. At the end of the corridor
there's a nurse sitting in a chair like one of those line

judges at tennis matches, staring at a line on the ground, testifying the whole time as to which balls fall on one or the other side. Because some are out and the others are in and there's no arguing about it. The afternoon's better than the morning, I suppose, because despite not being able to remember the morning clearly a slight but definite feeling of relief is flowing into each of the steps I take along the corridor. Like the condensation that disappears from the mirror in the bathroom when the windows are opened. Something that admittedly isn't going to change the world but is important enough for someone, this is the situation I'm in, who spends his days waiting for the arrival of little differences that distinguish one second from another before they're all swallowed up simultaneously by this magnificent black hole of my memory. The noise of the ping pong balls, for instance, or the sound of the TVs in the rooms give definite form to the minutes and the minutes are what count, basically due to my lack of awareness of the hours. The minutes are the middle pages of a book that is burning from both ends simultaneously. When the sound of the ping pong balls stops, that part of my life ends. The corridor itself has a flame at either end. What makes me walk so slowly isn't the fear of coming to the end but the fear of not having begun. All very tedious however you look at it. As tedious as a dead man facing a mirror. As tedious as a cross over an empty grave. Hugely tedious. I feel like one of those astronauts in hibernation on a journey lasting hundreds of years. While on earth people watch the summers follow one another, in here nothing happens. In here our nails don't even grow. Can you imagine anything worse? I'm sure you can, that's just a way of expressing it but can you imagine it? Even dead people's nails grow.

The nurse suddenly gets up from her chair, angry because

a ball has dropped out of play, or perhaps she can also feel
the heat of the flames that are burning up the corridor.

Meanwhile, a woman is still ostentatiously hiding behind
the drinks machine.

The rain beats against the telephone booth making a noise
that I can't hear from here, but making some noise all the
same. The box has one of those screens in it that let you see
the person you're talking to while the person you're talking
to can see you. As there's nobody using the box, just the
operator's face can be seen on the screen. A recording that
goes very nicely through the steps to be followed to use the
video phone. Now the operator's not doing anything. She's
watching the rain. That's just a form of words, of course,
because a pre-recorded image isn't capable of seeing the rain,
but even so, in some way, the operator watches the rain and
doesn't say anything. The road is completely deserted now
and as far as I'm concerned might always have been deserted,
because the first car I see, almost certainly at dawn, will be
the first one, as this is the first of the nights and the end of
it will mark the first of the days. Although I can remember
with complete ease many of the nights of the days and many
of the days of the old nights, I don't manage to capture the
nights of recent days nor the days of recent nights.

My pockets have holes in them.

Nothing of what they give me now is going to be there
tomorrow.

The white building has two storeys, it's not white on the
outside far from it, on the outside it's covered with big
yellow panels. The garden doesn't have a fence around it
or anything like that, here you're free to leave when you
wish, this is a hospital, not a prison. On the ground floor,

next to the large entrance hall, there's the dining room and the dining room has also got panels, but these ones are green like the grass in the garden. Normally, it appears, I eat alone in my room but today I've eaten in the dining room and I've even spoken with a woman who's desperately trying to get back some memories that have accidentally gone astray, because of the carelessness of Russian laboratories, according to her. Most of the former Russian mafias which spent their time trafficking in army surplus material and of course huge quantities of plutonium, are now involved in the clandestine trade in home-made chemical. The good lady tells me that Russian chemical has caused more harm in Eastern Europe than the floods in '99 and apparently the floods in '99 made more than ten million people homeless and killed at least several thousand poor wretches. The good lady also tells me that the poor wretches are always the first to be swept away by the current, wherever the water comes from. Nobody remembers anything, says the woman. Before asking me about my own memories.

'Me?'

'Yes, you, what have you forgotten?'

And although the question couldn't be simpler, the fact is that I don't really know what to say to this good woman, because during these days without memory, all the time I've been in hospital, my mind has shown signs of a chaos that is greater and different from that of the rest of men without a past, as old burnt out images have appeared while other new ones have disappeared. Something that has given my doctors a lot to think about and that they have taken to calling mnemonic anarchy.

What have I forgotten?

The very question is absurd and yet it's the question that flies along the corridors of this place when night falls. The question that flies around the closed rooms and the garden, over the heads of all those of us who stroll around gazing at the sky every time the rain lets up. It's also the question that floats in the swimming pool and the one that we'll take away with us when we leave here. On the way to the city at the end of the road or any other equally strange city.

What have I forgotten?

And how the fuck do you expect me to know this, my friend?

All I can tell you is that part of what I ought to have forgotten is still here and while you go crazy putting out new fires it's the old fires that flare up again with the strength of the images of old films.

What have I forgotten?

All my prayers, my parents' names, the shadow of the trees next to the fence of my school, the '78 World Cup, if I've ever been on a boat, bullet wounds if there were any, my children if there are any, their faces, the faces of a million women, for some strange reason not too many films, but some of course, numbers, the odd foreign language, mornings, afternoons, nights, the taste of many things and also the colour of many things, hundreds of songs, hundreds of books, favours, debts, promises, addresses, threats, streets, beaches, ports, whole cities, I've forgotten Berlin and I've forgotten Rome, of course I haven't forgotten Tokyo, I've forgotten yesterday, completely, just as I'll forget today and then tomorrow.

What else have I forgotten?

I've forgotten you, my lady, and I've forgotten the garden and the swimming pool and I've forgotten all the wounds on my own hands but regretting it a lot and you can't know how much I've been unable to forget her.

*   *   *

Today in the imprint implantation room I met a guy who's apparently the twin brother of another guy who turns out to share a room next to mine. We exchanged a few words in the waiting room which undoubtedly didn't mean much to either of us.

'Where are you from?'

'I'm not sure.'

'Been here long?'

'Three weeks.'

'What about me?'

'You've been here at least three weeks because you were already here when we arrived.'

'How's your brother?'

'All right, I suppose. He's always telling me things and he's got a story for each of my scars. You see this one?'

'Yes I can see it, a gash on your head the size of a finger.'

'I got that one going through a glass door in a country cottage on the outskirts of Prague.'

'Are you Czech?'

'So I'm told. Do you know Prague?'

'Almost certainly. What happened to the house?'

'My mother sold it before she died. From then on we lived in the centre, near the river.'

'Is it cold in Prague?'

'I don't know, they haven't told me. I suppose the winters are cold and that in summer you can go around in short sleeves until it's night.'

'I'm certain about that. There's nowhere in Europe that doesn't have a good summer. Or at least some nice summer evenings. Do you know Skagen?'

'I don't think so.'

'It's a little town in the north of Denmark.'

'Can you remember that or is it something that they've told you?'

'I suppose I remember it because, unlike you, I forget everything that they tell me.'

'What's Skagen like then?'

'Well I don't really know, but I do remember the sand dunes, huge sand dunes next to the beach, and I remember the Baltic Sea meeting up with the Atlantic. And the waves of one sea crashing into the waves of the other.'

'I used to spend my summers in Spain.'

'Really, I still remember Madrid as my first home.'

'I can't remember the Costa del Sol but apparently I had a great time there.'

'I don't doubt that.'

'People never sleep on Costa del Sol and somewhere there's a theme park with a wooden big dipper.'

'Probably in Fuengirola.'

'Probably.'

Then my friend looks down and gets lost amid his list of implanted memories with the innocence of those who feel at home wherever they are. When the nurse appears, my friend doesn't look at her and nor does he look at me, while I take my leave of him on my way to the re-implantation room. Some people develop an excessive affection for what they've lost. Of course I find it easy to say such things because I now remember Fuengirola perfectly well.

It's a lovely day today.

'Yes, it certainly is.'

'Have you walked in the garden?'

'I suppose that I must have, because my hands are cold and I'm still wearing my sunglasses.'

'What else have you done today?'

'I've been looking at pictures on the big screen.'

'Can you remember anything of what you've seen?'

'An experiment carried out in Holland aimed at reducing school truancy.'

'That sounds interesting.'

'It is. It's called the Vogler Project. It involves a campaign to show children how sad everyone is when someone misses school. Something like the Christmas tale of Mr Scrooge. When the ghost shows the old man Christmas present, past and future without him. A child was saying he was happier outside school than in it. That the feeling of being outside was in itself a better feeling.'

'Do you remember that sensation?'

'No but I can imagine what it's like. Anyway the poor boy sounded tremendously convincing.'

'You've seen other things.'

'That a question?'

'No, I know that you've seen them, I was there as well.'

'What other things?'

'Films.'

'Which one?'

'*North by North West.*'

'I can't remember it.'

'It's the one in which they mistake Cary Grant for a spy and kidnap him, the one that ends up in those mountains with the faces of the presidents.'

'Was Eva Marie Saint in it?'

'Yes.'

'I remember it now. Nobody can believe that a guy who's having his hands trodden on doesn't fall from a rock, and as for the plane, in the sequence involving the plane and the wheat field, you could just spot the trick.'

'Don't you like Hitchcock?'

'I don't like to be taken for a ride. I like *The Birds*. That really was good.'

'You could also note the trick photography there.'

'Ah, but it didn't matter there. It was all the fault of the mother who wanted to screw her son. Do you know the joke about the shrink?'

'No.'

'Well this guy spends years going to sessions with a famous New York psychiatrist and spends a whole lot of money on it, and one fine day the shrink says to him: 'My friend, I've discovered what your problem is, deep down you've always wanted to have sex with your mother.' The poor man is plunged into a fit of depression and replies: 'Know what, doc? I would have paid you double not to tell me that.'

In the afternoon a chronic amnesiac celebrated his birthday. They brought him a cake with forty candles on it but the man took them all off until only one was left.

'I'm not prepared to accept responsibility for the years that I can't remember.' That's what he said.

Sounds fair enough.

I went off to sleep thinking about Cary Grant. One of those old style actors who looks like a head screwed onto the end of a suit. A lovely guy, for all that.

Wretched progress in the re-implantation room, why deny it.

God alone knows how long it is since I was last in Madrid and yet on seeing the pictures of it on the screen, the crystal palace, the giant palms in Atocha station, the warriors armed with spears and the stone angels on top of the buildings in the Gran Via, I feel what a criminal feels when faced with someone else's crime, with a weapon that isn't his. Nothing.

Perhaps just a slight relief, on knowing that he's guilty of a different crime. Of course it's in the re-implantation room where you should start to weave the suit of memory from the threads that these good people have managed to assemble. Images, sounds, the odd song with which the patient must tie up the shoes of memory and leave walking over his own footprints. But for some reason that shocks the doctors, my mnemonic imprints light up and then disappear like planes in the sky lit up by the searchlights of fear during an air raid. That is, on, off, on, off. The neuronal decay with which we're dealing, I quote what my doctors say, is in an advanced state but of course this is not unprecedented. We have here a man who combs his hair in a different way every day, unable to remember his own appearance and we treated successfully a child who confused his mother with any woman appearing on television, whether it was Marilyn Monroe or one of those new cyber stars.

'What was he called?'

'Who?'

'The child, what was he called?'

'André.'

'Was he French?'

'He was Belgian. Does that have some bearing on it?'

'I suppose it does if you're Belgian.'

'The main thing is you shouldn't regard our natural concern as consternation.'

'What became of André?'

'He got back the image of his mother.'

'The image of his mother?'

'Yes, his mother had died in a plane crash.'

'So you replaced his dead mother in his mind with Marilyn Monroe or a Japanese cyber star, Riosuke, for instance.'

'The memory's obligation is to accept things as they are.'

At times it's impossible to bear things the way they are. Incidentally I don't know if you know that Riosuke was the first cyber star to end her own life, long before the copycat suicides of all those awful digital pop idols. What's more, I remember, however amazing it may seem to you, that when I was in Tokyo I saw Riosuke performing on the big screen in Shibuya, days before her virtual reality death, and I remember that an old song of Françoise Hardy's was playing in German, Wenn dieses lied erklingt, and I almost remember having cried, although I may equally be exaggerating this.

Of course I don't admit this to the doctors, but when I leave the re-implantation room, that is just an empty room with a large screen facing a very comfortable leather arm-chair, I can't help thinking about poor André, bombarded with magnificent images of his dead mother. All too often the work of all these people consists of dragging people back to precisely the places from which they've escaped. Back to the summer afternoons in Tokyo or back to the wreckage of a plane sunk in the middle of the Atlantic Ocean.

Running happily over the wet lawn in front of the hospital to celebrate with the rest of the patients that for the first time in endless days it's not actually raining. Of course this is a fact that I can't corroborate any more than I can the colours of the things that are around me. A marvellous leather football has appeared from somewhere and, when I see it appear, I chest it down skilfully and after a couple of touches I pass it to an adorable girl who runs after it as if there was nothing better to do in life. It's great to be out in the open and to see things from here. How green the lawn is and kick as hard as you like there's nothing to break here and having said this the girl kicks so hard that the ball goes over my head and flies past until it crashes into one of the glass doors to the building. Straightaway there emerges a formidable German nurse, who's really upset, so my friend and I start to run across the wet grass as fast as our legs will carry us and after falling over once or twice and feeling the water from the grass on our faces and, naturally, on our backsides, we reached an elegant formation of hedges and we hid behind them and we laughed like crazy people, perhaps that's not the most appropriate comparison, but the fact is that we laughed and looked at one another and although we hardly said anything to each other, I can't help touching her tits through a very Italian little smock, and in next to no time we're kissing and fucking happily away and god knows how long it'd been since I last fucked, but for a moment I cling onto this girl as if the whole world were spinning round and I was frightened of falling down with everything else, straight down to hell.

Then a big guy comes along shouting, asking where his ball is, and I tell him that I don't know what he's talking to me about but that in any case a leather football is a very important thing and he should take greater care, especially bearing in mind the tendency that we all have to forget, sooner or later, where we put everything.

On the other side of the hedge there's a lovely girl lying on the grass smiling. I naturally sit down beside her. We smoke a cigarette and fuck. When we've finished, the clouds close in politely over us as black as shoes.

Before I jump into the swimming pool the nurse tells me that despite my resistance I'm making progress, which is a betrayal of the senses. Just like at school, where however hard you try to avoid it, in the end, you do learn. Into the water then.

Once I'm dry, in the dance room, because it turns out that

they've got one of them here, I refuse to dance as if it were a matter of life or death and I stay in a corner watching how the others dance. And they dance well, some of them with real enthusiasm. Not contagious enthusiasm but enthusiasm anyway, and although some very attractive young men and women come over to encourage me to join in, the fact is that I am not encouraged to do so, because whatever is to happen and has already happened, one thing is certain, death won't catch me dancing.

And what is it that they're dancing to?

Well trance music from the DJs in London, sad music from the dives in Boca in Buenos Aires, red music from Spain, Strauss waltzes, Hungarian polkas, Arab dances, good music and silly music from the past and the future.

What about French songs?

No, there are no French songs.

And what is so good about French songs?

Well precisely because the French don't like singing and that's obvious, when they do sing.

The nurse comes over moving to the sound of a cumbia and, anyway, anyone can imagine how a nurse from Hamburg dances a cumbia.

Dance, says the good lady, when all's said and done, however much you dance today, tomorrow you'll have forgotten about it.

If I strangle you today, at this time tomorrow, undoubtedly, I'll also have forgotten all about it, but you'll understand that that's no excuse.

Of course as soon as I hear preparations for tea I forget about the dancing, because the fact is I could eat a horse. So I go out into the corridor again and stand there staring at the tray of doughnuts, but in the end I choose a piece of apple strudel, because if there's something that the Germans know how to make it's apple strudel and I ask the nurse if this hospital's German and the nurse says that of course it is and that we're only two kilometres from Berlin, so I take a piece of apple strudel and a fruit juice and a couple of serviettes and I polish it off in an instant.

I don't remember having gone to sleep and I was woken up by a clap of thunder. Am I one of those people who are frightened by storms or am I one of those who laugh in the face of flashes of lightning and sleep soundly?

Quite honestly, I don't know, but we'll soon find out.

The empty room, the sound of the rain, the first light of day, the voices of the nurses getting the breakfast ready, the TV sets on, the car engines, clean hands, the switched-off lamp, the open window. Every day is like this one.

In the re-implantation room, a river, a child, a fire engine, a cross, two hens, a Jewish wedding, Maradona, a woman at an airport. Arbitrary memories, a non-specific programme designed to establish immediate connections in anybody's mind.

In the changing room, next to the pool, a quick adventure with a Taiwanese boy, as slim as a girl.

In the dining room a woman has collapsed.

During the afternoon's stroll I counted three planes. The last of them made me think about a woman at an airport and a child and a river, but these memories aren't mine.

Facing the big screen, the pictures of a plane crash have reminded me of the wet grass on my walk.

Then it's time for dinner and at dinner a man asked me about his house and his father's face. In here people talk to you about things they come across just as in bars people talk to you about the things they've lost.

It gets dark so soon in here.

One of the nurses is called Anna.

I asked her what her name was when she came to bring me my helping of pills. She replied:

I'm called Anna, the same as I was yesterday.

'Allow me to explain to you what it's all about. Your immediate memory proves incapable of storing the information that we are trying to re-implant in it and your long term memory operates in a chaotic fashion, like the drum in a lottery from which certain numbers come out at times, and other numbers at other times, without us being able to establish a hierarchy in the importance of your memories or the importance of your inhibitions. The rest of your powers seem intact, once a painful period of memory loss has been overcome. The results achieved in the re-implantation room, it goes without saying, have been extremely disappointing.'

'I'm sorry.'

'It's not your fault. You're a patient not an election candidate. What we're setting out to do now, represents a considerable advance on the development of the Penfield Experiment.'

'The Penfield Experiment?'

'It relates to an investigation begun in 1963 by the great Canadian neurosurgeon W. Penfield and is based on psycho-physiological evidence of memory conservation. By applying weak electrical stimulis to the cortex of the temporal lobe in groups of epileptics, amazing results are achieved in the matter of recovering scenes corresponding to memories of past events. After a charge was applied to a certain point in this area, a patient was capable of finding a lost family memory. In the case of the first Penfield Experiment the patient found himself in an office. "I'm here," were his words. "I can see the tables. A man calls me, a man bending over a table with a pencil in his hand."'

'That doesn't seem anything to make a fuss about.'

'Another patient recently arrived from his country points out that he can hear people smiling. "My friends in South Africa."'

A woman who receives similar electric charges can hear a Christmas carol being sung, in her town, in Holland. She has the impression of being inside the church and she's moved once again by the beauty of the moment. Just as she had been years before.

'I don't want to go into a church again.'

'That's just an example. These flashbacks seem, in the words of the patients, to be "more real than a memory". They develop respecting the temporal order of the experience lived through, ending when the charge is interrupted, and they can appear again when the electric current is applied again in the same place.

'Despite its results, Penfield's line of investigation was not developed properly for decades.'

'Why not?'

'Endless controversy about the location of the mnemonic imprints. But we have taken up old Penfield's direction of enquiry again.'

'Why?'

'Because it works.'

'When he says "we", who's he talking about? "We" sounds rather disreputable.'

'I refer to Doctor Warthon Thiers's team.'

'That sounds much better.'

And that's how from one day to the next I see myself involved in the Penfield Experiment, although suitably modified by Doctor W. Thiers's prestigious team.

Incidentally, the city that can barely be seen from my window has indeed turned out to be Berlin.

THE DAYS OF
THE PENFIELD EXPERIMENT

I'm in Tokyo, on the hill of the love hotels. She's walking three or four yards in front of me. She's wearing a black, sleeveless dress and a short coat. She's wearing black, high-heeled shoes. On the hill of the love hotels there are thirty or forty small establishments that rent out their rooms by the hour. When you go in them, by the door, there's an illuminated panel with photographs of each of the rooms available. There's a key next to each photograph. When you take the key out of its slot the light behind photograph goes out. All the rooms are different. We go into ours and I close the door. She gets a beer out of the minibar. The carpet is a gold colour with a dragon embroidered in the middle. There are mirrors on the ceiling and on both sides of the bed. She's standing by the window now. The curtains are gold coloured, the armchairs are covered with blue velvet. The TV is switched off. The radio is on. An American song in the style of the 1950s big bands is playing, sung in Japanese of course. It smells of perfume. It's not the cheap perfume of a cinema nor the sickly perfume of a brothel. It's not that kind of perfume smell that hides something worse, just a slight, pleasant smell of perfume. Anyway it's not her perfume, this smell isn't at all like hers, it's the perfume of someone who occupied the same room before us.

She's in a hurry. She's very soon got to be somewhere else.

She says: I haven't got all the time in the world.

She says: You can't control everything. There're at least a million things that you can't change and they're all important.

She thinks I can understand what she's saying, but the fact is that I don't really know what she's talking to me about. I light a cigarette and she gets angry because she thinks that kissing a man who's smoking is like cleaning an ashtray out with your tongue.

She still hasn't taken her coat off but I know what her dress is like and I can already picture her shoulders.

It's hot. The windows are shut. If the whole building were in flames, all around this very room, it wouldn't be any hotter than it is now.

She says I'm never going to change the things that aren't in my control and probably not the other things either, those that seem to be within my grasp. Then she remains quiet for so long that I get frightened, like a child gets frightened when he wakes up in the middle of the night unable to recognise the sounds of his own house. She says I'm not capable of building anything and the future depends on what we build now, on everything that we haven't yet built. Then she takes off her coat and throws it on the bed. I switch on the TV and take another beer. The door to the bathroom is half-open. The bath is gold coloured. She's already half-naked. She almost doesn't look at me. She's hiding a dead animal in each hand. She's a woman imprisoned between memory and premonitions. Like a giant torn to pieces by two wild horses. Tied by her hands and feet to two horses which pull in opposite directions.

She says: This place is dreadful.

But I can't agree with her.

We're now at the door of one of those love hotels, in Shibuya district. We haven't gone in yet although it seems

certain that we're going to. The love hotels are squashed
in close to each other, all the way up the hill. We choose
a small French building at random. She asks me if we've
already been here before but I don't know what to reply.
She's wearing a red tunic dress tied at the waist with a ribbon.
She's wearing a black raincoat over her dress, despite it not
raining nor apparently having rained all day. We're looking
at the illuminated photographs in the panel by the door.
There are few rooms taken. I take out the key to a simple
room with light blue carpet and pictures of wild animals on
the walls, but she prefers a white room with a green quilt
on the bed. A room that looks like an operations room. I
replace the key that I had taken and the photograph, that
had vanished for an instant, lights up again. I take out the
key to the operations room and the photograph at once
goes out.

'Where have you been all day?'

I don't know where I've been all day. I'm not even aware
that the day's already over.

'I've been out for a walk.'

'All day?'

It's only three o'clock. I know this because there's a clock
in the corridor. A clock inside a picture frame with the
photograph of a waterfall. A light flickers inside the picture
and if you're stupid enough you might think that the water's
moving.

She repeats her question: All day?

For her the day's already over at three o'clock. That is, if
that's the way she wants it. It can equally well be the case
that at ten o'clock the day's beginning. According to what
suits her best. She controls the measurement of things.

'I walked through Yoyogi-Koen Park.'

'You don't like that park.'

'I do now. I like to sit down beside the river. In a place where we lay down until we got covered in caterpillars.'

She says she remembers the caterpillars and then she laughs. She laughs while I put the key into the lock. While we go into the room. And she's still laughing when I finally close the door.

She's frightened of accidents.

'Amongst the twisted metal of what was a plane a child can be heard crying.'

'What?'

'That's what the newspaper says. Amongst the twisted metal of the plane a child can be heard crying. There are photographs scattered around the dead bodies. People come back from their holidays loaded down with photographs. There are more photographs than can be seen on the ground. Images that are still inside cameras. Some of them can be developed, others can't. Some photographs will be burnt in the fire that follows all accidents.'

'Don't read those things.'

'Why not? The weatherman isn't followed around by rain.'

'What the fuck do you mean by that?'

'That testimony of the accident is always stronger than the testimony of the victims.'

'Not all planes crash.'

'Not all planes don't crash would be more exact. Are we going to carry on flying until it's our turn?'

She's got the annoying habit of reading the newspaper in the bath and the paper naturally gets wet and the bit that doesn't get wet gets damp with the steam and if that wasn't enough the newspaper prevents me from seeing her naked.

'Do you know what frightens me most?'

She can't know what it is because she doesn't reply.

'Your fear. And the enthusiasm behind your fear.'

'That's odd because what frightens me most is your lack of fear.'

'I'm as frightened as the most frightened person. Although I suppose that it's a different kind of fear.'

'There isn't a different kind of fear. It's always the same fear.'

'Not exactly.'

'Not exactly?'

'Not exactly. Your fear begins when planes take off and mine begins when they land.'

I'm now sitting on the bed in a room of a hotel in Roppongi. It's not one of those love hotels on the hill but a boring, small, austere Japanese hotel. The TV's on. They're talking about the copycat suicides of all those cyber stars. She's in the shower. I can hear the sound of the water from the bed. We've just fucked. I'm still naked. I imagine what my life would be like if she weren't in the shower, if she weren't going to come out of the shower at any moment. I imagine myself walking through the streets of Akasaka. Going into bars. Sitting under the bridges that carry the motorways and railway lines.

I imagine letting the hours pass sitting on the same bed. Watching TV without moving a finger, just out of the curiosity of knowing what time does with you when you do nothing with time. I imagine going into the Parko department stores and buying a shirt that she has never seen before and that she'll never see. I imagine the colour of that shirt with the same anxiety with which a child on a Monday morning travels, while sitting at his school desk, the impossible distance that separates him from Friday.

She closes the shower, but I know that she will still be

some time busying herself with all the creams in her little bottles.

Then a memory from my childhood turns up. I'm next to a windowpane with a stone in my hand. As I look at the unbroken pane of glass I can't imagine it broken. A second after I've thrown the stone the situation is exactly the reverse; looking at the broken glass I can't remember it unbroken. For the same reason I suppose that when you get across a bridge you're no longer sure of having been on the other side.

She eventually gets out of the shower and comes back into the room as if she'd never left it.

What a strange faith in the past. Her memories are infallible. The names of dogs and the names of their owners, the numbers of buses on the way to school and the colour of all the shoes she had when she was a child. A disturbing memory however you look at it. I can free myself from all of my ghosts and I'll still be at the mercy of hers. If she had a bullet taken out of her, she would wear it eternally hanging around her neck. She told me this herself.

Nobody knocks at the door of the rooms in the love hotels on Shibuya Hill; and so, when someone does knock, first of all we're alarmed and then, straightaway, we get dressed. When I go out into the corridor the woman who runs the hotel says something to me I don't understand but something that definitely means bad news. The door of the adjoining room is open, so I go over to see what the problem is and the problem turns out to be the lifeless body of a man immaculately dressed in a smart, cream-coloured suit, lying on the carpet in his own blood. With his veins cleanly cut by an elegant razor with an ivory handle, lying a few centimetres from the body.

I wait for a moment in the doorway looking at this man's

body with the amazement with which you watch a magic trick, knowing that it's all true and false at one and the same time.

She comes out into the corridor as well and also comes over to the door and looks at the dead man with the same amazement.

We naturally leave before the police arrive.

Today in Tokyo, hugely fascinated by the blue of the carpet while in the grip of recently taken staples, focusing on the pattern on the floor, following the lines in the blue carpet with the dedication with which a fortune-teller follows the lines in the hand of a giant. It now seems obvious that while one of the two sleeps, the other one inevitably traces the future in his own way. What do parents do when their children sleep? They try to decipher the signs. Tiptoe through the minefield, ready to dig up the mines with the point of a knife. That's how I behave, dragging myself across the carpet, with the healthy intention of defusing tomorrow's traps.

I get her overcoat out of the wardrobe in case it's cold tomorrow. But not her long, black Russian duchess's coat, but her short, grey French student's one, because it seems almost impossible that it's going to snow.

In case it rains I get out her rubber boots, but then I also get out her high leather boots in case it doesn't.

I take three different dresses out of her suitcase, with different temperatures in mind, all of them equally possible.

I look for her gloves but I can't find them. What I do find are her sunglasses and I tell myself that it'll certainly be the sun that we'll have to worry about tomorrow, and not the cold.

I go out into the corridor ready to look for all the emergency fire exits.

I would like to think that she does the same while I sleep.

Indeed, in the corridor I meet a nice Japanese man who's having a violent struggle with the ice machine. Let me help you my friend. These machines are inventions of the devil. My friend goes back to his room with the ice cubes carefully wrapped up in a bath towel. I get a beer out of the beer machine. I don't get anything out of the chocolate machine.

Back in my room I lie down once again on the blue carpet, and when the anxiety caused by the staples disappears, I go to sleep peacefully, just as an exhausted patrol can't avoid going to sleep in the middle of the jungle.

A summer that hasn't been at all happy. Yet when she finishes getting dressed I think that if this doesn't work, nothing will work.

Isn't Tokyo an impossible city? Aren't we climbing the mountain by the most difficult side?

Why do I need a suit anyway? But she insists, so apparently I have to have a suit and even a tie, and that's not a bad idea if I have to be completely frank because inside a suit I'm definitely another person and that's always a good thing.

Looking into the mirror in one of those amazing department stores in Shinjuku, I can't help admitting, eventually, that for all this time I have underestimated the importance of fashion. Now, suddenly, dressing well seems to me as important as speaking well, eating well, travelling well, living well, dying well. Tremendously important anyway.

Shall we try with another tie? says the solicitous Japanese

shop assistant, who deploys his English with the sluggishness of a snake charmer with a broken pipe.

Let's try it.

And she laughs of course. Because a man who looks at himself with apprehension in a mirror, wearing a new suit, arouses the same tenderness as a couple of newly-weds who move silently through a house for sale that they still don't know will be theirs.

Perfect, says the assistant when I have tied the knot in the tie.

Perfect, she says looking more at the man in the mirror than at me.

Perfect, I say to myself, in the end, looking at the same man. Seeing the same thing as them.

Afterwards we dine in a very smart French restaurant in Harajuku, then we fuck in the small room of our hotel in Shibuya and then, finally, we go to sleep.

She says:

'What letter?'

'The letter you sent home. There's no need for them to know what's going on.'

'And what's going on?'

'I don't know, I didn't read your letter. But I can't stand you writing the whole time. Not everything's important.'

'I can't tell now what's important. Later, with time, everything will assume its correct proportion.'

We're having lunch in a small sushi bar in Harayuka. I don't like her writing. She notes everything down. She writes on the serviettes and sends letters home. Letters in her own name. She preserves everything. Walks, trains, dogs, kisses, traffic accidents, pills. In fact I don't know what the hell she writes. But she writes. That's a fact.

She says:

'What are you so frightened about?'

'I suppose about myself in many years' time. Having to accept responsibility for whatever I do or say now, whatever it may be. To see that same face in whichever city I'm in. To come across that face every time I go back to Tokyo or Prague or wherever I might go afterwards.'

'And what about my face?'

'What's the matter with your face?'

'Does it also frighten you to come across it?'

Then I remember a photograph, taken next to the Saigon River. She's holding a reed in one hand and her other hand is clenched into a fist. Her face, though, is smiling.

I'm in the bath in The Liquid Room and there's a neo-punk band massacring tunes by the Carpenters and there's a Japanese girl of about fifteen lying on the floor almost naked and a Japanese boy as well, somewhat older, dressed in a leather jumpsuit. The zip is pulled down as far as his groin, his cock is out, and someone has just punched me because I notice through my top lip how my heart is beating and when I look at myself in the mirror I see some blood dripping down and the girl looks as though she's fainted, although she looks at me and the boy seems to have overdosed on heroin and she isn't there. She isn't in The Liquid Room. Nor in the hotel, but she's in Tokyo, of course, and so am I, although we're not together and I just hope that she's having a better time than I am, because all of this, that undoubtedly started out all right, is turning into a nightmare. All at once two heavies come into the bathroom, not without some effort, because the little Japanese girl lying on the floor almost blocked the door completely, and while the heavies are shouting and pushing I manage to take on board another handful of cocaine, just before one of them snatches the packet away from me. From there it's straight out onto the street. We cross the room at an amazing speed considering that there are so many people in there that it would be extremely difficult to pass a credit card from one end of the premises to the other. Before we reach the street one of my friends aims a headbutt at me which I can't escape. A small red tide sweeps through my head. Like one of those flags that are waved in front of your car when, for some reason, the race is abandoned. I don't really know why he headbutted me, because the fact is that I was leaving willingly, without even protesting. I suppose it's easier for these people, these poor brutes who work as heavies in bars, to headbutt you than not to. Just as it was easier for Hitler to invade Poland than to play the viola.

I'm sitting opposite the door to The Liquid Room and there are lots of people waiting to go in. All of them splendidly dressed, perfectly obedient, waiting their turn in the queue.

She left a message on my mobile more than an hour ago.

The message says:

I think about you all the time.

She's perfectly capable of having children. A gynaecologist from the international insurance company confirmed it this very morning. All that we need to know now is if I'm a genetically suitable man. Probably not, my father's a former alcoholic and my mother worked in a circus. Anyway we're ecstatically happy. Because a woman who knows she's capable of breeding is like a whale that knows it's capable of swallowing all the fish in the sea just by opening its mouth. Talking of whales, as we look for a smart restaurant in order to celebrate this news, I feel like a tiny Jonah trapped inside her. Her size and power intimidate me and at the same time, like Jonah, I can't help feeling myself strangely safe. Living inside her comforts me. The way that prison calms down cowards and the gibbet does the same for bad dancers.

The yellow flowers in the imperial garden at Fukiage are loaded down with good omens. She talks to me about a car journey from Los Angeles to San Francisco along the coast road. Naturally she was driving. I just held the road map. The hills of Big Sur reminded us of the hills of Ireland. Apparently we were incredibly happy during that trip. She wonders if we shall ever be so happy again. Once again I'm frightened by the clarity of her memories and the clarity of her premonitions. She's an army and I'm a disarmed man.

'I knew you would never use the kimono.'

She says this referring to the kimono that I got made in Vietnam, in one of the sewing stalls of Hoi An, near the river that goes down to China Beach.

I'm wearing the kimono. I'm sitting in a red chair in front of the TV, in my kimono of silvery and blue silk, but she knows that I'm not going to use it much more, and that probably, once I take it off, I won't put it on again.

'How can you be so sure?'

'You're not a man for a kimono. You've never been one and you'll never be one'

'People change.'

'No, people get worse. That's all.'

'Why didn't you tell me that?'

'What?'

'Why didn't you tell me that in Hoi An, before those adorable seamstresses took my measurements?'

'You were enraptured. You touched the silk like someone touching treasure.'

'I still like the fabric. It's a wonderful fabric.'

'You seemed to be just one kimono away from complete happiness.'

'But you knew that that wasn't true. You used to watch me sitting here two months later as you tried to get me used to this stupid kimono. You already saw the failure with the kimono as if you'd travelled to the future and had come back.'

'The fact that someone knows the future doesn't mean that they're capable of changing it.'

On TV there's an execution live from a prison in Arizona.

She looks for her wallet, counts her money, gives me a kiss and suggests that we should meet up in a couple of hours on the Bunkamura mezzanine, which seems a great idea to me, because on the Bunkamura mezzanine there are at least a dozen marvellous restaurants.

When she leaves the room I can't help feeling like a man dressed in someone else's clothes. Even so I remain for quite a while, very relaxed, in my lovely kimono.

I'm looking at the adverts on the screen in the taxi. It's already night. We pass very close to that ridiculous tower in Tokyo that is just like the Eiffel Tower. Thirty metres higher and thirty times more stupid.

I'm sitting in the bar of one of those baseball galleries in which the Japanese enclose themselves in little courts surrounded by high wire fences and with infinite patience hit the balls that a machine pitches at them. Ten little fenced-in courts, each one with a different speed of pitch. Most of the batters are drunken office workers. When they miss the ball their ties get wrapped around their faces. Some of them, despite everything, manage good hits, then they shout as if they were in the middle of a stadium, they're the spectators and the player at the same time. Almost all of them are alone.

I can't play baseball. I couldn't hit Panama with one of those bats, but there's something that reassures me in the way in which these people hit and miss and puff and wait for another ball and smash a ball against the fence. I like the idea of playing alone, at a game that nobody watches, in which the balls, wherever they go, misses or hits, never go very far.

There are also little golf courses like these, surrounded by metal fences, on the roof of many buildings. The Japanese love the tension of impossible games.

She's sitting beside me, she's got her eyes closed. We've been drinking. The office workers come in and out of the bar with their bats in their hands and they look at her legs. She's wearing a short skirt and high-heeled sandals. She's sitting on a red stool next to mine with her head resting on the bar. She's got lovely legs. For a moment I'd like to be one of those Japanese office workers who come out of the cages sweating, with their shirt sleeves rolled up, and who go up to the bar just to look at her legs.

'You know what your problem is?'

She's sitting on the floor, drinking tea and looking at her photos. I'm standing in the middle of the room, drinking beer. Naturally I don't know what my problem is.

'Your problem is you're not a reliable kind of person. You're not in the photos.'

'Which photos?'

'It doesn't matter which photos because you're not in any of them at all. It's just me in the photos. As if these were just my trips.'

I look at the photos spread out on the floor and it's true, I don't appear to be in any of them.

'Look through them. I remember that in Hanoi you took
a photo of me. It must be somewhere. And in the plane. You
took a photo of me in the plane. I'm certain of that.'

'Here it is,' she says, 'I've got a photo of you, sleeping in
a plane. That's all. It's as if I was travelling alone.'

'But you're not travelling alone. I'm here even if I'm not
in the photos.'

'You're here, that's true, but why aren't you in the photos?
Have you stopped to think about that?'

'I don't like photos of me.'

'You like photos of me.'

'Yes I like photos of you. It's photos of me I don't like.'

'That's the problem, do you understand now?'

'No.'

'Your problem is that a long time from now you'll be
able to deny everything, because you won't have left evidence. And that makes me question the faith that you've
got, in us.'

'There's something I don't quite understand.'

'What?'

'Well, in fact, everything. Will you take a photo of me?'

'I don't want to take a photo of you. I want you to be in
photos. I want you to stop struggling not to be in them. I
want to see you beside me, in Tokyo, ages from now.'

We've not yet had breakfast. She's on the floor looking
at her photos. I'm still standing drinking beer. I still don't
know what my problem is, but I suppose that I don't want
to be in Tokyo ages from now. I suppose that ages from
now I want to be somewhere else.

Suddenly the wind in Tokyo is so strong that she thinks
that there's someone hidden on the balcony, banging the
windows, but there's nobody on the tiny balcony. There's

no room for anybody, in fact. There would barely be room for a plant pot there, although it would be silly, to leave a plant in the care of the guests, because the guests in these hotels on the hill come in and out every two or three hours and they only come there to fuck.

We also come to do that, although of course we've got another hotel, a normal hotel, in which we talk, sleep and at times fuck as well, but in these hotels on the hill you can fuck better, because each time the rooms are unfamiliar. That's why we often come here to fuck on the floor and against the mirrored walls. When I open the door onto the balcony the whole room is turned around and the sheets lift up over the bed and the door to the bathroom shuts with such force that, for a moment, it seems as if the whole building is shaking. When I close the door everything is still again. She's naked and frightened and her hair's over her face, as if she had been driving an open-topped car. I'm naked as well.

'My God. For a moment I thought that we were going to fly out.'

Then she switches on a lamp next to the bed, because outside the sky has become dark so quickly that the cars in the street haven't yet had time to switch on their headlights, and the street lights, of course, are still off and everything has taken on a sinister tone, although in fact nightfall is a long way off.

'Come back to bed,' she says, 'perhaps we should spend the whole evening here and, if the storm continues, even the night and go back to the hotel tomorrow when all this has passed.'

I pause for a moment at the door to the balcony watching the people in the street, anxious because of this sudden darkness. Then I go back to bed and switch off the bedside lamp.

*   *   *

The Riosuke suicide occupies the large screen at Shibuya station. Riosuke is the most popular of the cyber stars. She doesn't sing songs, she just looks out from the screen while the music plays. Her hits have titles like 'My little tortoise never lies to me' or 'Different hells for different people'. Ten million Japanese adolescents copy her gestures. Now she's dead. The new stars control their own lives, they're not manageable programmes like those terrible warrior women who seem like whores from the old world, they're complex free programmes endowed with free will.

Riosuke's face fills the big screen in Shibuya station, the kids cry down on their knees while the police attempt to get them back to their homes. They've been crying for three days and nobody knows how much more they can cry.

Riosuke hasn't got the artificial beauty of the programmes that pursue fame like stupid performing dogs, using exactly the same tricks. Riosuke is only a normal adolescent, as pretty as the girls who lament her death on the floor of Shibuya station. Nobody knows what to say to Riosuke because Riosuke never said anything. She only walked up and down in front of her songs with the gracefulness of a princess in exile. She had an affair with a local boy and spent a year living with a very sad schoolgirl who has now hidden her own programme in some obscure part of the net. The way things work out, just her cat remains. But a cat, cyber or real, which as far as we're concerned is the same thing, is worthless as a witness.

I'm watching all this grief go by like an idiot watching a chance slip by, without any intention of seizing it.

Of course it's raining. The TV helicopters are flying over the square. The station is closed. The street is blocked. People

are frightened. All these children would give their life for
Riosuke. They probably will.

And where has she got to while hearts, from one side of
the country to the other, stop beating, following the rhythm
of Riosuke's own heart that has stopped?

Who knows. At times, in Tokyo, we spend whole days
apart just to see what effect that has on us. Like two idiotic
scientists trying small doses of poison.

I follow her in a drunken state through Narita Airport
carrying the suitcases, but she's high on flares and runs
around like a dervish and I'm coming down after a GPG and
the corridors in Narita are covered with shiny illuminated
screens that display lines by Kafu in six languages:

> *If I have to die*
> *Let me die then*
> *Before the winter comes.*

Happy lines that spread like the milk from a glass that's
been knocked over across an oilcloth table covering, and I
haven't slept, and I'm tired.

She's getting smaller and smaller as she reaches the end of
a corridor that's undoubtedly just the start of another one.
The noise from her shoes makes its own space, God knows
how, amid all the noises of the airport. What's more, if you
make a real effort to hear her walking, it's hardly possible
to hear anything else.

And where's she off to?

Not very far. Because the fact is I've got the tickets and,
when I take them out of the pocket of my jacket to check
them, I realise that the tickets are actually for another day,
and there are still three weeks to go before that day. For

some reason that escapes me at present, in the middle of
the previous night, due to the extreme effectiveness of the
amazing amphetamine derivatives, we decided that we were
about to miss a plane that was not even near to departure.

I find her looking at one of those little cemeteries that
they've set up in almost all airports for those who die in
plane crashes and who are not claimed by anyone.

The cemetery at Narita is just a room covered with little
memorial plates, like those monuments to the fallen that
they put up after wars. She's sitting on one of the benches
in rows in the middle of the room.

Don't worry, I tell her, we're not going to have to fly
right now.

She says: If my plane crashes, will you collect my remains?
Down to the very last little bit.

My words seem to satisfy her. We leave the cemetery and
leave Narita on the first train to Shinjuku. On the train we
drink beer and we kiss and we lie to a Japanese girl who
asks us how big the palm trees are along the Santa Monica
Boulevard.

She says she's not as slim as she was because women from
thirty onwards, even the slim ones, begin to take on the
shape of their mothers.

Why? Nobody knows that.

For what reason? In order to be mothers in their turn.

She's naked and I still can't see those centimetres that
according to her are making the curves around the premises bigger.

You're not looking properly.

That's what she says but she's wrong, because I'm looking
very carefully. I'm looking at the pelvis bones that she can
see disappearing. The line of her waist, that she sees filling

out with just one purpose. I'm looking, but I still can't see anything.

She says that women's bodies conceal their victories and their crimes from men's eyes and, for that reason, men are no use as witnesses. She says women are spectators at the parade of their own natures, caught between fear and amazement.

She believes that women, against their own bodies, are always alone.

She believes that willpower only has absolute rule over the simple destiny of men.

She says that probably it's just men who leave their bodies at death, while women remain fastened to theirs like sunken ships at the bottom of a river.

Then she gets dressed quickly because she's terribly hungry.

While we queue up at the door to a sushi bar, she tells me that at times she's frightened that she won't see me again and that this fear makes her feel all alone, even if I'm in the same room, sitting in front of the TV, with a beer in my hand.

Then she says: I'm not in Tokyo the whole time, I'm also in the cities in which I've been before and in the cities in which I shall be later on. You on the other hand are in Tokyo as if you had never been anywhere else.

The bar revolves around a conveyor belt that brings little dishes of sushi, like the conveyor belt in airports on which suitcases go round and round waiting for their owners. The people there, all of them Japanese, eat quickly and in silence.

When we go out into the street again it's cold.

Who knows what things will be like after Tokyo? It's not strange that someone who finds himself suspended in the middle of a period of strange happiness should equally reject murmurs from the past as those from the future. Just as the mother of a family closes the doors, so that nobody should get in, and the windows, so that nobody should get out, with just the same degree of concern. That's how I'm living these days by her side: closing all the traps that lie around us. Closing all the doors of all the hotel rooms, like the watertight compartments of a ship that has already got a leak and which, despite that, is trying not to sink.

What's she thinking about all this time?

I don't know. She doesn't say. And if she does say the noise of my fear is, as always, too great and that's why I can't listen to her.

Is she ill or tired? Something's definitely changing, because her days are soon over and then she collapses onto the bed and says she can't breathe, and of course all the air in the street is insufficient and our walks through Tokyo get shorter and shorter, and the city is shrinking around us. Who knows? Isn't it love itself that you fear most, when you're in the midst of love? If that weren't so why all this distrust in the cities of the future?

Why do I insist upon thinking about her like a gentle light that is going out, when in fact she could kick me out of the room, out of any room?

Love is really a frenzy of the imagination.

In any case, there would be no harm in checking the dose and quality of my stimulants, because I'm unable to answer so many dark questions and because I've got the feeling that with the tip of my toes, I'm treading on the heels of my own boots.

In the end I fall asleep next to her, although she of course has already been dreaming for hours about God knows what other equally dangerous things.

*   *   *

'Careful with our home!'

'But we haven't got a home.'

'But we shall have one.'

We're in one of those motels on the love hill. The carpet is yellow, the walls have a black satin finish. There's a mirror next to the bed. While we were fucking, I've realised that she was looking at herself the whole time. She wasn't looking at me. She just looked at her own body and of course my body was at the end of her body, but she didn't look that far. She watched her own movements with the surprise and interest of a person who sees someone close to them fucking. Like someone who watches his sister fucking.

Now she's talking about the house that we'll have. About the garden full of dogs, at least two of them, about the lake facing the garden, because we once spent a few weeks in Berlin in front of a lake and she decided then that it was the best way of living, with high ceilings, with plaster mouldings, with the room of the son that we haven't got. While she's talking I am going through the rooms of that non-existent house with the same fear as if they were real.

I ask her about the colour of the walls and she tells me that the walls, for the time being, are white.

When I ask her about my possessions, she tells me my possessions are still packed up, but hers have already been in their right places for weeks.

There are flowers in glass vases and carpets from Azerbaijan beside the beds.

I can't see anything of mine. It may be that my things are still packed, but it could equally be that I don't live here.

We're both naked. She's thinking about our house. She thinks I don't respect her plans. She doesn't know how cautiously I peer into the rooms I describe. She has no idea of the effort I put into looking for my place. Of the suspicion with which I look under the lamplight on one side then the other of our own shadows.

While we get dressed, I leave the house that we don't yet have and I return to the room in which we are. Nobody's house. One of those magnificent hotel rooms that disappear as soon as you close the door, on the other side.

My father, when he was a child, used to play football in Alcalá Street. Every two or three goals a car would pass by. My grandmother went to buy milk and the Pasionaria in person grabbed her by the arm and enlisted her support for a demonstration. My grandmother has always been right-wing but she paraded with her milk pitcher with the dignity of the early communists. Now I'm in Tokyo and I'm the invisible man. My grandmother wouldn't survive for a week in Tokyo. My father's ball would bump into the helicopters. History moves slower than science.

She's sitting next to the window. Tokyo's the city on the other side and I suppose on this side as well. When you're in Tokyo, Tokyo is everywhere.

She says: My mother lived in the mountains of Mikuni and used to ski to school every morning. My grandfather used to dance in the lounges of the *Queen Mary*. I suppose that neither of us were born for that.

'When you're alone do you think about me?'

'Yes, although not all the time. At times I leave you in the hotel and I feel like someone who leaves the cinema halfway through the film. I'm out, but I know that the film carries on.'

She then says that at first she needed to be alone, despite wanting to be with me and that now in contrast she needs to be with me, even if she wants to be alone.

'When you leave me in the street I go round and round

the shops and I try on all those dresses that don't really suit me and I talk to the salesgirls until I drive them crazy, until they all lose their smiles, and I try on shoes of all sizes although my foot is obviously always the same and I look at other women as if they were crazy and then, when I look at myself in the mirrors, I can't avoid the same fear.'

'It's not your fault, everyone here shops with great conviction, and it's difficult not to be dragged along by this. In Tokyo people shop for the same reason that in Mecca they pray.'

'Some day they'll close down all the shops and we'll have to go up there, where a superior being will cast an eye over the Visa receipts.'

'That's true, darling, but it won't be tomorrow.'

Then she moves away from the window and takes out of the wardrobe some beautiful shoes that I'd never seen. They look so good on her that, when she leaves the room, I have no alternative but to follow her. There's no denying that Tokyo's an incredibly good place for buying shoes.

Red days are calm ones. To be on red means the temporary suspension of the natural suspicion aroused by all possessions, other people's and your own. All people and all streets. To be on red, means to halt the constant tide of catastrophes. Like the peace of heroin without the exaggerated faithfulness that heroin demands. Like blue needles without all that canned sadness. Like sunny days without the ridiculous arbitrary nature of sunny days.

We're at the Akasaka aquarium looking at the fish, that's why you go to an aquarium. The smiles of the sharks seem as delightful to us as the amazement of the children. We go along the glass walls, we kiss very near to a red bream, we appear accidentally in the photos of strangers and we stick religiously to our own concerns. Red days are days that aren't included in the absurd order of the other days.

When the aquarium closes we walk next to the railings of the closed parks. For some reason unknown to me she dresses better than other women, despite the fact that she undoubtedly buys her clothes in the same shops as them. I've developed a meticulous love for each and every one of her things. That's why I am so fond of packing her case for her and carrying it like the possessor of a treasure. Love is as real as other things are imagined. Like the warmth that one feels when looking at the names of cities that you've never visited. Like the sea on maps or the nightmares of astronauts.

Tourists wave from the boats on the Sumida Gawa. Tourists have the annoying habit of greeting other tourists in the same obligatory way as soldiers greet other soldiers. The tourists don't know that I've always been in Tokyo and that I've never been anywhere else. The noise of the helicopters drowns out the noise of the water and the noise of the boats. The monorail is full of sleeping office workers. The music from the giant videoscreens wakes the dogs, and the students trust only their mobile phones.

For once, she's amazingly happy.

Red days conceal the hell of everything.

And now she's talking endlessly about afternoons in Hoi An, in Vietnam, riding on bicycles on the way to China Beach through the ricefields, avoiding the oxen, and she says those are precisely the best days of her whole life. After the infinite green of the ricefields, the cement of Tokyo, that seems to erect a palisade at each step you take, is unbearable to her. We walk all day long like soldiers. She's exhausted. So am I, it goes without saying, although I refuse to admit that she's right. A couple are like a boat, there has to be one of them on either side. If you put all your weight together, the boat turns over. It's true, in any case, that the Vietnamese used to speak to us and the Japanese didn't, that's why it's easier to feel abandoned and at the same time, and this is the strange thing, imprisoned.

She would like to carry on the journey right away, but I for some reason prefer to stay in Tokyo. She, of course, has lived here and she's not surprised by any of it, and it's that surprise, I suppose, that keeps me so entertained. She is not resentful to me about anything. She just talks about Vietnam with the excitement of someone who has found, when they least expected it, where they least expected it, a new home.

The train crosses the park. The carriage has dozens of children in it returning despondently from school.

In Sakuradamon a few children get off the train, while a few more get on leaving us almost as we were before.

Now she tells me that she prefers bicycles to trains although of course she prefers trains to planes.

'What about you?'

'Me?'

'In which order would you put them? My order is: bicycles, trains, planes. Which is yours?'

'Well, first of all planes. I like planes a lot.'

'And then?'

'I think that it would be: planes, bicycles, trains.'

'Fucking marvellous, we don't have a single preference in common.'

'No.'

'Anyway, I don't think that's what's going to break us up.'

She's wearing a blue, long-sleeved t-shirt that we've just bought in one of those gigantic fashion stores in Ebisu Nishi and she looks great, on the other hand just like everyone around us, because the young people in Tokyo dress divinely. On her t-shirt is written:

ARE WE HAPPY?

Are we?

I suppose so.

Why wouldn't we be?

We are drunk on sake, surrounded by coloured trainers and perfect haircuts, no sign of any religion is to be seen, of whichever type, in the more than fifteen streets we cover, nobody says anything we can understand, the shops are all open and the banks are all closed. Heaven must really be something very like that.

When this city ends others will come and what good summers and cold winters we'll see in other ports and what kisses we'll give each other in the shadow of Polish freighters and at the top of the highest tower of the city of casinos and on the hills of Big Sur and in the deep valleys that surround Prague, and it'll be so big a love that the days will become short and the nights long and if all this will come to pass, inevitably, why do I feel that the world comes to an end when on putting two fingers into her vagina I discover the old rubber barrier?

Where are the children that we were looking for to adorn our future house? Where is the little monster that was coming, from God knows where, to enliven our garden? I can no longer hear him running along the passage. I can no longer see him run up sweating kicking his first proper football. I can no longer see the patches of paint around the little table where he does art. I can no longer see the clouds and the whales and the giant rats and the rest of the absurd things that he paints. The fact is that I can no longer see anything.

Why did I put my fingers in there?

Because the cocaine has produced one of those half erections, as stupid as a scared army.

She's bathed her feet in the rivers of Vietnam, she's listened to the stories of the old soldiers from the Cu Chi tunnels, she's crossed the squares of Mexico without looking at the murderers of women, hiding from the sun beneath a straw hat, but now without informing me she's allowed the best of her promises to be false.

I know that she'll have a child, but I know that it won't be now and it won't be mine.

I watch how she comes and while I watch, perhaps because when she's protected behind her diaphragm she's a different woman, I finally achieve a wonderful erection, wonderful is certainly an exaggeration, but the fact is that the owner of an erection always has all the self-belief necessary. So we fuck there on the floor which is red. Red carpet throughout the room and even in the bathroom.

I come against the rubber barrier.

Like a fool halted in front of the closed gates of heaven.

Now we're in one of those love hotels in the Shibuya hills and I'm lying on the floor, having taken swift bullets just arrived from the laboratories in Shiba, and she's still in bed and beside her there's a boy asleep. One of those devilish Japanese adolescents poisoned by the smoke of the strip shows of the port of Yokohama. The swift bullets keep me transfixed on the floor like a christ nailed to the carpet. The swift bullets of Chiba ransack you inside with the fury of grave robbers and they take everything in their way, first all the worst and then all the rest.

Now she says that she wants to leave because, for some reason unknown to me, women die off quickly after fucking with strangers.

She gets dressed very quickly and I dress slowly looking at my own clothes with the surprise of someone who attempts to set up a video recorder following the instructions for a washing machine.

We go down the hill in silence until we reach Shibuya station.

We go back to the hotel by taxi. The screen in the taxi is broken. We watch the darkened screen until we reach our destination.

You have to love me a lot more.

I naturally carry on as if I'd not heard her. Then she closes her umbrella and it probably all ends there.

From the windows of the monorail the lights of Shinjuku can be seen and the darkened heart of the imperial palace and the sleeping elephants in the new Ueno Zoo and the switched on mobiles of the drugged children of Shibuya and the flashing lights of the planes and the constant ill feeling of the war veterans and the reborn beauty of widows and condensation on the hotel windows and the absurd light from TV sets and blood under crashed cars and the black sky and the red price of sales tickets and the yellow light of child pornography establishments and artificial snow and the metal heads of golf clubs and the blue light of taxis and the white cotton gloves of traffic policemen and the small street stalls selling noodles and adverts for tobacco and the faces of the new Hollywood stars hanging over the streets of Ginza and the graves in Yanaka and the fish in Shinobazu Lake and steel suitcases in Akihabara station and the bones of sick models in the doorway of the clubs in Roppongi and the candles lit for the death of Riosuke in Hibiya Koen Park and the terror of sailors in Russian ships and the cold on cement bridges and faith in casinos and the weariness of trains and the fortune of dogs and a knife, two rivers, and a hat, nothing else.

Doctor W. Thiers finishes gathering together his things. Around him six other eminent neurologists raise and lower their heads as if they were drinking at an invisible watering-hole.

The Penfield Experiment is over.

'Tell me, Doctor, have we made much progress?'

'We've definitely made progress, but we haven't got very far.'

Doctor Thiers goes on to explain to me that all the material brought to light by means of the Penfield Experiment will of course be kept strictly confidential and it won't be able to be commented upon by any of the co-workers beyond the area of their own speciality. This means that nobody will have access to the recordings made in the past days, nor to the data revealed by them. I didn't really understand this last part, probably because my brain is still recovering from the manoeuvres of these good people; anyway Doctor Thiers doesn't mind explaining to me the more obscure points of his explanation.

'Nobody, my friend, not even you yourself, can get to grips with these glimmerings of memory. That could adversely affect your recovery and that's not what we're about.'

'What are you about, to be precise?'

'We're here to turn over the earth. Nothing else. You've got the seed inside you and you've got to make the plants grow. You've cut down what was in the fields and you'll make them grow again. It's the natural process. We're the gardeners, and you're the garden.'

What good explanations this gentleman gives. It's a pleasure to see how he illuminates with his images the pool of my perplexity. They all look at him with such respect. If I weren't so tired I'd give him a hug.

'Please forgive my lack of enthusiasm, Doctor Thiers, but I'd like to sleep now, because I feel as if my head's been split open and you've filled it up with stones.'

'Forgive me, my friend, for not putting your rest before any other consideration. Sleep as much as you can and dream, for sleep is the best cure. But remember, if you can, that all the stones that you've got inside there are the ones you already had. And that we have gone in there and come out cleanly, without disturbing anything, without taking anything that was yours and without leaving anything of ours.'

Having said this my good doctor shakes hands with me with the suspicious air of conviction of a second-hand car salesman and he leaves, dragging behind him his half-dozen doctors with the same unhurried joy with which the train of a bride's dress is dragged along on the way to the altar.

Go to hell Doctor Thiers.

A sweet nurse accompanies me to my room and leaves me there, surrounded by my possessions, which are of course the belongings of a stranger.

Through the window, in the distance, a city can be seen. The lights of a city. The lights of the cranes above the darkness of the wood. From the city to here, there is a road and along the road, from time to time, some cars come.

Of course I don't know how long I've been in this place, but, of course, I'm certain that it's time for me to leave.

The chemical in hospitals is excellent but it's not yours. You submit yourself obediently to the rhythm of their capsules, to the elaborate design of their cures, to the morality that controls the limitation of euphoria, but you're never in control. The owner of the chemical is the owner of the present. Let's pick up once again then the reins of our own destruction. Farewell to hospitals. Farewell to induced sleep. Farewell to the magnificent apple strudel. Farewell to all that.

I feel like a man who walks out unharmed from among the wreckage of a crashed plane and says to himself, not without a certain relish: Right here is where my life starts.

PARIS BAR

'It's not that straightforward my friend. We've had a hell of a time finding you and an even worse time trying to reclaim you, although as far as this is concerned, clearly, we haven't been too successful but anyway you're not the first agent we've lost, nor of course will you be the last. Anyway what worries them isn't your mental health, and forgive me for being frank, but certain merchandise lost at knife-point in Bangkok Airport although right now you don't know anything about that.'

'No sir, nothing at all.'

And I say that because I really don't know what this man is talking to me about and because, in any case, it seemed to me that my ignorance about this was more acceptable to him than my innocence.

'Ah. Here come our beers.'

And this was true because, at once, an Iranian waiter who comes and goes talking to himself leaves a couple of beers on the table and, needless to say, I grab mine with real relish and with a single swig I down half the bottle.

'That's some thirst, my friend. I suppose that it's some time since you've been near a good beer.'

'Yes, a long time, sir. Although I couldn't tell you how long.'

'Of course, and that's precisely the burden you've got to bear, although I suppose, and forgive me once again for being frank with you, it's entirely self-inflicted. Which brings me back to what we were talking about. Our doctors are unanimous in establishing that a memory loss like yours is only possible with the help of our miraculous chemical and that each one of the beautiful holes in your memory is directly connected with the disappearance of our valuable merchandise. Even so, we haven't been able to get out of you sufficient information to undertake what our lawyers consider a risk-free legal action. I trust you realise that at this moment the greatest risk for us is the negative publicity that is generated every time we take public legal proceedings against an agent who's blown it. On the other hand, the death of our agent in Bangkok was immediately linked to the wild activity carried out in that area by the fanatical Guardians of Memory originating in the American West. That's the way things happen, and to our great regret, we have no option but to believe your innocence, since the results of the mind recovery procedure have been disappointing and since you've even undergone the Penfield Experiment without shedding any light upon the dates and events with which we're concerned. In short, my friend, you're free to leave Berlin whenever you wish and to do what you want with the rest of your life, as long as you remain outside our operation. As for the chemical brotherhood, that's all over for you. As a legal agent you're irrevocably dead and as an illegal agent, if you decide to follow this poisonous path, your days will be numbered. Your identity card will bear for eternity the label SICA, that is to say, suspected of illegal chemical activity, which makes you legally liable to be stopped, searched and deported at all the frontiers of the free world. I'm sorry to sound unpleasant, but that's the way things stand. We haven't been able to nail you but at least we're making sure that you can never screw things up for us again.'

Of course half of the many things that this man is telling me sound like gibberish, although if we've learnt something in these days of violent chemical infringements it's that ignorance of where the fault lies doesn't rule out crime, far from it. In any case and despite how unpleasant this conversation filled with words of reproach and vague threats might seem, my only possible response is to be over the moon, because here, in Berlin, there's no more fun place than the Paris Bar, with old Michelle at the door and girls drinking champagne halfway through the afternoon and this turn of the century atmosphere that equally challenges reason and memory.

'And now, so that you see we're not monsters, I'm going to give you some personal communications that we've received in your absence, although it has to be said that there aren't many of them and they're on the gloomy side.'

The man gives me an envelope and I naturally put it away without looking at what's inside, because only madmen rush to seize bad news.

'Just one more thing – and here I'm displaying greater concern for you than you deserve. According to the report drawn up by our specialists in the memory institution your neuronal situation is critical and the light which has been flickering over the ruins of your memory can go out, once and for all, at any moment so I do recommend that wherever you go you try to follow the right treatment and indeed, from now on you'll simply have to bear all the expenses yourself. Once we failed in the search for the information that we needed to string you up by the balls officially we stopped giving a damn about the confusion reigning in your memory.'

What an unpleasant man and what calm efficiency. If it turns out in the end that there's a hell, I have no doubt that these elegant bearers of bad news will have their place reserved there, even in front of murderers, because murderers have shown when all's said and done a bravery about which these loathsome bureaucrats know nothing and a belief in their own crimes that these pygmies have decided to place, by contrast, in other people's crimes. Anyway, although there's no doubt that I'm in a fucking difficult situation it's equally certain that my friend isn't going to have it any easier when the day comes for him to pay his outstanding accounts.

The fact is the Paris Bar is full of the best of Berlin. Film stars and hungry aspirants to stardom, cocaine salesmen who brave the stares of strangers with the tenacity of whores, whores who dance with the arrogance of mad women, drunken office workers and proud sober waiters, German counts and French duchesses, the best of the best of the worst of Berlin society, and this boring unarmed executioner who accompanies me doesn't see any way of giving up on this stupid business for one moment.

'We trust that you'll leave Berlin at once. And please don't hold it against us if we advise you to leave New Europe at the first possible opportunity. However little you may remember, you'll now know that our destinies are united.'

Having said this, my good friend tightens the knot in his tie as if he were putting in order his whole life, he says goodbye and leaves, having hardly touched his beer. Needless to say both these things really delight me. A bit of calm and an extra beer are just right, when the future is uncertain and the past impossible.

In the envelope there are only two notes.

The first is from my mother, a woman whom I definitely don't remember.

'I hope you're well,' says the good woman, and then she gives me directions to my sister's grave.

The second note is even shorter:

'COME BACK. K.L.KRUMPER.'
Although this latter message of course includes a city marked on the map of Arizona.

Berlin's fortune is the fortune of the rest of the world. At least as far as believers in the chemical brotherhood are concerned. The Berlin laboratories control the destiny of the souls of those who have surrendered themselves to the sentimental tide of the new and more incredible compounds. As an old football trainer said the day before being sacked from his job. The future? I'm the future.

That's how free men live. Controlling their own spirit. Like the owners of thousands of obedient horses.

The rest carry on at the mercy of old curses.

I spend the night in a hotel near Checkpoint Charlie, the open wound between the two old, frozen Germanies. One of the many scars in this city that's still clinging onto the pain of memory. And in the hotel, in the middle of the night, all that can be heard is a woman praying in perfect French, perfectly incomprehensible to me but equally devastating, because all prayers, the ones that you know and the ones that you don't understand, are made of the same faith. Not faith in yourself, but faith in everything else. Faith in the power of what lies outside you.

Something that happened today and which for some reason I haven't yet forgotten:

In a café in Alexanderplatz a waiter called me by my name. Later on in the street I posted a postcard on which it only said:

'I think about you all the time.'

A postcard with the photograph of the Flamingo Hotel in Las Vegas and the address of some place in Tokyo.

Dawn breaks in Berlin over a burnt wood. Near the

airport, next to the road, there's an old abandoned plane. Tokyo's so far from here that it's impossible to go there. It's even impossible to think about Tokyo any longer. Just the way it becomes impossible to think of the name of a dead dog.

GOOD FRIDAY

The man with the tattooed face has no alternative but to run ahead.

There's a little receptionist with just one arm dancing in a hotel reception.

I woke up in Madrid, at a complete loss, like a guy who on coming out of the water can't remember where he's left his clothes. There's a French film on TV. A man is having his face tattooed in a barrack hut of the Spanish Foreign Legion. 'Whatever happens I'll never be able to go back home now.' That's what the tattooed man says. The fear that he's got now will save him from fear in the future. Like one of those vaccines against an allergy. Poison against poison. A good film anyhow.

In the hotel reception there's a receptionist with just one arm dancing to music on the radio.

The penitents stoop to get the Holy Week float out through the church door. Two thousand kilos of Christ. They almost scrape their knees against the floor. The ladies dressed in black carry red carnations and walk slowly in front of the float. People weep and applaud in the street when they see the procession of Jesus the poor Nazarene. The Nazarene penitents are dressed in purple. A purple tunic and also a purple hood. Many walk barefooted in order to sprinkle the act of penance with blood of their blood. Spain washes away the eternal guilt. I'm at home but that doesn't mean anything any more. To give things back to an amnesiac is like sending letters to a blind man.

In the Philippines people are nailed to the real cross with real nails. In Cuba penitents drag themselves on their knees to the shrine of St Lazarus more than twenty kilometres from Havana. In Guatemala just the children are pure enough to carry the Holy Week floats. Christ continues to choose his disciples at random. The number of mistakes made is increasing at an alarming rate.

In Sevilla the rain has brought the Macarena herself down to earth, while in Murcia the Brotherhood of Veracruz is already dragging around the Christ of the Blood.

And doesn't the Christ of the gypsies go upright on his way to Sacromonte? Isn't the Christ of the Good Death upright as well? Faith in Spain, once again, appears irrevocably impenetrable.

In Malaga it's also raining but that doesn't stop the *saetas* from being sung, and in Larios Street there can be heard with the clarity of a clap of thunder:

Who has crowned you with thorns?

In Madrid, in a pious club in Huertas Street, one of those bars full of faith that show on TV screens events from Christ's passion relayed live from every corner of the world, the only question possible is still the same:

Can nobody ever halt the faith of these people?

What the hell keeps Spain nailed to the faith of the past?

Almost certainly, the lack of faith in the future.

In the Gran Vía, the white zone extends from Alcalá Street as far as the Plaza de España. The white zone is the area of free chemical circulation, in which you can buy, sell and consume whatever you want, without having to be tested by the black guard, state security squads charged with regulating distribution in the sad outlying areas of the city. Despite the lack of a river with the abundant dignity of important rivers, Madrid has managed, finally, to have two river banks. I naturally spend the whole morning without leaving the Gran Vía. I leave the hotel to have a couple of martinis in Chicote's. Later, from the Puerta del Sol, I survey at a distance the murmur of the Good Friday processions. In the doorway of the Capitol Cinema I take a photo of a cheerful South African tourist. Through the viewfinder of his camera I see the skies open slowly over the Torre de Madrid, a splendid building. I know that I was born here and I imagine that in the days when this was my home I didn't find much reason then to leave the Gran Vía, because only the Gran Vía resembles the cities that appear in dreams. The bronze angels, on top of the buildings, bless these streets and away from here the whole city certainly disappears. Just as children disappear in parks when their mothers can no longer see them.

Back to Chicote's for another martini. Americans look at the photos of other more famous Americans on the walls. Chicote's with its wonderful art deco décor, is the only centre that this city needs. The harmony of this elegant bar challenges the madness of this impossible country.

In a strip club in Barco Street, behind the Telephone Exchange, a very sad Hungarian ballerina swears eternal love to me. The next girl who comes along, despite having been born in Guinea, swears exactly the same to me.

I spend the afternoon fucking a couple of Koreans in my room in the Emperor Hotel.

The boy asks me if you can screw on Good Friday, I tell him sincerely that I don't know, but after fucking him I tell him that apparently you can.

The girl kissed me as if we were engaged.

*   *   *

God alone knows how big the Almudena Cemetery is. Where it starts and where it ends. I spent the morning going round and round among the graves, trying to follow my mother's directions. I joined up with two funeral parties. There were a lot of people in the first one, but nobody was very sad, almost certainly because the priest made it very clear that we were there to celebrate the end of a dark road and the beginning of a shining path. In the second there was just a very old man burying a dog. Of course it's perfectly illegal to bury animals in a Christian cemetery, but the man had a spade and great determination. As far as I'm concerned you can bury an empty beer can if that makes you happy. I carried on searching among the tombstones. Some of them are simple and humble and others are baroque and absurd, adorned with equestrian statues and angels armed with trumpets. It's such a beautiful day that it almost makes you sad to think that all these people are dead. In the end I managed to leave the flowers on my sister's grave. This act marks an end to my connection with this land.

Tomorrow Arizona.

K.L. KRUMPER AND
THE BIRDS OF WINTER

At Phoenix Airport I was of course kept under arrest for six hours on account of a fateful instruction, attached, apparently for eternity, to my identity card. Suspected of illegal chemical activity. After a thorough search which was truly humiliating I emerged into the burning hot Arizona sunshine and hailed a taxi.

From my hotel room in Tempe you can see clearly all those absurd planes going up and coming down like letters sent and letters returned, hundreds of aircraft, taking off and landing on the cement runways. I suppose that they're made of cement, it's not that I'm an expert. Anyway, it's curious to realise that there's always exactly the same impossible number of people trying to come in and go out of the same place at the same time. As if the number of promises made was exactly the same as the number of promises not kept. The number of enlisted men, the same as the number of deserters. And I'm thinking about this as I take a beer out of the minibar and then straightaway another. I'm clean, which naturally can't be very good. I spend a moment overcome by the natural sadness of things, until I manage to get one of the men in the hotel reception to sell me some innocent mildly euphoric stimulants. Then I put on my swimming trunks and go down to the pool because I've got the feeling, and at once I confirm this, that I like swimming a lot.

In the pool, a very nice Uruguayan lawnmower salesman asks me if I'm on a business trip and I tell him that I am, although in fact I still don't know with which kind of business I'm involved. Then he tells me that Arizona is an incredibly bad state for lawns and that the representatives of his company must be crazy if they expect to fulfil their sales quota here. He also shows me a glossy catalogue of lawnmowers and it has to be admitted that they're dazzling machines that force you, even if you don't want to, to envy greatly the owner of a garden.

Back in my room I look over K.L. Krumper's map. If everything goes according to plan, and I can't see why everything wasn't going to go according to plan, that's just a form of speech, tomorrow at midday I should be in Quartzsite in one of these communities of old people that moves across the desert in their own mobile homes in pursuit of the sun during the winter. A million old people camping out on the banks of the Colorado River next to the frontier with California.

What a beautiful day and what an unpleasant surprise. That's the way bad news always travels, crouching like a poisoned present, like the pointed shadow of flowers, like the resentment hidden in the hearts of dead animals, like the postponed revenge held tight by children in their fists as they sleep. Anyway, I digress from the subject in hand, something strange happened on the journey to Quartzsite. It seems that your mother has turned up dead in a small hotel, near to Maricopa, less than fifty kilometres from Phoenix. I'm drinking a chocolate milkshake in Denny's, one of those roadside restaurants that serve breakfasts lunches and dinners 24 hours a day 365 days a year. My driver waits by the car. On the other side of the motorway there's an ambulance and two police cars stopped outside a motel belonging to the Best Western chain. A Mexican waitress called María de la Luz, God knows why, says that the woman who always won has been killed and that her lifeless body is still lying on the floor of her room. María de la Luz also says that the woman who always won was on her way through bound for Las Vegas and that her tips and her luck were famous throughout the state and probably in six or seven other states as well. When I ask her if she knows what happened, María de la Luz replies that she does, that she knows exactly what happened.

'Murderers of women. They're everywhere. The murderers of women are equally unaware of the good fortune and misfortune of us women. The hatred of centuries runs through their veins. The hatred of all the religions created by men. The hatred of all the magazines filled with naked women kept by boys under their beds. The hatred fed by the fear of all men.'

I imagine that this good woman has certainly got right on her side.

Later, María de la Luz goes back to the kitchen for a turkey sandwich and two beers and carries on with her job as if she hadn't said anything.

When I go back to the car there are six female soldiers belonging to the League for the Survival of Women lying on the ground, next to the ambulance, as a mark of protest. They are wearing t-shirts stained with blood. Two police photographers go into the reception like a couple of lost tourists. A TV helicopter flies around the motel looking for somewhere to land. On the women's t-shirts, under the blood, is written:

DEAD WOMEN.

We hit the road again, on our way to Quartzsite. They still haven't taken your mother's body out. At one of the motel windows, through the curtains, you can see the flashes from cameras going off.

Old men on horseback, all at a trot, with their amazing cowboy hats and a group of old violinists on the back of a pick-up truck, livening up the festivities.

I've reached Quartzsite in the middle of the rodeo. Barbecues, dancing and flags. Thousands of caravans drawn up around the town. All over the desert. Beer stalls, mobile medical units, sunshades, folding chairs, balloons, dogs, snakes, shotguns, revolvers, palm trees and satellite dishes. I suppose that's how everything ends up.

I leave my car at one end of a sunny avenue. My driver turns round and walks away. One of these old horsemen, one of these old ladies dancing, is K.L Krumper. Now it's just a matter of finding out which one, and what the hell he or she wants of me.

A lady armed with an ancient gun, complete with telescopic sights, tells me that she's always been a wonderful shot and that her mother gave her her first rifle as a fifteenth birthday present and that since then she's always travelled with a weapon concealed on her. She also tells me that her own daughter calls her the 'mad woman of the desert' and that she was driven over here by the cold of Minnesota.

'The cold here grabs you from behind and splits you in half if you let it. Lots of us come to the desert to escape the cold, and that's why they call us the birds of winter. My daughter's got a stupid husband, but that can happen to any of us, the problem is that my daughter's letting the stupidity soak into her like the rain.'

This magnificent shot, who's apparently had five husbands, has decided to park her caravan some distance from the rodeo because she doesn't like to see the old men falling off their horses and breaking their bones.

'The doctors here really make a packet. They come from all over the country to patch us up, like those mechanics who specialise in cars that haven't been in production for years. They're experts at impossible repairs. They know the names of all those components that can no longer be obtained. There are also warlocks, gravediggers and quacks, but fortunately we're free of fortune tellers. Nobody wants to look at the short term. In Quartzsite, we all know the future. Want a beer?'

'Well yes, lady, I would.'

So the good lady gets out a couple of cans and we sit down under the awning that she's got fastened to her caravan and we have a quiet drink, like two new friends who've undoubtedly got lots in common, but who don't yet know exactly what.

'Know something? I feel really sorry for women who've only just had one husband, because they'll only have one memory. I on the other hand have five wonderful memories. And let me tell you I still sit in the corner with the single women when the dancing starts.'

Of course it goes without saying that I ask her if she's ever forgotten anything.

'No, sir, nothing of importance.'

Then she tells me she doesn't believe it's proper to forget, but she's nothing against those who decide to forget everything, since no two lives are the same, nor two sorrows different.

As the sun is setting, the woman decides to set about cleaning her shotgun. Although I can't honestly see what one thing has got to do with the other.

Incidentally, she doesn't know anything about a person called Krumper.

* * *

'My friend, you'll see many of these oxygen cylinders in Quartzsite City, they're like lucky charms. And if that doesn't work we've always got the cryogenic plants in Prescot Valley. Anybody is able to gets his bones frozen there. Now that nanotechnology is finally paying off, with those nanorobots the size of a molecule capable of rectifying the damage caused by the cold, only idiots and poor people allow their bodies to die for ever. And Catholics as well, of course, they believe that by reproducing like rabbits they've done their bit in this world and they can't wait to get to the next one. They're some people, the Catholics; they pass through this life like someone waiting, silently, in front of an abandoned station. They're ready. As for me I've got my dear wife frozen in the SICUR laboratories and I hope to get together enough money to join her when the time comes, and mark my words that time always comes.'

Having said this the man goes off dragging his oxygen cylinder. A man determined not to perish in this war.

I visit ten or twelve more caravans. Ex-lawyers, ex-policemen, ex-joiners, ex-wives, ex-husbands, an alarming number of people still in love with people who have already died, practising addicts, alcoholics, ex tennis champions, Elvis imitators and an insurance salesman capable of convincing a Democrat that Kennedy committed suicide.

No sign of Krumper.

The days go by in the desert and only God knows how many of them.

'Fifteen,' says a nice Hungarian emigrant who's rented me a bed in his caravan and who has a hand made of graphite with which he would be capable of playing the piano if he had ever learnt to play the piano or if at least there was a piano near by. 'You've been here fifteen days. Fifteen days since you left your hotel. I've kept an exact count, but I don't intend to take advantage of that amazing facility of yours for forgetting everything and charge you over the top. Although it would be very simple to do, because you leave cigarettes burning and bottles open and you're always asking me the same things and every night I have to bring you back, because you're wandering lost amongst the caravans like a ghost.'

'You can't imagine how grateful I am to you for that.'

'Don't mention it. It's actually a great pleasure to see how you find all the days so different, considering that I find them all the same.'

The Hungarian now sets about dinner. Now we dine. Now we put out the light and we go to sleep. The TV is left on because my friend is convinced that at any moment, in any part of the world, something important might happen.

K.L. Krumper is a Mexican girl. I don't know why but I thought it would be different.

'How old are you?'

'Twelve, but I haven't always been, of course.'

Krumper's caravan is less that a hundred yards from mine. But for some reason I've been taking thousands of steps in the wrong direction. Like one of those impossible puzzles that children do, the ones that always have such simple answers that they make you feel stupid.

'I didn't know you were looking for me,' says the girl, 'these old men are all very jealous. If I had known I would have sent for you a lot sooner. The old man has been waiting for you for a long time, as he did for the others, but just as happened with the others he didn't have much faith in you actually arriving. Because the old man sends his messages all over the world, like a shipwrecked man sends papers rolled

up in bottles. And you know those messages usually end up
in the bellies of fish.'

'What about the old man?'

'Old K.L. Krumper, of course.'

So my friend takes me inside the freezing caravan, where
there's just a blue monitor and a woman who's also Mexican
preparing food.

'Would you like some Aztec cake?'

'I'm not very hungry.'

'Of course you want some. You've not eaten an Aztec
cake like this one, however much you've travelled.'

'That's certainly true lady, although there's no way of
telling that now.'

The child goes over to the monitor and naturally old
Krumper appears on the screen.

'Is he your father?'

'No, sir,' says the girl smiling, 'this man is me as well.'

The man on the monitor isn't Mexican, he looks more
like an old German general. The man on the blue monitor
is sleeping but he wakes up at once.

The man on the monitor says:

'Sit down, my friend, and allow me to explain some things
to you.'

The last two days have been terribly hot. The old people
hardly venture out of their caravans. Some of them spend
hours soaking in their small inflatable pools. Like meatballs
in a plate of soup. Others have showers naked. They wear
coloured eyeshades and carry sunshades. The heat overwhelms them. It overwhelms me as well. Old Krumper, on
the other hand, is unaffected by the heat. So is the Krumper
girl. The Krumper girl runs across the desert and laughs at
the naked old people.

'It's my blood,' says old Krumper from his blue monitor.
'They transplanted my brain into the body of that Mexican
girl destroyed by a cerebral coma. But I'm no longer myself,
at least not completely. Blood takes its own decisions. The
new blood from that girl dominates my old brain. That's why
I spend all day playing around the settlement. Opening fire
on the old folk with my water pistol. I don't want to go back
to the caravan until it's already dark and then I fall asleep
exhausted. I ask that old woman to make a bit of an effort,
there's lots to do, but she doesn't listen to me. It's my blood.
The arrogance of a dead man can't match the arrogance of
blood.'

I ask old Krumper how long he's got left. Because I don't
know who's caring for him, I don't know who the life of his
reincarnation programme depends upon.

'My life's now dependent upon her, my friend, and she
knows this and refuses to look after me any more. When I
bought that girl in a coma, I designed the programme so as to
live under her care. My old body was wracked with cancer.
Now that Mexican child doesn't need me and that's why she
no longer cares for me. The programme is degenerating . I've
nothing left. The blue light of the monitor is growing faint.
So that the person I am is going to die anyway. Afterwards
it'll just be her left. The girl's killing me. Her blood is taking
control of operations. Her blood is going to bury me in this
desert.'

I naturally ask old Krumper why he was looking for me.

'You see, my friend, I've been working on the development
of chemical against memory for the last six decades. Since the
last days of the Second World War. Why? Don't ask stupid
questions and in that way you won't have to listen to stupid
answers.'

Of course, I didn't ask anything.

'During the withdrawal of the occupying troops, a hand grenade thrown by the French resistance destroyed almost all of one of my corneas. In June 1947 I spent a week with my eyes bandaged in an ophthalmic clinic near to Göttingen. On returning to Hanover, when they finally removed the bandage, I saw from my window some labourers working on the ruins of a bombed-out building. The labourers were demolishing with sledgehammers, one by one, the bricks of the old building with infinite patience. I got my sight back gradually in time with the blows of the sledgehammers. From my bed I allowed myself to be carried along by the noisy euphoria of the demolition, until one morning there only remained a few labourers, totally exhausted, holding their sledgehammers on an empty site.'

'Where's all this leading?'

'Patience, my friend.'

'By the way, do you happen to have a cigarette? I like to watch people smoking.'

Of course, I light up a cigarette at once.

'This wretched girl doesn't even smoke, but anyway, that's what young people are like, always going against your wishes. Where were we?'

'Hanover.'

'Ah yes . . . Hanover . . . Now seeing absolutely clearly the feeling of peace sweeping through those labourers as they finished their job, I decided to place all my faith in the demolition of the past in the same way that other men throughout Europe decided at the same time to place all of theirs in the construction of the future. You have to remember that in those days I was just one more of the millions of soldiers surviving from a vanquished army. Belonging to a dead Germany, defeated by shame. I had lived through the occupation of Paris and I had come back

from Paris expelled by the American troops. We came back
to Germany in the slow trains defeated, like strangers ejected
from paradise by strangers. The destruction of the past then
seemed to me the only possible hope.'

Now the blue light is flickering like the light of a candle.

'Then the summers and the winters passed in succession,
but you realise that neither one nor the other change
anything. At the end of the eighties I was working for the
old American enemies in the development of the chemical
eradication of sexual impulses. You have to be aware that
amongst the insects that live in communities, the workers
are asexual, suffering this restriction to benefit production.
It's not strange, therefore, that the CIA should employ its
best chemists in such far-fetched projects. The appearance
of the AIDS virus offered, to be sure, a more effective
response to the difficult matter of sexual instincts. Fear is
a chemically-wonderworking monster, so that the funds that
supported our research were diverted, as fire is diverted in a
wood when it reaches a place that is already devastated. A
search for the end to the virus has forced them to return to
the path that we left at that time, but that's another story.
The fact is that in those days I was already immersed in
the certainty that the chemical solution is the only solution
possible for the soul. I suppose that you'll agree with that.'

'Yes, sir. I agree completely.'

'Perfect. But, please, don't interrupt me, I'm losing my
train of thought. Temporarily halted, but still master of the
trust that the all-powerful German chemical industry had
placed in me, I finally came across the spectacular advances
achieved by the Russian KGB in the field of retrograde
amnesia with veterans from the war in Afghanistan. This
is going to surprise you but, contrary to popular belief, it
wasn't the collapse of the Wall which put paid, once and for

all, to the old guard in Russia, but the discovery of the soul.
Quite some people, the Russians. Too sad for revolution.
Addicted to nostalgia. Have you heard their songs?'

I'm not sure if Krumper expects a reply. For a moment I
think about Russian songs, but I'm incapable of remembering any.

'Horribly sad those songs. If you don't cry when you're
among Russians, then you're never going to cry. Anyway,
as I was saying, while they were trying to obliterate the
mnemonic imprints in the soldiers returning from the front,
while they were trying to eliminate the killings of children and other horrors like those that would plunge the
young combatants beyond help in the black sea of guilt,
the Russian researchers bit off more than they could chew.
It turns out that after exposing their men to painful processes of hypnosis with the aim of locating the dreadful
memories that had to be erased, like the unworthy pages
of a book that was otherwise glorious, an old Communist aspiration, those in charge of Operation Lacunae, as
the task was called, came face to face with even older
memories, with the experiences gone through by soldiers
in other wars, in other lives. Needless to say, the KGB
reacted with horror at the discovery of souls that finally
appeared inside their soldiers after having left the lives of
other men. The guilt that they were attempting to over-
whelm stretched back to the beginnings of time, like a
serpent sunk in the mud of centuries which would appear
and hide away and that would continue appearing and
hiding away for God knows how long. This discovery,
my friend, destroyed the backbone of those who had built
the revolution upon faith in the impossibility of there being
a soul.'

Now old Krumper stops for a second to gather strength,

like an old man at the end of a journey. After a while, of course, the old man carries on.

'It was terribly cold that winter, and Germany was recovering from its shame in the warmth of reunification, and the Wall came down, stone by stone, like the old building demolished by the sledgehammers of the labourers outside my window in the days after the war, and against that background, assisted by the advances achieved in the fight against Alzheimer's Disease and the unstoppable progress in the field of serotonin and neurotransmitters, I finally developed the first effective chemical solution to the tyranny of memory. Imagine what a triumph! What a victory over the stupidity of our own natures! If it weren't for me, people would still remember! With no cure for it! Anyway, let's not get carried away by euphoria.'

For a moment, old Krumper sounded like the Wizard of Oz, one second before Dorothy's little dog finally drew the curtain.

Why do I remember The Wizard of Oz when I'm not capable of remembering my father's name? God alone knows. In any case, whatever Krumper and I feel now, it resembles euphoria as much as a toothbrush resembles a neutron bomb.

'And this is where you all come into it, my friend, you executioners of memory. I've followed your footsteps with the concern of a father and I've followed the havoc that you've wrought with the fear of a creator of monsters. That's why you've come here, like some others before you and like many others after you. Because unlike you, I've never forgotten anything, so that I have preserved for all these years, like a complete idiot, the treasure of guilt.'

Hardly surprisingly I have a terrible headache, because this good man, who is simultaneously a light that is going out and a scatterbrained Mexican girl, has insisted on dragging to a half-dead town, lost in Arizona, soldiers wounded in his holy war against memory and I sincerely fail to see how so much effort is going to help him or us.

'There's nothing that I can do to help you and, it goes without saying, nothing that you can do for me,' says old Krumper, 'but in all wars there's a moment when you wonder what you're firing at.'

'I suppose that we've been firing at everything.'

'I suppose so. In any case, you've arrived too late. If you want to know anything else, you'll have to talk to that child who carries my brain around in this new century. But I warn you she's an impossible girl.'

Now the blue old man closes his eyes, because he's an exhausted programme. The Mexican woman has now finished preparing the food, but nobody seems to be hungry. The caravan is in silence. The Mexican woman looks at the wonderful Aztec cake as you look at things when they're of absolutely no use. The Mexican girl is sitting on the floor reading an anthology of Robert Lowell, *For the Dead of the Union and other poems.*

Old Krumper opens his eyes, returning from that brief sleep of old people who fear death more than sleep itself.

'These Mexicans are always like that. First they all talk at the same time and then nobody says anything. When everything's quiet, I can hear the humming of the monitor. When I cannot hear it any more, everything will be over.'

'What about the girl?'

'Ah naturally the girl will stay. And that wretch is going to live at least another hundred years. Just imagine what I'll see then. The horror and glory of another century. And a lot of wine. The Mexicans drink better than the Germans. And when they drink they sing better songs. There's nothing worse than those German songs, heavy like tractors and boring like tractors. But tell me, my friend, what the hell are you doing in this ghost town?'

'It was you who called me.'

'Yes, I called you, but that's no longer of any importance. It was but it is no longer. You have to realise that the whole of life is a process of acceleration. Do you remember when you were a child? Of course you don't remember, it's just a way of saying things, but as a child an hour spent sitting on a chair in grandma's entrance hall, any grandma, yours, if you like, an hour spent sitting, is like a week, then a year. Hours for a child are eternal. Hours for a man, on the other hand, fall down from the sky like rain and there's nothing you can do to stop them. Hours for an old man are still quicker, they go past you at the speed of light. A day goes by in the blink of an eye. What was important a second ago now seems ridiculous. When it's time to put out the light, children are quiet and they sleep and that was an end of that. That would be great! My mother had some temper!'

'Your mother?'

'Yes my mother, a terrible tyrannical German woman. If we didn't go to sleep at once, she threatened to sell us to the coal merchant. You probably can't remember your mother. You see the trouble I've saved you. Do you know what time it is? Not that it's important, but even so.'

Before I can reply to him, old Krumper switches off again, like the last candle on a birthday cake.

The hot air from the desert sticks to your body and makes you forget the artificial cold inside the caravan. And that's how it will always be. New dreams over old nightmares and over the new dreams even newer nightmares.

The eternal spiral of resistance. Blood is cleaned from the

sword while you wait for the next battle. Fear is the only thing that's never forgotten.

Let me tell you how the beginning of this story ends. After eating, with my good Hungarian friend, something resembling a pile of sausages covered with pastry I sat in a folding chair until the absurd colony of Quartzsite disappeared for a few seconds to reappear shortly after, already transformed into any other thing, magnificently lit up by the light of the moon. Like an army that surrenders all its weapons at the approach of another army. The change of guard between the heart of all dead things and the heart of all living things.

Night is just the end for the sleeping animals of the wood.

THE TIRED HEART

The cold of desert nights always catches you unawares. It's all the same whether you can remember it or not. That's when the old men wrap themselves up and go to bed.

I'm going back to Phoenix tomorrow.

Arizona has finished.

The Krumper girl said to me:

'Old Krumper's blue light has gone out forever.'

The Krumper girl has also told me that a French mechanic, expert in the repair of helicopters, has given her her first kiss and that the cock of this enthusiastic mechanic seemed to her like an elephant's trunk, the monstrous extremity of an absurd animal.

Everything is finishing and everything is beginning at the same time. The miracle of cryogenics has given Krumper a little Mexican body capable of carrying around his guilt with unforeseen expertise.

Indeed, contrary to popular belief, Walt Disney's brain was never frozen. At least that's what this child assures me.

Bad news for Donald Duck.

The Krumper girl told me, before going off to dance, that a long time ago when she was still younger, even before the Second World War, the order that she most liked to hear in old ships was:

'Visitors, please leave the ship.'
Only after this order is given can the journey begin.

New York, 4 July 1998